Also by Amanda Nelson

Novels

Claire and the Missing Heir

Novellas

Claire and the Class Hare

Claire and the Artist Pierre

BY AMANDA NELSON

LAUREL ELITE BOOKS

Chapter 1

I'm sitting in my best friend's kitchen, trying to recover from the awful afternoon I just had. It was torturous. Instead of spending one of the last beautiful fall days outside enjoying the weather, I was trapped inside for hours.

"I still can't believe the children all agreed to go to the art museum, and therefore, the tie-breaking vote rule did not apply. We had the perfect system in place, and now this betrayal," I complain.

"The perfect system being that the majority rules on our outings, and in the event of a tie, you get the deciding vote?" CC, my best friend, asks while stirring something delicious-smelling on the stove. She's also putting guacamole, sour cream, salsa, pico de gallo, and cilantro lime rice into bowls. I consider getting up from the huge banquette I'm sitting at to help her, but based on past experience, it would not end well, so I remain seated.

"Well, yeah," I confirm. "I mean, what siblings agree with each other? It's a perfect system. They can't agree, and then I get to choose." Why did they want to torture me that way? I wonder silently. An exasperated sigh from CC implies I did not, in fact, wonder silently, but aloud. I often say whatever I'm thinking without realizing it. The struggle to keep my thoughts in is never-ending and usually unsuccessful.

Dean, CC's seven-year-old, appears as if by magic to start setting the table. He has to reach around me to finish, but he manages it with minimal issues, so I don't bother moving. As if some inaudible dinner bell has rung, CC's other children stream into the kitchen like a blond-haired, blue-eyed horde. On their way to join me at the table, they help Dean by grabbing the various bowls CC had filled.

Jake, CC's gorgeous husband, comes through the back door just in time to grab one of the giant skillets holding the chicken fajitas, while CC grabs the other. Yum! I think, both about the fajitas and about Jake. He is six feet of muscle with gleaming blond hair and laughing blue eyes. CC's friendly welcome-home kiss deepens, but since they've already put the skillets down, I ignore them and start loading my plate.

"Dinner and a show." A rude voice interrupts what's turning into quite the make-out session. Since CC and Jake are looking at me with a mix of exasperation and resignation, I realize it was my voice. I guess I didn't ignore them after all. Unrepentant, I smile and take a big bite of my fajita.

"What did you all do today?" Jake asks, taking a bite of his fajita.

"Mom and Aunt Claire picked us up from school and we went to the art museum," Kyle, their thirteen-year-old, who has a smear of something purple across one cheek, answers with a surprising show of enthusiasm. Kyle rarely shows outward interest in what's happening around him, but he can draw everything in his sketchbook in astounding detail. Not much gets past him; he just doesn't often engage. He's also a dead ringer for Charlie Brown's friend Pigpen. His dark-blond curly hair resembles a bird's nest, with stray curls peeking out here and there from the unruly mass. "We got a tour too. It was so amazing."

It was not amazing. I flash back to how the tour guide told us all about the artists. I mean *all* about them, in excruciating detail. She droned on and on about the long-dead artists and their evidently traumatic lives.

CC shoots me a look full of reproach. Apparently, I've once again lost the struggle of keeping my inner thoughts from becoming outer words.

"I can't wait to go back tomorrow for Pierre's art show opening," Kyle adds, choosing to ignore my interjection. This is news to me. I squinty-eyed glare at CC, who is studiously avoiding my eyes.

"We're going back tomorrow?" I question in what some might call an accusatory manner. Kyle nods enthusiastically, ignoring my tone.

"He's even going to be there for the opening," he continues, excitedly.

I debate whining to get out of spending more time trapped inside an art museum, but before I can decide, CC says, "They're serving fancy appetizers." Hmm, I do like fancy appetizers.

"Wait, do fancy appetizers mean fancy clothes?" I ask suspiciously. I'm more of a cutoffs- or jeans-and-a-funny-T-shirt kind of girl. Like the shirt I'm wearing today. It has a picture of several art easels, one of which has a sash that reads THE BEST, and underneath the picture, EASEL-Y THE BEST is printed. I thought it was perfect for our art museum outing today. Nobody even commented on it, let alone complimented me on it. I sigh heavily in disappointment that people can't appreciate a good pun.

"Yes, Claire. It will be fancy clothes," CC says with a hint of exasperation. "Remember, we picked out that nice dress last week? The emerald green matches your eyes so well." I ponder this turn of events while eating another fajita. I did look terrific in the dress, and I do like fancy appetizers, and I love Kyle and want him to be happy.

"I guess we can go," I concede grudgingly. Although I suspect my permission is not required, and regardless of my thoughts on the subject, we'll be attending the art opening. It sounds like we'll be missing our standing Friday night line-dancing plans. I contemplate this as Ann, CC's ten-year-old, drones on about some basketball game she beat the neighborhood boys in, and Dean rambles on about his newest Rube Goldberg project. These are common topics of conversation, so I don't bother listening. The kids monopolize the conversation so nobody else can get a word in edgewise.

Ann and Dean wrap up their monologues, as all the children finish eating and trickle out of the kitchen. Eve, their two-year-old, calls my scruffy terrier mix Benji to join them. He abandons me without even a backward glance, happily trotting at her heels. I frown after him. You would think he would show a little hesitation when abandoning the person who feeds him.

"Have you heard when your office will open again?" Jake interrupts me before I can work up to a good, aggrieved rant about Benji's abandonment. "It's been almost two weeks now, hasn't it? I still can't believe Brandon hired an outside construction company. Everybody knows Woodall and Sons is the best around."

I answer his list of questions. "No, I haven't heard. Yes, it's been two weeks. Brandon's intelligence and decision-making have always been lacking. I'm conflicted on how I feel about it. I mean, I like not having to go to my soul-crushing office job, but I miss the paycheck." I don't *need* the paycheck, I admit to myself. I inherited my paid-off house from my parents, and I basically eat every meal with CC and her family. I have very few expenses, so I've been putting most of my paycheck into profitable investment accounts for years, and years, and years.

I sigh so deeply that, had there been any papers nearby, they would have fluttered away. "I talked to Brandon yesterday, but as usual, he knew nothing. You would think his dad would have stepped in before the remodel started, but he seems to have more faith in Brandon than I do," I say. Not that that would be hard, since I have practically no faith in Brandon.

"Have you thought about using this time to look for a different job? Maybe one you don't hate?" CC asks, handing me a glass of iced tea. I drop my head onto the table.

"I hate job hunting," I whine, not bothering to pick my head up. "Especially here. Everybody knows me personally. Either we grew up together, or they knew me as a child. It is *so-o-o-o* awkward."

"You could always work with me," Jake offers. "We could use a good office manager." I pick my head up to stare deeply into his beautiful blue eyes while I consider his offer. On one hand, it would be a paycheck. On the other hand, working with my best friend's husband might be an issue. On the other other hand, I bet Jake is a great boss. On the other other other hand, we could carpool.

Geez, I'm running out of hands fast. "I'll think about it," I finally say.

"I'm a great boss, and we can carpool." Jake tries to sway me with my very own points. Maybe he's reading my mind. I think really hard about chocolate. I close my eyes and envision Jake bringing me a big bowl of it. I hear a rustling sound and open my eyes to see a candy bar in front of me. It worked!

"Claire, you always want chocolate, and besides, you're still saying everything you think out loud," CC says as she finishes her iced tea. Shoot, I think—or say, who knows. Not giving it another thought, I eat my candy bar.

While I'm enjoying the last bite, there's a loud crash from upstairs, followed by a chorus of "We're fine!"

Despite the children's shouted assurances, CC and Jake jump up and head upstairs to investigate. Benji races down the stairs, passing CC and Jake on their way. I hope he wasn't the cause of the crash. I eye him suspiciously, as if I could determine his possible part in the commotion. He barks sharply at me, seemingly unconcerned by my scrutiny. He looks at me expectantly from where he's waiting by the back door. When I don't immediately comply with his demand to go home, he barks again, this time adding a foot stamp. He can be so bossy.

"What?" I ask. "Did you do something upstairs?" He stamps his foot again, adding a little huffy breath. I sigh and get up to head home to bed. I'm not sure if he did anything wrong, but a little space never hurt anybody. I just hope that whatever caused the crash couldn't be traced back to me or my dog. I also hope that Agatha, my bloodhound, and Blackbeard, my cat, have left me some space in my bed. I'm doubtful.

Chapter 2

The next morning, I stagger zombie-like into CC's kitchen, desperate for coffee. CC is standing at the counter, holding a mug ready for me. Taking it from her, I drink half of it in one gulp. Frowning at me, CC gets another mug out of the cabinet and pours herself a cup. I wonder what her problem is. Maybe she isn't a morning person either.

"That was *my* cup of coffee," CC says. An only child can be possessive like that. They never had to learn to share. "You're an only child, too," CC says, still frowning at me. It's as if she's reading my mind, I think, as I finish my coffee and hold my mug out for a refill. CC, still frowning at me, refills it. She's learning to share. It just goes to show you're never too old to learn. Her frown deepens, so I take my now-full mug and retreat to a barstool. It seems prudent to put some space and a physical barrier between us. I grab a muffin from the mostly empty pan in front of me and take a big bite. The house is quiet since the kids are already at school. An advantage of not working is sleeping in.

I consider the consequences of not working. Eventually, I might run out of money. It would take quite a while because I have a very large savings account, but it's still a possibility. Maybe. It's a very, very large—some might say obscenely large—savings account. Also, I'm finding that my days drag on. I'm not used to having so much free time. It's not like I have a bunch of kids to take care of. My pets are mostly self-sufficient. Agatha sleeps all day and all night, and Blackbeard seems displeased by my presence.

Only Benji enjoys my being around more, but there are only so many times I can feign appreciation for the gifts he presents me. Most recently, he presented me with a flashlight, of all things. I didn't even know I owned a flashlight. He loves bringing me things, which is never helpful and sometimes embarrassing. Even now, the memory of him presenting my red lacy bra to the sheriff heats my cheeks with embarrassment.

"Have you given any more thought to working for Jake?" CC asks, interrupting my thoughts.

"He just asked me last night," I remind her. "That's not a lot of time for thinking."

"I think you should do it. You hate working at the insurance company. I'm sure Jake pays better, and you wouldn't have to deal with Brandon or Steve." I consider her words. I do dislike Brandon. He's on a power trip, is an inept boss, and has the intelligence of a goldfish. I also dislike Steve. However, after the sheriff talked to him, he'd been keeping his hands to himself, so I didn't have to put up with the harassment anymore.

"I don't know, CC. I spend all of my non-working hours with you-all. Do you think spending all day with Jake would be too much? Besides, everyone would say I got the job because I'm your best friend."

"I thought you liked spending all your time with us." The slight hurt in her eyes makes me feel guilty, but I don't want to wear out my welcome. "We have spent every spare minute together since kindergarten. If you were going to wear out your welcome, it would have happened *long ago*." CC answers my inner thoughts. Wait, maybe they are outer words again. Shoot, I'm still struggling with keeping my thoughts in.

"The emphasis you placed on 'long ago' is hurtful." I glare at CC. I open my mouth to give her another piece of my mind, but when she refills my coffee cup, I take a huge swallow instead.

Finishing my coffee, I realize I'm alone in the kitchen. Huh—I wonder where CC went. The sound of a vacuum from somewhere upstairs tells me either she's upstairs vacuuming, or a very tidy burglar broke in. I conclude it's probably CC. We don't get a lot of burglars here. There are too many busybodies watching everybody's business for anybody to get away with burglaries. I decide to beat a hasty retreat back to my house in case CC asks me for help cleaning.

I putter around my house trying to be busy, but not really doing anything. Benji is my shadow, randomly presenting me with various objects, including a throw pillow, a phone charger, and a rubber duckie. I briefly wonder where the duck came from, but decide one of CC's kids probably left it.

I finally give up on trying to appear productive and curl up on my overstuffed couch to reread one of my favorite books while Blackbeard tries to crush me to death. Not for the first time, I wonder if he is part panther. He is approximately thirty pounds of sleek, muscled, black-furred purring disdain. I always get the distinct impression he barely tolerates me, even though I am the one who feeds him, and who also feeds his love of water by letting him shower with me. He is so weird. I'm still not sure how Jane convinced me to keep him.

"Lunch is ready," CC calls from my back door. I carefully slide out from under Blackbeard. He glares at me for disturbing him. His one green eye is full of contempt. When his tail starts twitching, I back away several steps, turn, and rush out of the room. There's no point in aggravating him further or making myself an easy target.

I breeze into CC's kitchen as if I didn't just fear for my life, and head straight for my plate at the banquette. Since there aren't any leftover fajitas, CC made us club sandwiches. She also put chips and sliced pears on the plates. Yum! She is so good to me, I think happily, taking a big bite of my sandwich.

"Remember, we're getting our hair done at two," CC reminds me. "So don't dawdle over lunch. You still need to get dressed." CC is already dressed. As always, she looks like she's ready for a photo shoot. Her blond hair is pulled back from her face with a wide headband that perfectly matches her fuchsia shirtdress. As always, I compare my look with hers and feel lacking. I look down and realize I'm still wearing my pajamas. Usually, they're old yoga pants (that have never been to a yoga class) and an old T-shirt, but today they're a matching set I got for Christmas last year. The pants have an all-over print of a moose covered in chocolate sauce, and the shirt has a picture of the same moose with CHOCOLATE MOOSE printed beneath it. I smile at the joke. Chocolate moose is like chocolate mousse, and I love chocolate mousse.

"Hurry up, we don't want to be late," CC says. She's already finished her sandwich. I obligingly return to eating. CC is normally a very nice person, but she has a terrifying side as well. Shoving the last slice of pear in my mouth, I head home to get dressed.

I choose a pair of worn, but not yet holey, jeans and a fabulous V-neck T-shirt. This one reads I'M HAIRLARIOUS and has various hairstyles on some of the letters as if the letters are heads. I have a shirt for every occasion, I think happily.

CC is waiting for me in my driveway. She eyes me up and down, but refrains from commenting on my outfit. We, of course, take my car to our appointment. She's a turquoise '67 Impala. My dad and I restored her when I was in high school. She's something special, and she reminds me of my dad. Plus, I avoid riding in CC's minivan, also known as the Mommobile, whenever possible.

I find a parking spot right in front of the salon, which, considering it is two o'clock on a Friday afternoon, isn't surprising.

Saturday is a more common time for manicures, hair styling, and, most important, small-town gossip.

Tina, the willowy redheaded owner of the salon, greets us warmly. Every visible inch of her is covered in freckles. I assume the parts not visible are also covered with freckles, but I don't have firsthand knowledge of that. We are ushered to a pair of salon chairs.

"What are we doing today?" Tina asks, running her fingers through my hair in what I assume is a professionally assessing manner. Her slight frown tells me she's professionally unimpressed with my hair.

"We're going to that art show opening tonight, so something classy, but not too fancy," CC answers for both of us. "Something that has …" She's searching for words. "Staying power," she finally finishes, eyeing my head in a judgmental way.

"Rude," I tell her. Shoot, I was supposed to think that, not say it. Tina nods while continuing to run her fingers through my hair, shifting it first one way and then another. At this point, I'm sure my hair isn't up to her standards. She tilts her head, then pulls a narrow binder off the nearby shelf. She flips the pages quickly, barely glancing at each page.

She finally stops, pinballing her eyes between the page and my head. Making a face, she flips a few more pages. "How about this one?" she asks, showing CC.

"It's my hair, don't I get a say?" I ask.

"No," they both answer at the same time.

"Hmph," I say, crossing my arms—some might say petulantly— over my chest and settling back in my chair.

CC scrutinizes the image and then my head. She nods slowly and smiles. "Yes, I think that will be perfect," she says. "It's simple but elegant. It will highlight her beautiful bone structure. And it looks sturdy, so it'll probably last all night," she adds rudely.

Having decided on my hair, Tina begins flipping pages again and shows CC another page. "How about this one for you?" she asks.

CC smiles again. "Tina, it's perfect," she declares happily.

I spend the next hour staring at myself in the mirror as my plain brown hair is combed, styled, and secured to my scalp with what I estimate to be a million bobby pins. Some of which I'm sure puncture my brain based on the force used to secure them, and the pain they cause.

I can't argue with the results, though. My hair no longer seems plain and boring. It gleams where it's swept off my face in a smooth wave. It's loosely braided—or knotted, I can't tell which—at the back of my head. Interspersed through the tresses are sparkling bobby pins and jeweled hair combs. I look stunning. CC was right, it does highlight my bone structure. I'm a knockout!

CC also looks great, but she always does, so that isn't surprising. Her honey-and-gold hair has at least a dozen braids of different sizes. They crisscross and overlap each other in what should be a disaster, but instead is breathtaking. The hair that isn't braided is left in loose, flowing curls down her back. Our eyes meet in the mirror as we examine Tina's handiwork.

"Jake and the sheriff won't know what hit them," Tina says, smiling. Her satisfaction with her work is obvious. My smile falters at the mention of the sheriff. We have a history which generally shows me in a less-than-stellar light. I didn't mean to hit him with my car, run over his foot, slap him, hit him with two different doors, and punch him in—well, never mind where I punched him. The point is, we have a history. Not for the first time, I wonder why the sheriff spends so much time around me, since it usually results in bodily injury to him. I haven't seen much of him recently, so maybe he's learned his lesson.

"Thanks, Tina!" CC says as she stands up from her chair and moves to the counter. I follow her more slowly, partly because I'm still contemplating the sheriff, and partly because I'm trying not to disturb my hair.

"Don't worry, sweetie. Your hair isn't going anywhere. I made sure of that!" Tina reassures me as she rings up our total. Feeling slightly better, I move more normally. "Just be sure to keep the car windows rolled up," she adds, as if I have no common sense.

I have some common sense, I think. CC and Tina's expressions tell me I might have said it out loud. Dang it!

Settling into my car carefully, I roll my cracked-open window all the way up, staring pointedly at CC the whole time. She ignores my antics. Sighing heavily at her lack of response, I start my car, carefully back out of my parking spot, and head home.

"You look like a princess!" Eve, CC's two-year-old, exclaims as we walk into CC's kitchen. Her head of golden curls and big blue eyes surrounded by long, thick lashes make her look like an angel, but her looks are the only angelic thing about her. She can throw a tantrum that could deafen the whole town when she's even slightly displeased. "Except for your clothes. They don't look like princesses at all."

That was a little judgmental, I think, frowning at her. Any princess would be proud to wear my awesome shirt.

"Don't worry. We have princess clothes that we are going to put on right now," CC tells her, as she guides me toward the stairs. She doesn't even give me a chance to grab a cookie off the plate in front of Dean. He wouldn't have noticed. He's too busy fiddling with a piece of wire, a clothespin, and a tiny spring. I don't have time to wonder what he's building this time, as CC continues to propel me through the kitchen and up the stairs. I just hope whatever it is doesn't cause me bodily harm. I still have flashbacks to the omelet machine he made me. Spoiler alert: It didn't make an omelet, but it did give me a goose egg.

We reach CC's bedroom, and she stops dragging me long enough to open her closet and pull out our dresses. Getting my shirt and then my dress over my hair without disturbing it is a bit tricky, but with CC's help and criticism, we manage it. While CC puts on her dress, I take the opportunity to inspect my reflection. The emerald-green chiffon dress is cut low, but not too low, across my chest. Ruffled off-the-shoulder sleeves, more like wisps than sleeves, fall nearly to my elbows. The bodice is gathered across the front to my left hip, accentuating my trim waist. The skirt falls in soft waves when I'm standing still, but every time I move, it sways around my ankles. I've always thought of myself as average, maybe even plain, especially compared to CC, but the way I look in this dress has me reassessing.

CC joins me in the mirror. Her dress is a sleeveless black sheath that hugs her curves. Since she resembles a pinup model, there's a lot of curve hugging going on. The bodice is cut modestly straight across her chest. The black lace overlay rises a few inches above the sheath's neckline, extends into long sleeves, and ends in a scalloped hem several inches below the sheath, at mid-shin.

"Wow! You look amazing! Are you sure we have to go out tonight?" Jake asks from the doorway behind us. His eyes hold a lot of heat and a promise of something more.

"Thanks," I say, "but you're married to my best friend, so that's kind of inappropriate." Not giving up, he crosses the room—and pulls CC into his arms. Huh, I guess he was talking to her the whole time. Maybe that's why he was looking at her.

It's impossible not to watch their kissy-face smooching since they're right next to me, and the full-length mirror is in front of me. I'm starting to feel like a voyeur. Deciding I should leave before clothing might be removed, I head downstairs. I'm pretty sure they don't notice.

"Now you look like a princess," Eve says, looking up from her coloring. I smile warmly at her, swaying slightly to make my dress swirl. I debate the risk of messing up my dress by eating one of the cookies from Dean's forgotten plate.

I've just decided any crumbs will be easy to brush off and am reaching for a cookie when Kyle joins me. I almost don't recognize him. His usually unruly mop of curls is carefully combed. He's also dressed in slacks and a button-up shirt, which incredibly don't have any unidentified schmutz on them; nor is there any on him for that matter. It's a miracle!

Before I can comment, possibly saying something hurtful, CC and Jake come down the stairs. Jake is wearing a tuxedo that emphasizes his broad shoulders, trim waist, and muscled frame. His blond hair is mussed like always, in that way that celebrities spend thousands of dollars to achieve, but in Jake's case it's caused by him distractedly running his fingers through it. It only enhances his good looks.

"Frank, we left pizza money on the counter. Be sure the kids are in bed by nine," CC says while kissing goodbye whatever blond-headed child is closest to her.

"Don't worry, Mom. I can handle it," Frank, CC's sixteen-year-old, says, catching Eve in midair as she tries to jump from the banquette onto Jake's back. Jake ushers CC, Kyle, and me out the door before Eve can plan her next move or throw a tantrum at being thwarted. As the door closes behind us, I hear Eve suck in a deep breath. I fear it is in preparation for her eardrum-rupturing screams, so I walk a little faster toward my car. It might resemble a jog more than a walk, but my self-preservation has kicked in. Past experience tells me I'll still be able to hear her screams even from my driveway. I'm proven correct when the eardrum-rupturing screams begin. CC, Jake, Kyle, and I increase our pace, almost running now, to try to escape the tantrum.

"Frank can handle it," I say, opening my car door and hopping in. "But if he can't, at least I will be far enough away that I won't hear it." CC doesn't say anything as she slides into my passenger seat, but her expression shows both relief and guilt at leaving Frank to handle Eve alone. Jake and Kyle are stuck in the back, but seem relieved to be leaving the tantrum behind, and don't complain. With the roar of my engine, which doesn't quite drown out Eve's piercing screams, we are off!

Chapter 3

I pull up to the museum valet stand and watch the two valets jostle to see who gets to park my sweet ride. The victor opens my door, while the loser opens CC's door. His face, when he gets a good look at CC, indicates he's feeling better about not being able to drive my car. When CC smiles her thanks at him, he gets that shellshocked look most men get around her.

Meanwhile, Jake and Kyle have opened their own doors. Ha, losers! Jake, well used to the worshipful looks his wife gets, ignores the valet's reaction and holds out one arm to escort CC, and one arm for me. Kyle trails behind us as we ascend the steps and enter the large reception room. It is already full of people. Men wearing suits and tuxedos mingle with women draped in gorgeous gowns in a rainbow of colors. Sparkling chandeliers cast a soft glow on the flowers spilling from vases placed around the room. Most important, waiters weave through the crowd with trays of fancy appetizers. Sadly, none of them are weaving near me.

"Don't worry. I'll handle it," Jake says close to my ear. He deftly maneuvers us through the crowd until suddenly a waiter is right in front of me.

Score! I think (but based on the surprised expression on the waiter's face, I probably said). I don't let this stop me from grabbing a mushroom cap off his tray. Quickly shoving it into my mouth, I'm able to grab a second one before he can move on to other guests. Chewing with relish, I scan the room for more waiters.

Spotting one, I indicate our target to Jake. He begins casually leading us toward the waiter. I eat my second mushroom cap in preparation for my next tasty morsel. Reaching the waiter, I see he has only two crab-topped crackers left on his tray. I grab the first one and shove it in my mouth to free up my hand to grab the second. I would simply use my other hand, but it's still tucked into Jake's arm, so I make do. Having shoved the whole cracker in my mouth, I probably resemble a hamster with full cheek pouches, but I managed to get both crackers, so I don't care.

While I'm scanning for the next waiter, my gaze settles on the very broad, very muscular shoulders of a tuxedo-clad man approximately twenty feet to my left. I let my gaze roam over him. He's tall like Jake, so, over six feet. His brown hair gleams with hints of mahogany and chestnut. We approach Mr. Tall, Dark, and Hunky as Jake works his way toward another waiter. When we're only a few feet away from him, he turns toward us. His gaze locks on me and his eyes widen with recognition, quickly followed by appreciation. My own eyes widen in shock.

"Sheriff, how nice to see you again. I didn't realize you were coming tonight," CC says warmly. I'm trying to swallow the giant cracker in my mouth without looking like I'm swallowing a giant cracker. I don't feel successful, but the sheriff's eyes are still taking in my dress. Well, probably me in the dress, but either way, he isn't looking at my face. With an audible swallow, I clear my overstuffed cheeks just before the sheriff's eyes meet mine again. His eyes hold that look that causes my temperature to rise and my feelings to get all muddled.

"You look amazing," the sheriff says. "You both do," he adds, sparing a brief glance for CC before laser-focusing on me again. I don't trust myself alone with the sheriff when he's looking at me like that, not even in a room full of people. For support, I tighten my hand on Jake's arm, only to realize I'm no longer holding Jake's arm. In fact, turning to my right, I realize Jake isn't even standing next to me. Where'd he go?

"I think he took CC to get a drink," the sheriff answers, making me think I might have said my thoughts out loud again. Luckily, all my thoughts seem to have fled, so it's unlikely I will make that mistake again, at least not in the foreseeable future. "You really do look amazing tonight," he repeats, shifting closer to me.

"So do you. Kind of like James Bond," I tell him, sneaking a quick up-and-down of his impressive physique. His smile implies I haven't been as sneaky as I thought, and my cheeks color slightly at having been caught.

"Did Kyle drag you here tonight?" the sheriff asks, probably taking pity on me.

I nod, then cock my head to the side. "Well, come to think of it, I think CC tricked me into coming." I mull this over. "Yeah, I'm pretty sure she tricked me. We bought this dress last week, but she didn't say it was for an art show. I only found out about the show yesterday." The sheriff runs his gaze down my body again at the mention of the dress, and his eyes heat even more. Yikes, when he looks at me like that, it makes me feel warm all over. The sheriff's cocky smile makes me realize I've said that out loud.

"I'd better go find CC," I say a little desperately. Suiting actions to words, I turn on my heel and practically run to CC's side. Feeling better with some distance between us, I heave a sigh of relief.

"Dominic, can I get you a drink?" Jake asks. Silly man, the sheriff's still on the other side of the room.

"That would be great," the sheriff answers from directly behind me. I refuse to turn around. It's probably for the best since it feels like he's standing extremely close to me, and turning around would put our faces too close for comfort. For my comfort, anyway—I'm not sure about the sheriff's comfort.

Remembering the cracker in my hand, I pop it into my mouth, not just because it's delicious, but also to give me something to do. When the sheriff reaches out his hand for the drink Jake offers him, his arm brushes along my side. I suck in a shocked breath at the contact.

Unfortunately, I still have the cracker in my mouth, and when I suck in my breath, I also suck the cracker down my windpipe, which blocks the flow of oxygen. The sheriff quickly wraps his arms around me from behind. He puts his fist just under my sternum and jerks it sharply toward my backbone. This has the desired effect of clearing my airway. However, since the sheriff keeps his arms wrapped around me, my breathing does not return to normal.

"Relax," he murmurs in my ear. "Let's not make a scene. It will just look like you're my date." This is probably reasonable and meant to save me the embarrassment of almost choking to death in front of a crowd, but I'm struggling to think straight as he holds me pressed against him.

A commotion near the front of the room begins drawing attention. Without seeming to move, the whole group congregates near the podium, leaving the back half of the room empty. I try to use this distraction to extract myself from the sheriff's embrace, but somehow I'm still wrapped in his arms when we join the edge of the group.

Everyone is staring at the slender woman behind the podium. Her light-brown hair is slicked back into a no-nonsense bun at the nape of her neck. She is wearing a purple taffeta dress that bells out from a banded waist. She also has a stunning multi-strand amethyst necklace that catches and reflects the light with her every move. It almost looks like she's sparkling.

I'm not sure how I feel being trapped in the sheriff's arms. On one hand, I'm very comfortable in his embrace. On the other hand, I'm very uncomfortable in his embrace. A soft chuckle stirs a stray curl near my ear. I close my eyes, mortified that I said my thoughts out loud. Again.

"Welcome, everyone. Thank you for joining us tonight. I'm sure you will enjoy ..."

I tune out the droning welcome speech and instead hyper-focus on being wrapped in strong arms and held against a muscular body. I have a lot of different feelings about being in the sheriff's arms, but the one that stands out the most right now is one that I probably shouldn't be thinking in a room full of people.

"It's him," Kyle breathes reverently from beside me. "It's Pierre." I drag my focus back to the woman at the podium. A dark-haired man now stands beside her. I suppose he would be considered attractive. He's slender and well-dressed with a neatly trimmed goatee. I cock my head to study him better. The sheriff takes this as an invitation. I feel his lips skimming lightly along my now-exposed neck. My breathing suddenly becomes very irregular.

"Thank you for coming tonight," the man says, stepping up to the podium. His French accent makes my nose wrinkle, but I'm not sure why. He talks about his inspiration for his art and some other boring things. I notice Kyle is enthralled. CC and Jake seem to be listening almost as intently as Kyle. I guess I'm the only one bored by his speech.

When the room applauds decorously, the sheriff finally drops his arms from around me. I subtly shift away. Just kidding—I'm not subtle. I practically run toward the ladies' room. I need some space to think. I didn't know we were at the holding-and-neck-nuzzling phase in our relationship. I thought we were still in the I-accidentally-injure-him-and-he-expresses-his-displeasure-with-my-actions-often-at-a-high-volume stage.

Leaning on the counter to support my weakened knees, I realize I'm not able to think. My brain is still scrambled. The bathroom doesn't provide enough space for thinking.

Several minutes pass before CC joins me. "Are you planning to hide in here all night?" she asks with a knowing smirk. I can always count on my best friend to support me in my time of need, I think sarcastically. CC rolls her eyes at me, indicating I said it, not thought it.

"I don't think being held and nuzzled by an incredibly sexy single man is a 'time of need,'" she counters, scrutinizing her perfect reflection.

"I didn't know we were at the holding-and-nuzzling phase in our relationship. I thought we were still in the I-accidentally-injure-him-and-he-expresses-his-displeasure phase," I tell her. "Although the holding and nuzzling are much more enjoyable than the yelling." CC doesn't respond. She links her arm with mine and drags me out of the bathroom.

Her lack of sympathy makes me question whether she is really my best friend. When she deftly intercepts a waiter, I decide she really *is* my best friend. I grab two skewers of meatballs in my one free hand. Debating the merits of trying to eat them one at a time, or both at the same time, I decide that both at the same time will be less likely to result in spilling on my dress. Just as I shove both of them in my mouth, I spot the sheriff heading straight for me.

Not ready to face him again, I turn to beat a hasty retreat—and slam into someone. His slightly clammy hands grip my elbows to steady me and also keep me all but pressed up against him. My startled gaze fixes directly on the storm-gray eyes of Pierre.

"I am fortunate indeed to have in my arms the most beautiful woman present," he says. His accent makes it sound more romantic than it should, but it also rubs me the wrong way. I don't know why. Usually, a French accent is sexy, but from him, I get a slightly icky feeling hearing it. Luckily, I manage to keep these inner thoughts in, so I don't embarrass myself further.

"I'm so sorry," I say. "I should have been watching where I was going." I offer him an apologetic smile while trying to subtly place a respectable distance between us. He seems reluctant to let me go. He's forced to drop his hands when I step back, less subtly than I would have liked. His eyes rove over me, warm with interest.

Feeling slightly uncomfortable with his continued interest, I cast about for something to say. I realize Kyle is now standing next to me, so—a little desperately—I wrap my arm around his shoulder, bringing him into our little bubble. "Kyle, I know you were hoping to meet Pierre. Pierre, this is Kyle. He's a huge fan of your work."

Pierre spares a glance for Kyle before returning his gaze to me. "You have a son?" he asks with a hint of something I can't identify. I'm not sure if it's disappointment, anger, or possibly disdain; whatever it is, it definitely isn't a happy feeling.

"Kyle is my nephew," I clarify. "He's the reason I'm here tonight. He was dying to see your exhibit."

Pierre's expression clears as he smiles at Kyle. "Then I owe you a debt, for without your interest in my art, I would not have met this lovely lady." He raises my hand to his lips and kisses my knuckles. His goatee tickles, but I manage not to make a face. It takes great force of will, which isn't usually my strong suit, but I manage it.

My hand is suddenly snatched away from Pierre's. Perplexed, I look down to see it completely enfolded in a strong, long-fingered hand. Following the arm to the shoulder, and then the face, I'm shocked to see the sheriff.

"There you are. I've been looking for you," he says as if he has the right to possess my hand. "Kyle, how are the murals going?"

I abandon my glare at the sheriff to stare in surprise at Kyle. "What murals?" I ask. "Why don't I know about your murals?"

Kyle fidgets slightly at my ire. "I'm painting murals at Town Square Park," he admits.

Wow! I think. I knew he was talented and destined for great things. This is only the beginning. I'll be able to say I knew him when. Kyle's shy smile tells me I probably said all that out loud. Oh well, at least this time it isn't embarrassing.

Kyle answers the sheriff. "It's going well. They're set to be completed for the town Halloween party next weekend."

"Young artists are such a gift. Watching them grow into their talent is truly inspiring," Pierre cuts in, a little condescendingly, drawing our attention back to him.

"Kyle, your mom wants to introduce Claire to somebody. Why don't you tell Pierre about your murals?" the sheriff says. "It's great that you like to encourage young artists," he adds to Pierre, leading me away.

"I don't like him," the sheriff tells me gruffly, still holding my hand. Before I can form a reply, he guides me into an empty room off the main hall. I frown as I realize he probably made up the story about CC wanting to introduce me to someone. He just wanted an excuse to whisk me away.

"CC didn't want to introduce me to anybody. You just wanted an excuse to whisk me away," I accuse. His wolfish smile confirms my suspicions. It's becoming a habit, this smiling of his. When I first met him, I didn't think he even knew how to smile, but now he smiles fairly regularly. It's usually when I've done something embarrassing, but hey, I bring joy to all.

"Guilty as charged," he confirms, pulling me into his arms. "You really do look incredible, although I kind of miss your punny T-shirts." His chocolate-brown eyes stare deep into my own.

I think he might kiss me. I don't know how I feel about this. We've had several near misses with the kisses. The rhyme makes me snicker. Ignoring my snicker, the sheriff slowly leans closer, bringing his mouth within centimeters of mine. Nervously, I lick my lips. His gaze drops to follow the path of my tongue.

"Ladies and gentlemen, Pierre's exhibit is now open," a cultured voice says over the loudspeakers. The sheriff ignores it and continues slowly closing the slight distance between our faces. When his lips gently touch mine, my mind goes completely blank.

When he lifts his head, who knows how long later, my thoughts come rushing back in. He kissed me! He actually kissed me! And it was incredible. His satisfied smile says I might have said that out loud. Shoot!

Deciding to flee my embarrassment, I realize my hands are clutching the lapels of his tuxedo. Forcing my fingers to uncurl and my legs to stiffen from the jelly-like consistency caused by his kiss, I take a careful step back, making sure my legs will support me. Sighing in relief when I don't crumple, I turn and practically run away. Feeling the sheriff's hand settle at my waist, I realize I'm probably not moving as fast as I think I am. Darn jelly legs!

Joining the crowd perusing Pierre's art collection, I pretend a nonchalance I don't feel. "Claire, are you all right?" CC asks, materializing at my side and staring in concern at my face. Apparently, I don't look nonchalant either. Shifting her gaze to the sheriff, who still has his hand on the small of my back, her concerned expression clears.

"I have to check on Kyle," she says and disappears into the crowd. My mouth drops open in shock. She just abandoned me in my time of need.

"Don't worry, I'm still here," the sheriff murmurs in my ear. His lips graze my ear, and I instinctively tilt my head to give him better access. Remembering I'm not sure if I want him to have better access, I straighten my head again.

An excited murmur sweeps the crowd. Fearing they are all watching the sheriff seducing me, I panic. Luckily, nobody's looking at us. They're staring at a curtained section of the wall. I guess I overestimated how interested a room of people are in me.

Pierre stands to one side of the curtain, near a braided cord. "And now—the moment you've all been waiting for!" he announces with an off-putting air of self-importance.

"The moment I've been waiting for does not include Pierre," the sheriff murmurs in my ear. I don't have time to respond—it probably wouldn't be anywhere near an intelligent response anyway—before Pierre tugs the cord to pull the curtains, revealing a blank wall.

"Huh, not really my idea of art," I say, eyeing the plain wall. It looks just like the rest of the walls around the room.

The crowd's initial silence is replaced by surprised murmurs. Pierre seems to sense something is wrong. He turns to look at the blank wall. His first expression is one of shock, which quickly turns to outrage.

"My masterpiece! Where has it gone? Who has taken it?" His accented voice echoes around the room, silencing the murmuring crowd.

Pierre's outburst causes the sheriff to raise his head from where his lips are skimming my neck, which was possibly angled to allow him better access. Sighing heavily, he releases me.

Moving quickly to secure the scene, he orders the two security guards to lock down the museum. "Nobody in or out, including the staff," he commands. "Everybody, I'm Sheriff Dominic Armstrong, and nobody is leaving until I've taken their statement." Wow, he sounds so professional and commanding. It's very sexy, I think. I might have said it, but nobody was near enough to hear, so I'll never know.

Taking everybody's statement is a long drawn-out affair. The sheriff's deputy joins us, but he's more of a deputy-in-training, so he isn't as helpful as one might hope. His experience is more in parking violations than statement taking.

You'd think that since the sheriff knew us personally, we would have been released first, but apparently, necking with the sheriff doesn't come with crime scene perks.

"You were necking with the sheriff?" CC asks with a delighted smile. Shoot! Inner thoughts became outer words again! "Do you think you should call him by his first name since you're kissing him?"

"Who's kissing who?" Jake asks, appearing at my side.

"Claire is kissing the sheriff," CC tells him, snuggling into his arms. She hasn't even paused to consider if I want it to be public knowledge or not. Jake and CC seem pleased by this turn of events.

"Well, if we're being honest, the sheriff—Dominic," I correct myself, "kissed me." CC has a point. Kissing probably requires a first-name basis. I'll have to work on that. Since CC and Jake are having a silent conversation, probably about me and the sheriff, I'm not sure they hear my clarification.

I fidget as I glance around the room. I don't know what I'm looking for, but when my eyes fall on Pierre conversing, rather intently in my opinion, with the woman from the podium, my suspicions are roused. I don't know why that piques my curiosity, but it does. I suppose the artist *would* want to confer with the museum woman about the missing painting, but something about it seems off.

Wanting to hear what they're talking about, I move toward them. I try not to look like I'm sneaking up on them, but I'm probably not successful. Fortunately, they're too focused on each other to notice me. Unfortunately, they finish their conversation and go their separate ways before I can hear anything.

Before I can decide which one to follow, a waiter comes by with a tray holding bruschetta topped with prosciutto and what I guess to be mozzarella. Since both hands are free, I manage to snatch three of them before the waiter can escape.

I glance around the room, looking for more waiters while I chew. Spotting several on the other side of the room, I frown. Why aren't they on this side of the room? I wonder. As they circle, one of the waiters makes eye contact with me. He immediately does an about-face and melts into the crowd. Huh, it seems they're avoiding me. Not one to be denied, I search the walls of the room. Spotting a swinging door to my right, I head that way.

Despite my best efforts to intercept a waiter on my way to the door, I am unsuccessful. They all spot me with enough time to divert and disappear into the crowd. Rude!

I swing open the door and narrowly avoid hitting a waiter in the face. Aha! I think. Here are the fancy appetizers. Based on the fact that everybody in the kitchen is staring at me, I probably said it instead of just thinking it. Taking advantage of their shock, I begin snagging whatever treats I can reach and piling them onto a plate I find nearby.

"You can't be in here," an extremely large man says from the other side of the room. His intimidating scowl is enhanced by the large knife he is using to chop vegetables.

"Don't worry, I won't be long," I tell him, grabbing a few more morsels for my plate. When he heads toward me, still holding the knife, I whisk myself back out the swinging door, clutching my towering plate.

My catlike reflexes are challenged when I almost run into the sheriff—Dominic, I correct my thoughts. I think we are both relieved that I don't hit him with the door. It wouldn't have been the first time. It wouldn't have even been the second time. The sheriff—I mean *Dominic*, I correct myself again—eyes my heaping plate, but refrains from commenting.

"I'm ready to take your statement," he says. A pad and pen appear, as if by magic, in his hands. I pop a shrimp into my mouth and chew with relish. "Did you see anyone near the curtained area?" he asks.

I nod while swallowing. "Yup, I sure did."

His eyes fly to mine, surprised. "Can you describe them?" he asks, his pen poised above the notepad.

"Let's see, he's about my height, has dark hair, a goatee, gray eyes, and a French accent."

The pen stops scratching against the pad about halfway through my description. "Pierre? You saw Pierre?" he asks in what I can only describe as a testy tone. Maybe he's hangry. The waiters do seem to avoid certain people. Maybe they avoided him, too. I thoughtfully offer him a bruschetta from my plate. He ignores my offer scowling, implying he isn't hangry, just angry.

"You might have seen him, too. Although you did seem inordinately interested in my neck, so maybe not," I say, taking a bite of the bruschetta he didn't accept.

"Did you see anyone, *besides* Pierre, near the curtain?" he asks through gritted teeth. I shake my head, chewing another bite. "Did you see anyone acting suspiciously?"

I frown, considering. "Well, when you were doing your sheriffing stuff, I saw Pierre and that woman in the purple dress talking. It seemed weird."

"The artist of the missing painting talking to the museum director doesn't seem weird," he states, putting away his notepad and pen.

"I know it shouldn't be weird, but their expressions just seemed ..." I struggle for the right word. "Weird," I finish weakly.

Sighing, the sheriff—Dominic, I mean—guides me back to CC, Jake, and Kyle with a hand at my back. By the time we reach them, my plate is empty. "If I have further questions, I know how to reach you," he says to our little group. "I'll let them know you're free to go."

Chapter 4

The ride home is quiet as we all silently contemplate the evening. Who stole the painting? Why did Pierre rub me the wrong way? Why did the waiters avoid me? Is there a recipe book for fancy appetizers? Jake's snorted laughter from the back seat tells me I might not be contemplating silently. Sighing deeply, I focus on keeping my mouth shut.

"Do you think the sheriff will find Pierre's painting?" Kyle asks softly from the back seat. "I was hoping to see it in person. Pictures don't do his use of texture justice."

Nobody seems to have an answer for him.

"I'm sure he will," CC finally says. "He found Mr. Johnson's killer and rescued Jamie."

"Umm, *I* found Mr. Johnson's killer and rescued Jamie," I remind CC. "Remember, you were there too."

"Don't remind me," Jake says. "That was the worst night of my life. You two could have been …" He pauses, searching for the right word. "Hurt."

He probably chose the word to spare Kyle. We could have been *killed.* Uh-oh! Did I say that out loud? Panicked, I look at CC, but since she isn't glaring at me, I feel confident that my thoughts have stayed in, for once.

Entering CC's dark kitchen, I realize it is later than the kids' nine o'clock bedtime, and they're probably already sleeping. But hearing a gaggle of giggles filtering down the stairs makes me think the kids are not asleep after all. With a militant expression, CC heads up the stairs, not even bothering to turn on the kitchen lights.

After I bump into the counter and a barstool, Jake flicks the lights on. I half fall, half sit on the barstool I bumped into. Suddenly, I feel exhausted. When a beer appears before me, I happily take a deep drink. The events of the evening are catching up to me. I continue sipping my beer as I contemplate the events of the evening.

What a mystery, I think. Why did the sheriff, I mean Dominic, show such interest in me? And why was he nuzzling my neck? And he even kissed me! Wait, I don't think it, I say it. Shoot!

"I'm pretty sure he did all those things because he likes you," Jake answers.

"But why tonight? And more important, why does he like me? Every time we're together, I seem to cause him bodily harm," I say plaintively. "He also yells at me on a regular basis," I add, plunking my head on the counter in defeat.

"I think the yelling is because he cares, and you and your antics drive him crazy with worry," Jake tells the top of my head, since my face is pressed into the counter. "Besides, he's a big strong man. He even has military training. I think he can survive you." I suppose he means it to be comforting, but I find it patronizing. Deciding I'm not going to hear anything that would make me feel better, I finish my beer and head home.

My hopes that Agatha and Blackbeard have left my place on my bed unoccupied are dashed when I see both of them spread across my mattress. Blackbeard twitches his tail at me with an attitude of contempt. Meanwhile, Agatha's snores cause her jowls to flutter as she lies melted across most of my mattress. They've left me about two feet of space. Sadly, it's divided on opposite corners.

I sigh heavily. Heading into the bathroom, I begin pulling the millions of bobby pins from my hair. An hour later, I pull out the last one and add it to the huge pile on my vanity. (The clock tells me it's more like ten minutes later, but I stand by my original estimate.)

Luckily, Agatha's rolled over at some point, leaving me enough room to slide into bed. I quickly take my dress off, put my chocolate moose pajamas on, and slip into the space before she can roll back. No sooner have I claimed my space than she rolls again. Her muzzle is pressed to my cheek as her chainsaw-like snores threaten to deafen me. I sigh. Why does she sleep silently all day, but once in my bed, she snores loud enough to wake the dead?

I sigh again. Sleep will not come easily tonight. Not just because of Agatha's snoring, but also because I'm still thinking about Dominic—the sheriff, I correct myself. (Wait. I was right the first time—Dominic.) We almost kissed once before, but that was ruined by some college boys and a soccer ball; my lip throbs at the memory. I mean, there had been something simmering between us, but tonight it seemed like he'd forgotten all the unfortunate incidents from our past interactions. I suppose some of those incidents might have caused some damage to his brain, resulting in memory loss, but that seems improbable. The most likely one was when I slammed a door into his temple—accidentally, of course. I thought he was a murderer. Luckily, he only needed four stitches, and he seemed fine afterward, so it probably didn't cause any brain damage.

What was different about tonight? I wonder. The only thing I can think of is that I wore a gorgeous dress, and according to Eve, I looked like a princess. Maybe he has a thing for princesses. That doesn't bode well for a relationship between us. I very rarely look like a princess. I usually look more like an overgrown kid with my punny T-shirts and messy hair. My office attire makes me look more professional, but it still doesn't make me look like a princess. He said he liked my punny T-shirts, though, so maybe there's hope for a relationship.

Now I have a new worry. Do I want a relationship with him?

I weigh the pros and cons. Pros: He is gorgeous. He saved me from a murderer, kind of. He didn't make a huge fuss about me hitting him with my car, slapping him, running over his foot, flipping him like a rag doll, hitting him with two doors, or punching him in the testicles. I wince at the list of injuries but continue: He's a good kisser. He understands my place in CC's family. He yelled some nice things at me once. His grandma owns the best bakery around. Maybe I would get free brownies if we were dating.

Cons: He often expresses his displeasure at my actions by yelling. (Although I might have deserved the yelling, so maybe that shouldn't count as a con.) If we had a relationship and it ended, how would we divide our friends? He and Jake are close, and he gets along with all of CC's family, so that could get messy. Also, if we broke up, his grandma might not let me have any brownies, even if I pay for them. My con list doesn't have much on it, unless we break up.

Exasperated with my thoughts, I roll over and try to get some sleep. Instead, I replay the events of the night. Well, the parts that involve Dominic and his lips on me. I feel a little warm just remembering those parts. I wonder how it would feel to have his lips on me all the time. Jake and CC are always kissy-face smooching, and they seem happy about it. I was pretty happy about Dominic kissy-face smooching me. Besides the panic, it was incredible. This time, my sigh is wistful. I finally drift off to sleep, imagining what the future might hold.

Chapter 5

Waking up to the sun streaming through my window, I realize I'm smiling. I must have had some good dreams. I try to remember what I was dreaming about, but I can't. Deciding that coffee might help my memory, I stagger upright and head next door to CC's.

Jake is manning the griddle, where several pancakes wait to be flipped. A plate nearby holds a stack, so I snag that along with the cup of coffee next to it. Taking a quick drink, I realize it's only half full. Jake sighs, reaching to refill my mug before grabbing one out of the cabinet for himself and filling it. Weird—I'll never understand how somebody can start their day without coffee.

"I did start my day with coffee." Jake answers my apparently spoken thoughts. I briefly wonder what happened to it while I raise my mug to take another swallow. CC had a similar problem yesterday, I recall. A thought suddenly occurs to me. I don't have any syrup! Jake shakes his head as if I've disappointed him, but since I bring joy to all, that can't be right. Despite his possible disappointment, he hands me the syrup bottle and starts a new batch of pancakes.

My happiness is short-lived as the telltale clicking that precedes doom can be heard approaching the kitchen. It's too late to escape.

The kitchen door swings open, revealing a bear. He's monstrous. His demonic eyes lock on me like a heat-seeking missile.

A whimper of fear slips from me. It only seems to excite him as he lumbers toward me.

My hopes for salvation soar as Jane, CC's eleven-year-old, who has a remarkable way with animals, enters the room. My hopes are dashed as she ignores the bear now trying to crawl into my lap while I sit at the counter. She just takes the plate of now-ready pancakes next to Jake.

Finally, I wrestle the bear, or as I often refer to him, "the danger floof," to the ground. Now that he's no longer trying to force his affection on me and is lying panting on the floor, I can concede he resembles the Newfoundland he is. Although, with Jane, a bear was a possibility. She collects all kinds of animals, including wild ones like deer, birds, raccoons, tortoises, and once a beaver. I lost a porch post to that beaver. Luckily, Jake fixed the post before I could get hurt.

Mopping up the last of my syrup with my last bite of pancake, I realize all of CC and Jake's children, except Nell, who's still at college, are now in the kitchen eating pancakes. I briefly wonder when that happened and how I didn't notice, but when Jake refills my mug, I decide it doesn't matter and take a deep drink.

CC sweeps into the kitchen looking ready to take on the world. A few of the braids from yesterday are still evident in her high ponytail. She has on a pair of palazzo pants with a bold floral pattern running down the outside seams. Her shirt is a coral boatneck that matches the largest of the flowers on her pants. She seems like she might have plans for today. I'm afraid her plans might include me.

"Get dressed," she commands me as she accepts a cup of coffee from Jake. "In something nice," she adds before Jake distracts her with some kissy-face smooching. I debate whether I have time for another cup of coffee. It looks like the make-out session might last a while.

"Now," she snaps out during a brief pause in the kissing when Jake flips the pancakes. Sighing, I slide off my barstool and head home.

Not sure what CC's plans are and how nice I'm expected to dress, I stare at my choices. I decide on a pair of wide-legged denim trousers and a light-blue wrap shirt. Surveying the results in the mirror, I concede that I clean up nicely, except for my hair. It resembles a rat's nest tangled around my face. Frowning, I pluck out a few stray bobby pins I must have missed last night and head into the bathroom to try to tame the mess. Armed with only a hairbrush, I'm not sure I'll be victorious, but after only ten minutes, I manage to contain it in a loose braid.

Heading back toward CC's, I see her and Kyle standing beside my car, so I divert to the driveway. "Since we had to cut our evening short last night, I told Kyle we would go back to the museum today," CC says as she slides into the passenger seat.

This sounds suspicious. We did not cut our evening short. We were there all night. Well, not all night, but it was late when we got home. And how come Kyle doesn't have to wear something nice? He's dressed in old jeans and a wrinkled T-shirt. He also has what appears to be grass clippings in his unruly mop of hair. Before I can argue that we didn't cut our visit short, CC offers to drive us in the Mommobile. I shudder slightly at the thought and hop into my driver's seat.

The drive to the museum takes longer than it should because everyone in town is outside, and small-town rules say we can't simply drive by. Luckily, we're able to just wave and call out greetings.

Most people are afraid to approach any car I'm driving. In the past, there have been a few unfortunate events involving pedestrians, my car, and an occasional ambulance.

After we park at the museum, Kyle practically skips up the stairs to the entrance, in contrast to his normally reserved actions. I might be dawdling behind, trying to soak up as much of the beautiful fall day as I can before I am, once again, forced inside. I'm forced inside faster than I hope, since CC loops her arm through mine and drags me along in Kyle's wake.

His happy skipping ends when we get to the doorway of the exhibit hall—the police-crime-scene-taped doorway.

"We probably should have anticipated this," I say. Kyle's slumped shoulders make my heart hurt. The kid is great, and he rarely asks for anything. He deserves whatever makes him happy. He just wants to see some paintings. It isn't like he wants to take over the world.

I peer past the crime scene tape into the room. Nobody is even in there, so why is it still taped off? I glance around and, not seeing anybody, duck under the tape and into the exhibit hall. CC's and Kyle's shocked and horrified expressions tell me they aren't likely to join me. Solving my problem, I grab Kyle's hand and yank him into the room. His quick reflexes cause him to duck so he doesn't disturb the crime scene tape.

"You wanted to see the art. Here's the art," I tell him, gesturing all around us. At first tentatively, but then with more confidence, Kyle moves toward a large canvas. It's full of blues and greens with a hint of white. The colors swirl and overlap each other. It reminds me of water. It's actually very pretty. I'm not sure how Pierre achieved it, but it's wild like a stormy sea, but also calm like a lake.

Suddenly, I'm interested in the other paintings, and I eagerly move on to the next. This one is all oranges, reds, and yellows. It looks like a fall day. Moving on again, the next painting is a mix of pinks, purples, reds, blues, and greens. At first, I'm not sure what it is, but then I realize it looks like a wildflower meadow. Huh, these are pretty good.

Moving on to the next one, I'm presented with a blank wall framed by curtains. "Oh, yeah, the stolen painting," I say.

"Yeah, the stolen painting," a voice says from right behind me. My shriek of surprise echoes back at me as I spin around and come face-to-face with a scowling sheriff. Well, not quite face-to-face, because he's several inches taller than I am. My eyes are more in line with his mouth.

"Didn't you see the crime scene tape?" he asks. It sounds like he's already decided I saw the crime scene tape and ignored it, so I don't bother answering. Besides, I'm distracted by the sheriff's—Dominic's, I correct myself—lips. I'm remembering what those lips were doing last night.

Sneaking a peek at Dominic's eyes does nothing to help me focus. He's so close I can see those beautiful flecks of copper in their chocolate depths.

"I tried to stop her, Sheriff," CC calls out. I peer around the sheriff to see CC and Kyle on the other side of the crime scene tape.

"Traitor," I hiss at her, returning my attention to the angry man in front of me. He appears to be silently counting to ten. It's taking a really long time. I read his lips to see what number he is on. It looks like "vudy-boo." Huh, that isn't even a number; no wonder it's taking so long.

"Why are you here? At my crime scene," Dominic asks through gritted teeth. Evidently, he's given up on counting to calm himself.

"CC told Kyle we would come back to see Pierre's paintings. We didn't get much of a chance to see them last night. What with the crime and all." I gesture to CC, trying to deflect the sheriff's anger, but he's still focused on me. Casting about for another distraction, I ask almost desperately, "Do you have any leads on the missing painting? Has it been recovered? Any suspects?" I was instrumental in solving the last crime. He probably needs my help this time, too. His expression darkens further. None of the smoldering looks from last night in sight.

"You are not a detective. Stay out of my investigation," he grits out. "Or I will arrest you." It doesn't sound like a threat. It sounds like a promise. In fact, it sounds like he would like to arrest me anyway. Deciding a strategic retreat is in order, I duck under the crime scene tape, grab CC, and bolt for the parking lot before handcuffs can become involved.

"What's the rush? What happened with the sheriff?" CC asks as I practically run to my car, dragging her along. I assume Kyle is following us, but I don't slow down long enough to check.

When I reach the relative safety of my car, I glance in my rear-view mirror to make sure Kyle is with us before I drive away. I continue ignoring CC's questions. Mostly because I don't want to think about, let alone talk about, "the sheriff" and "handcuffs" in the same sentence.

CC's pointed silence and even more pointed glances tell me she won't be letting this go. Dagnabbit! Can't she cut me some slack? I was almost arrested. Well, maybe not really, but I think I still deserve some slack.

Trying to avoid CC's interrogation, I bolt into her kitchen as soon as I park my car. For once, there are no children present. How could they all abandon me in my time of need? I've always been there for them.

Both kitchen doors swing open simultaneously CC comes through the one from the backyard and Ann comes through the one from the hallway. "Ann," I practically shout in relief, "how's your day going? Tell me everything." Ann's expression changes from surprised to thrilled. She loves bragging about her sports achievements.

"The Jenkins twins challenged me to a race, but even with a five-second head start, I still beat them both. Then Sammy challenged me to a rock skipping contest. His rock only skipped three times. Mine skipped six." I tune out the rest of her stories but feign interest to keep her talking. Luckily, she doesn't require a lot of encouragement. Suddenly realizing she's wrapping up her list of wins, I panic.

Just as Ann finishes, Dean enters the kitchen. "Dean," I practically shout in relief, "how's your day going? Tell me everything." I get a feeling of déjà vu, but Dean begins describing the complicated system of pulleys, blocks, wind spinners, wooden arms, and various other items that reaches from the wooden play structure to a spot behind the garage. According to Dean's description, once completed, it will push the swing so Eve won't need somebody to push her. Sadly, once he finishes describing his project, he heads to the backyard, presumably to keep working on the swing-pushing contraption. I hope it turns out better than the omelet maker. Eve might not survive a swing-pushing machine gone wrong.

"Don't think I don't know what you're doing," CC tells me, placing, carrots, celery, butter, a container of chicken stock, two huge bags of noodles, a container of shredded chicken, a block of cheese, and two loaves of bread on the counter. "Once lunch is over, we're going to discuss everything." It sounds a little threatening, especially since she's holding a large knife that she's using to slice the vegetables. At least I have some time to come up with a plan to avoid the discussion.

Sadly, even though making lunch took time, I'm unable to come up with a plan to avoid the discussion. All too soon, the children and Jake finish their lunch, leaving CC and me alone in the kitchen. I think about making a run for it while she's clearing the table, but dismiss the idea. She would just hunt me down.

CC returns with a glass of lemonade for each of us. Settling across from me, she looks at me expectantly. The silence stretches out uncomfortably.

"So, what's going on with you and the sheriff?" she asks, breaking the silence.

"I don't know," I tell her honestly. "I mean, nothing changed until last night. You've seen us when he hangs out with Jake and when he comes to dinner and such. Nothing was different. I saw him around town a couple of times after the incident at Mr. Johnson's, but it was all normal. And then we went on that one disastrous date a couple of weeks ago. Who knew shirts were so flammable these days?"

"I still can't believe he took you to a hibachi grill. You would think he would have more self-preservation instinct than that," CC muses with a pointed look. I glare at her, but have to admit to myself that I agree. There had been way too many incidents resulting in injury to him to make choosing somewhere with an open flame a smart idea.

"What do you think changed?" I ask CC, hoping she has more insight than I do.

"You haven't seen him since the date?" she asks.

"Not really. I've kind of been avoiding him since then," I admit. "I saw him walking his puppy once, and then there was the time I accidentally rammed his cart at the store. Also, the time I almost hit him with my car at Bake My Day. But every time, I ran away before he could say anything. And I haven't seen him at all for the last week or so." I try to remember if those were all the near meetings, but I decide it doesn't matter. They were near meetings, not actual meetings.

"He acted like you two were seeing each other. And I mean dating, not chance sightings." She wiggles her eyebrows at me suggestively.

"Who's dating?" Jake asks, coming in the back door. I didn't even realize he'd gone outside.

"Sheriff," CC answers him, looking surprised. That seems odd. Why would she be surprised? We were talking about it for some time.

"CC, Claire." The sheriff's warm voice washes over me. I close my eyes, trying to control my rioting emotions. When I feel a large body slide onto the banquette next to me, my emotions riot even harder. My breathing also turns erratic, my pulse skyrockets, and I feel warm all over. I still am not brave enough to open my eyes and face the sheriff. (I need to get used to thinking of him as Dominic, especially if we are going to be kissing.)

"We are going to be kissing?" Dominic whispers hopefully in my ear, as if he didn't threaten me with arrest mere hours ago.

"I didn't mean to say that out loud," I admit, still with my eyes tightly closed.

"You don't mean to say half of what you say out loud." Dominic keeps whispering in my ear, causing me to shiver. "It's one of the things I like about you." My eyes fly open, and I turn my shocked gaze on him. He is so close that my nose all but brushes his.

"You do? You like that I can't keep my inner thoughts in?" I ask, shocked.

"I always know what you're thinking, and since your thoughts are more jumbled than Eve's toy box, I appreciate the insight." His eyes are warm on mine, and a smile lurks at the corners of his mouth. A mouth that is very close to mine.

"Why are you so close to each other?" Eve asks from across the table. Snapping out of the hypnotic state Dominic's presence put me in, I whip my head around and stare at Eve. She's standing on the chair where CC was sitting when Dominic arrived. I briefly wonder where CC went and when she left.

"I thought I had something in my eye," I boldly lie to Eve. I silently congratulate myself on my quick thinking.

"Maybe I should check again," Dominic says wickedly.

"It's better now," I say without bothering to look at him. "Where's your mom?" I ask Eve, perhaps a little desperately. Being alone with Dominic isn't safe. Although we were in a room full of people last night, and it didn't stop him.

"I don't know," Eve answers. "I want a cookie."

That came out of nowhere, I think, but now I want a cookie, too.

"Well, you're in luck," Dominic says, opening a box on the table in front of him.

When did that get here? I think. Dominic's private smile makes me realize I said it out loud, so I continue, "Are you a witch? Or would it be a warlock?"

"My grandma made these just for you-all." Dominic nudges the box toward me, and I grab a chocolate chip cookie. Then he turns the box toward Eve. As she carefully selects her M&M cookie, Frank, Ann, Kyle, Dean, and Jane spill into the kitchen ahead of Jake and CC. They are each holding at least one pumpkin.

I suddenly remember today is pumpkin carving day! "This is going to be so fun!" I say happily.

"This is so thoughtful of Rose," CC gushes. "If you see her first, please thank her for us." She smiles warmly at Dominic.

Geez, she is such a kiss-up. I show my displeasure at her by scowling at her. I also grab another cookie, beating Eve to the chocolate-dipped shortbread. I figure CC deserves a tantrum, and I can just take my cookie home and put in my earplugs. Eve's puckered Kewpie-doll lips look like they are about to open to emit eardrum-rupturing screams.

"Eve, this one has rainbow sprinkles," Dominic says. She immediately snatches it, smiling happily at him. I scowl as I chew the last of my cookie. How is he so good at preventing Eve's tantrums? I wonder. He's still new here, and Eve is not an easy child. I've often wondered if "Eve" is short for "Evil." I consider slipping away to my house to muse on my confusing thoughts, but Dominic's large, muscular body is blocking my escape. Plus, I want to carve my pumpkin.

Once everybody has their pumpkin in front of them, the carving begins. I spend the next hour or so engrossed in carving. I go classy and save my pumpkin's guts so I can make it look like it's vomiting.

Finally finishing my pumpkin, I look around to see what everyone else has carved. Frank and Ann went with the classic smiling jack-o'-lantern. Kyle has somehow both carved and scraped the top layer of skin off of his pumpkin to make an impressively realistic Frankenstein's monster face. Jane carved her pumpkin to look like an owl. Dean's pumpkin has several googly eyes stuck to it above a sharp-toothed smile, and wires arching over the top. He's somehow rigged it so that a visible electric current jumps from one wire to the other. It's very impressive. Eve, who isn't allowed to use a knife, told Jake how to carve her pumpkin. However, she lost interest halfway through, and Jake had to finish on his own. I just hope he didn't mess it up. Eve will be mad if he did. Dominic has carved a traditional jack-o'-lantern face, but he turned his pumpkin on its side to use the stem as a nose.

"Not bad," I say grudgingly. He just smiles at me. With the carving completed, the kids take their pumpkins to their porch. I carry mine to my porch and carefully place it so the vomiting guts spill off the step. Stepping back to admire my work, I realize Dominic has placed his pumpkin on the other side of my steps.

I don't know how I feel about this level of intimacy, I think. Wait, I said it. I close my eyes in mortification. Dominic wraps his arms around me and pulls my stiff body into his. "It's just a pumpkin," he tells me. "I can think of far more intimate things." I shiver. Both at the feel of his breath against my ear, and also at my thoughts about what those more intimate things might be.

I don't know how long we would have stood there, but we're interrupted by Dean.

"Sheriff, do you want to see my swing pushing invention? It isn't done yet, but I'm getting close." His hopeful expression is hard to resist.

"I'd love to," Dominic says, releasing me to follow Dean. I practically bolt for the safety of my kitchen.

I press my back to the closed door as if keeping an invading horde from entering. Benji appears, wagging his tail and proudly presenting me with my TV remote. I sink to the floor and allow Benji to climb into my lap. I find his presence a comfort and a distraction from my thoughts.

Some unknown time later, the door I'm still leaning against thumps as if someone is trying to open it.

"Auntie Claire? The door is stuck. Are you okay?" Jane calls through the door.

"I'm fine," I say, climbing to my feet and opening the door.

"Dinner's ready," she says, eyeing me with concern. I follow her silently back to CC's now pumpkin-free kitchen. The rest of the family joins me at the table, and everybody fills their plates with pork chops, roasted vegetables, and applesauce. Jane manages to snatch the steak knife Eve was reaching for and place it out of reach. Eve frowns, but when Jane scoops a large serving of applesauce into a bowl and hands it to her, she happily digs in.

Ann and Dean vie for Dominic's attention. They talk over each other about inventions and sports competitions, not allowing anybody else to get a word in. I've heard all this before, so I tune them out. Instead, I contemplate deep thoughts while eating. Why has Dominic been avoiding me? Why did he stop avoiding me? Does he really like my T-shirts, or was he just saying that he liked them?

"I wasn't avoiding you. I had to go back to the city for a week. Besides, you kept running away. Now I'm back. And I love your T-shirts," Dominic says. Dagnabbit, I wasn't thinking, I was speaking. My embarrassed gaze flies around the room seeking a distraction, but CC and her whole family are gone. It's like they could teleport, and they decided to use this magical skill to abandon me in my time of need. I didn't even notice them finishing their dinner. How long was I musing?

A bang on CC's back door causes Dominic to slide out of the banquette and assume what I can only describe as a battle-ready pose. I frown. Why is he so jumpy? If he's going to hang around me, he'll have to get over that; loud noises and disasters seem to follow me. Seeing Benji appearing and disappearing in the door's glass, he relaxes his stance and opens the door for him. (Benji can't open CC's doors like he can mine, because she has doorknobs and not the lever-style handles I have.)

"I suppose it's an ingrained response to my time in the military," he answers. Either I spoke my thoughts out loud, or he can read my mind. Since CC keeps saying nobody's reading my mind, and it's always me saying my thoughts out loud, I assume I said them. I'm about to ask about his time in the military when I spot what Benji is proudly presenting to Dominic.

"Benji," I hiss, sliding out of the banquette and trying to snatch his prize before Dominic can accept it. I fail. Dominic takes my red lace bra from Benji. The same red lace bra Benji presented to him a few months ago.

"I have fond memories of this," Dominic says, smiling wolfishly at me. I have memories of that bra, too. Mine are more embarrassed and less fond. That bra was a contributing factor in the unfortunate testicle-punching incident. As if remembering that part, Dominic shifts uncomfortably. Taking advantage of his distraction, I snatch the bra from his hand.

"Well, it was nice to see you again, but I have to go," I lie as I bolt out the back door, across CC's and my yards, and into my kitchen. I lean against the closed door and try to regain my composure. It doesn't work.

Chapter 6

Despite the sun shining through my curtains, I remain in bed. Sleep was a struggle last night. I spent most of the night replaying everything that happened with Dominic, my feelings about everything that happened, what I hoped might happen, and what I feared might happen. I'm a complex person with complex thoughts. I debate the pros and cons of staying in bed forever.

Pros: Nobody would hear my inner thoughts become spoken words. Benji could fetch me whatever I need. My bed is comfortable. I've already staked a claim, so Agatha and Blackbeard can't claim the whole bed. I wouldn't have to face Dominic again.

Cons: Benji isn't reliable with fetching helpful items. My bed doesn't have a coffee maker. I would eventually miss CC and her family. I wouldn't see Dominic again.

A knock on my partially open bedroom door surprises me. Nobody knocks on my door. They always just barge in. I'm too shocked to say anything. I watch as the door slowly swings open, revealing Dominic. Now I'm even more shocked.

"I did knock," he says. "Benji let me in. I would have rung the doorbell, but I remember how much Agatha hates that." Well, that's true. The doorbell causes her to bay like a thousand hell-hounds. Besides her snoring all night, it's the only sound she makes. When I still don't say anything, he continues. "CC sent me to get you. Breakfast is ready." We stare at each other silently for several seconds before my brain finally starts working again.

"What? Why? What?" Okay, maybe my brain still isn't working.

"CC was worried you hadn't come for coffee yet, so she sent me to get you," he answers, as if that made sense.

"Why were you at CC's for breakfast?" I finally manage to form a coherent question.

"She invited me." As if that answers my question. He pushes off the doorframe he was leaning on and stalks toward me. My brain once again shuts down. There are no thoughts in my head at all.

"Are you going to get up? Or should I join you?" he asks wickedly. This kick-starts my fight-or-flight instincts. Luckily, I choose flight, so Dominic is unlikely to be injured. I jump out of my bed on the far side with only a slight stumble as my feet briefly tangle in my sheets. Keeping the mattress between us seems like a good idea until I see his eyes darken to that smoldering look they do so well. Deciding that a room without a bed is a better idea, I practically bolt out of my bedroom and down the stairs. I'm already at my back door when I hear him coming down the stairs behind me.

His laughter follows me across CC's and my yards, but I reach the relative safety of CC's kitchen without further embarrassment. That is, until I realize I'm wearing my bear-bottom pajamas. They have a picture of a bear with the word BOTTOM printed below it across my bottom. I close my eyes in mortification and swear I will never wear them again, even though they were a gift from Nell.

Sliding into the banquette so the picture is hidden, I pretend nothing is wrong. My bright-red face is harder to hide. The table is filled with an impressive array of breakfast foods: eggs, toast, English muffins, sausage, bacon, and hash browns. There's also a cup of coffee in front of my place. I take a big swallow, using the mug to hide my still-flaming face. When Dominic slides into the banquette next to me, I squirm in embarrassment.

"Why are you late?" Eve asks, shoving a whole piece of bacon in her mouth.

"I slept in," I mumble. "It *is* Sunday." I emphasize the word is to highlight how ridiculous her question is.

"I thought you were dead," I'm touched by her concern. "Too bad. Now I can't have Benji," she finishes.

I'm no longer touched. "You spend way too much time hoping for my death," I tell her, glaring. She ignores me and keeps shoving bacon in her mouth until CC moves the plate away from her. I manage to snag a couple of pieces as she passes the plate to Dominic.

"Any news of Pierre's painting?" Kyle asks hopefully. His wire-rimmed glasses are askew, and he has a smear of what I guess is peanut butter across one cheek. I look around, but don't see any peanut butter. Not for the first time, I wonder how he gets so messy.

"I can't discuss an ongoing investigation," Dominic answers, but then shakes his head, indicating there's no news. Kyle wilts slightly, but doesn't comment further. He returns his attention to his ever-present sketch pad. I wish I could see what he's drawing, but since he's across the table from me, I'm left wondering.

Something brushes my foot under the table. I sneak a peek to see which of Jane's pets it is. "Meg!" I exclaim happily to the adorable chocolate merle puppy now chewing on my foot. Jane found an Australian Shepherd mix a couple of months ago, and the dog promptly gave birth to five puppies. Meg was my favorite from the very first day, but Jane gave her to Dominic. I still haven't forgiven her. It doesn't matter that I already have two dogs. Or that I didn't want the hassle of training a puppy. It's the principle of the thing.

"Come here, baby," I croon as I awkwardly hoist Meg into my lap. I may have bumped my head on the table, but Dominic's hand cushions the blow, so it doesn't hurt me too much. His sucked-in breath and shaking of his hand indicate it might have hurt him, though. I ignore his theatrics because I have an adorable puppy licking my face, so nothing else matters.

"Claire, not at the table," CC admonishes while she begins clearing dishes. Since Dominic is blocking the near side, I would have to scoot all the way around the table to get out, so I ignore CC. Dominic reaches over and scratches Meg behind one ear.

This feels suspiciously like a family, I think. Wait, no, I said it. Shoot! Feeling Dominic's body vibrate with suppressed laughter, I decide that scooting all the way around the table isn't such a bad idea after all. I begin scooting. It's even harder because I'm holding a squirming puppy set on licking my face, but I manage it.

"I think Meg needs to go outside," I say as I beat a hasty retreat. I breathe a sigh of relief, having escaped Dominic and my embarrassment. My relief is short-lived, as Dominic joins me in CC's backyard. Meg is happily running around amongst the flowerbeds, sandbox, various bird and squirrel feeders, and a discarded bike.

"If I didn't know better, I'd think you were trying to avoid me," Dominic says, managing to snag my arm before I can move out of reach. He reels me in like a fish and wraps his arms around me. "I think we need to discuss a few things," he says seriously.

"What things?" I ask suspiciously. Before he can answer, the baying of a thousand hellhounds fills the air.

"Agatha," we both say as I slip from his arms and hurry across the yards.

I don't bother closing the back door behind me as I grab my picnic-basket-shaped cookie jar and rush to the front door and Agatha. I reach into the jar and grab a dog biscuit. I wave it in front of her nose to get her attention. She snatches it from my hand and starts crunching it. Before she can resume her deafening howls, I toss a handful behind me. Agatha and Benji chase after the bouncing and rolling treats, each trying to eat as many as possible as quickly as possible.

Taking advantage of their distraction, I open my front door to see Pierre standing on my porch. I step out and close the door behind me to prevent Benji from deciding to present any gifts when he finishes his treats. Pierre's mouth is twisted in a way that implies he's unimpressed with my dog's welcome. However, the way he eyes my army of skeletons, posed like they are attempting to break into my house, makes me think they might also be the source of his disdain. I love Halloween and went all out with my decorations this year.

Seeing me, Pierre's face clears momentarily—until he takes in my pajamas, and once again his expression sours.

"Pierre," I say, surprised, "what are you doing here?"

"I could not go another minute without seeing your ..." Here he pauses, eyeing my pajamas again, before he forces out, "Beauty." His accent is thicker than I remember. Not knowing what to say, I remain quiet, possibly for the first time in my life. Apparently taking my silence for interest, he continues. "I was hoping you would do me the honor of joining me for dinner tonight."

"Tonight? Dinner?" I ask, struggling to form a coherent thought. I'm not sure what to say. "Has your painting been found?" I blurt out.

"No," he says with a mix of emotions. If I had to guess, I would say anger, sadness, frustration, and something I'm not sure of. "But dinner with a beautiful woman would lift my spirits in this time of darkness."

"Unfortunately for you, she already has plans with me," Dominic says from behind me. I glance over my shoulder to frown at him, but he is staring at Pierre, so he probably doesn't notice. Before Pierre can say anything, Dominic places his hand on my hip possessively. They engage in a staring contest, a silent battle of wills.

"What about tomorrow?" Pierre transfers his stare from Dominic to me.

"Sorry, we have plans," Dominic answers. Pierre clasps my hand, the one not holding the cookie jar, and raises it to his lips.

"Whenever you have time, I would be honored to have dinner with you." His goatee tickles my knuckles as he kisses the back of my hand. Before Dominic can snatch my hand away from Pierre, I pull free. I barely resist the impulse to wipe the back of my hand on my pajamas. Before either man can say anything else, a banging on the door behind Dominic distracts us.

Dominic opens the door before I can stop him. I fear a repeat of the red lacy bra incident, but Benji is holding one of my shirts. He looks at Pierre, then turns to present my shirt to Dominic. Accepting the shirt with a quick pat, Dominic reads it, and a smile twitches his lips. I manage a peek at the T-shirt's design. On it are a seal saying BOOOOOO! and the words SEAL OF DISAPPROVAL printed below.

"What a perfect shirt," Dominic says.

Realizing I never answered Pierre, I struggle to think of a way to let him down gently. Even if I wasn't dating Dominic—possibly dating Dominic, I correct my thoughts—I wouldn't be interested in Pierre.

I'm not sure *why* I'm not interested in Pierre. He is objectively good-looking, he has what should be a sexy French accent, and Kyle would love having another artist around, but Pierre makes my skin itchy. Worried I might be thinking out loud again, I cast a quick look at Pierre and Dominic. They are busy glaring at each other again, so I feel confident I haven't said anything yet.

"I have a pretty busy week, but if I have any free time, I'll let you know," I lie to Pierre. His disappointed expression causes a twinge of remorse. I'm worried I might have hurt his feelings. Out of the corner of my eye, I see Dominic's satisfied expression, so I elbow him sharply. There's no reason to rub salt in the wound.

"We have to go," Dominic tells Pierre with only a slight wince from my elbowing. Without further ado, he deftly steers me inside and firmly closes the door on Pierre. Luckily, Benji is fast, so he makes it inside before the door closes.

"I don't like him." Dominic frowns. "How did he know where you live?"

I take advantage of his distraction and scoot up the stairs to put on something less embarrassing than my bear-bottom pajamas. Returning downstairs, I'm surprised to see Dominic leaning against my kitchen counter. I'm further surprised to see him holding Blackbeard. Blackbeard isn't a fan of strangers, or people in general, and only likes attention on his terms. Also, he weighs about thirty pounds and is quite the armful. Luckily, Dominic is strong and appears to be able to handle him. Blackbeard glares at me through his slitted green eye, purring happily as Dominic absently scratches his chin.

Dominic smiles at my T-shirt. It has a picture of a steamer basket with two dumplings in it, and another one held in a pair of chopsticks. I'M ALL THAT AND DIM SUM is printed around the picture. At least somebody in my life appreciates my awesome T-shirts.

"Did you tell Pierre where you live?" he asks, leaning against the counter.

"No. I barely spoke to him. Not that it's any of your business." I fold my arms defensively across my chest.

"I think it *is* my business," he counters, stalking toward me. His heated gaze holds a promise of something I'm not sure I'm ready for. I back up until my back hits the wall behind me. Blackbeard finds himself pressed between our bodies when Dominic keeps walking. His angry grumble prompts Dominic to set him on the floor before bodily harm can occur. (I mean, bodily harm to us. I'm sure Blackbeard would come out without a scratch.)

"I think everything about you is my business," he continues as if we hadn't both been almost attacked by an angry panther. Most people call Blackbeard a house cat, but I'm not fooled.

Dominic leans closer in what I assume is preparation for kissing me. I panic. For once, my reflexes don't fail me, and I duck out of the way. Unfortunately for Dominic, while ducking away from his kiss, I manage to bump into his knee, causing it to buckle. I watch in horror as his face slams into the wall and he crumples to the floor at my feet. When I think of a sexy man at my feet, it looks nothing like this. In my imagination, it involves more worshiping and less swearing in pain.

"Oh, my gosh! Are you okay?" I ask, bending toward his prostrate form. I fight the urge to wring my hands helplessly. He is stretched out on my floor, holding one side of his face.

When he doesn't say anything, I drop to my knees beside him. "Let me see," I say, trying to pry his hand off his face so I can assess the damage. A slight tug of war ensues as I try to remove his hand, and he tries to keep it where it is. Finally wresting it free, I lean close to what I can now see is a rapidly discoloring eye. Not again, I think or say. (I have more important things to worry about than my inner thoughts escaping.)

I have horrible flashbacks to when I hit him with a door a couple of months ago. "Why does this keep happening to me?" I wail in despair.

"I think it keeps happening to *me*," Dominic clarifies. "You always seem to escape unscathed." Before I can jump up to get some ice for his swelling face, his large hand wraps around the back of my neck and pulls my lips to his. I forget everything except the feel of his mouth moving on mine.

We might have gone on kissing forever, but Benji barks sharply in my ear. Surprised to find myself draped over Dominic like a blanket, I turn to look at Benji. Dominic simply moves his lips to my neck.

Spotting what Benji has brought me, I jump to my feet. Based on Dominic's grunt of pain, my knee might have slammed into some part of him. I snatch up my red lace bra and hide it behind my back before Dominic can recover. Why does Benji keep bringing it to Dominic? How does he keep finding it? After the last time, I hid it in the back of my dresser drawer.

"I'll get you some ice," I say, scampering like a scared puppy to my freezer. I shove my bra in the freezer when I reach in to grab several ice cubes. I wrap the ice cubes in the towel I snatch off the counter and then turn to hand it to Dominic. He's still on the floor, although now he's sitting with his back pressed against the wall.

I eye him cautiously, remembering the other incident that occurred the last time I blackened his eye. Let's just say it involved punching and his testicles. His wince makes me think he is also remembering, or I said that out loud. Sighing heavily, he heaves himself to his feet and holds out a hand for the towel-wrapped ice.

"I really am sorry," I tell him. I carefully hand him the ice, trying to avoid further injury.

"I know," he says as he places the towel against his face. His uninjured eye stares at me intently. His expression could be lust, anger, or pain. Maybe all three.

"Oh, it's definitely all three," Dominic confirms. Darn inner thoughts need to stay in.

"Auntie Claire, Mom says you need to hurry or we'll be late." I look toward the voice and see Ann standing in my open back door. Her blond hair is in two no-nonsense French braids.

"Coming," I call, beating a hasty retreat. "Wait, late for what?"

"The Family Sports Festival," Ann calls over her shoulder.

CC and her whole family are gathered around the Mommobile, so Ann and I head that way. Ann joins CC, Jake, Kyle, Dean, and Eve as they load into the minivan.

Frank, Jane, and Dominic's puppy are already in my back seat. Benji, who I just now realize has followed me, jumps onto Frank's lap. Quickly sliding into the driver's seat, I crank the engine and smile as my baby rumbles to life. Putting the car in reverse, I start to back up, only to slam on the brakes when my passenger door opens. Dominic receives a glancing blow from the door as he slides in. I gape at him in shock.

"I thought I made a clean getaway. Are you following me?" I don't even bother to keep these thoughts in.

"Jake invited me to join the sports festival," he answers, as if that makes sense.

"It's the *Family* Sports Festival," I tell him, strongly emphasizing the word family. He just smiles at me, still holding the ice-filled towel to his eye.

We might have remained locked in a silent battle, but as CC's Mommobile pulls out, Eve yells, "Last one there is a rotten egg!"

Chapter 7

"You're a rotten egg," Eve declares as I pull in next to CC's Mommobile.

"I would have beaten you, but the sheriff kept threatening to write me a ticket for speeding and reckless driving," I tell her as I climb out of my baby. I give my sweet ride an affectionate pat on her roof to let her know I still love her, even though the sheriff wouldn't let me show her off.

"It wasn't a threat," Dominic says as he climbs out of my passenger seat. "You are a menace." He sounds angry, but before we can argue further, CC gasps.

"Sheriff, are you okay? Claire, what did you do to him?" she asks, rudely assuming I've done something. She's right, but it's still rude to assume it was my fault. She rushes toward him with worried-mom energy. Carefully removing the towel-wrapped ice, she scrutinizes his face. I can't help but wince when I get a good look at it.

"At least his eye isn't swelling shut like last time, although I suspect he'll be sporting a shiner by tomorrow." When everybody turns to look at me, I realize I've said my thoughts out loud, again. Before anybody can comment, I grab a folding chair from the back of CC's minivan and head to the fields. Benji trots along at my heels, and I assume CC and the rest of her family trail behind me. If there were any mercy in this world, Dominic would stay by the cars. Or better yet, leave.

"No such luck," Dominic says from my left side. "You're stuck with me." I ignore him, mostly because I don't have an intelligent reply. The silence doesn't have time to get awkward as people start calling out greetings.

"Claire, sweetie, so nice to see you," Angelica Garza says as she comes toward me. She is several inches shorter than I am, but her strong presence makes her seem taller. Her dark hair is pulled back in a French braid. Streaks of silver in her hair reflect the sun, only adding to her beauty.

"Sheriff Armstrong, what a pleasant surprise. I didn't expect to see you here today," she says, turning toward him with a warm smile. "Is your eye all right?" she asks, in concern, before casting me an accusatory look. I don't know why everybody assumes I'm to blame. I'm starting to find it a little annoying.

"It's fine, just a little bump," he tells her. "I wouldn't miss the Family Sports Festival." He casually drapes his arm around my shoulder. Angelica's eyes and her smile widen at the move. I can almost hear the gossip mill revving up.

"Well, I hope you have fun," she says, practically sprinting off to share her news. My shoulders slump when I see she's run to Missy. Missy has been the biggest gossip in town since we were in middle school together. Dominic just tightens his grip, pulling me closer as we begin walking again.

"You know the whole town will be talking about us, right?" I ask him as he propels me on.

"I'm pretty sure they already were," he says with a lack of concern. I risk a glance at his face. He's left the ice in the car, so I have an unobstructed view of his discolored eye. Luckily, it doesn't look swollen, so it probably won't affect his depth perception.

I notice a lot of people are looking our way and then talking amongst themselves. Before anybody can work up the courage to approach me for further gossip, the mayor uses a megaphone to address the crowd.

"Welcome, everybody, to the seventy-sixth annual Family Sports Festival." He drones on about community involvement and family values, but having heard this speech every year for as far back as I can remember, I tune him out. A polite round of applause from the crowd draws my attention back to the present.

"Come on," Ann says, appearing at my side and dragging me out from under Dominic's arm. "The hula hoop contest is starting soon. You can't be late." I quicken my pace, partly to keep up with Ann, and partly because I'm excited. I'm very good at hula hooping. I've won every year since I was thirteen. My victory is assured.

"Are you ready to lose?" I taunt the other hula hoopers while readying my hoop at my waist. Even though most of my competitors are children and teens, I plan to crush them. Before any more trash talk, the starting whistle blows, and we all begin to gyrate, keeping our hoops circling our waists.

A few participants' hoops immediately fall around their ankles, disqualifying them. As the minutes pass, more and more hoops hit the ground. Finally, the second-to-last hoop falls, and I whoop in victory. Ann jumps up and down in a circle around me, sharing my joy.

"I enjoyed watching that," Dominic says with a lascivious smile as the crowd disperses, heading for the next contest. Since it's a relay race, I'm not in this event. Running isn't my thing. I join the spectators to cheer on Ann, Jake, Frank, and Kyle.

Ann starts the first leg of the race. She's miles ahead of the other runners. Okay, it's probably only several yards, but it's still an impressive lead. She passes the baton to Jake, who maintains the lead. He might even add more distance between himself and the second-place runner. Frank gets the baton next. He loses some of their lead, but he's racing against the track star, so that's to be expected.

I'm screaming encouragement as I jump up and down beside Dominic. Unfortunately for him, on one of my jumps I land on his foot. His grunt of pain is mostly lost in the cheers from the crowd.

Kyle shoots across the finish line with an amazing show of speed. Most people discount his athleticism because of his quiet, artistic nature and his messy appearance, but the kid can run!

Ann's victory dance is epic. She won whatever athletic contest she was in, so she had a lot of practice with her victory dance. She's still dancing when the crowd and I walk away and head to the field where the tug-of-war ropes are lined up for the next contest.

Teams of four find their places amongst the ropes. Angelica, her husband Luis, their daughter Tessa, and son Rick grab one end of a rope, and Jane, Dean, Jake, and I grab the other. Just as the whistle blows, starting the contest, I see Jake standing next to CC. Then who's behind me?

I don't have time to wonder since the whistle blows and we all start tugging the rope. We are slowly dragging Angelica and her family closer to the line. With one final heave, we drag them over it.

The sudden slack in the rope causes us all to tumble in a heap. Like dominoes, Jane falls into Dean, who falls into me, knocking me back onto a large male body. I know that body. It's Dominic. Luckily for me, he cushions my fall. Unluckily for him, he cushions my fall. I'm surprised he isn't yelling at me for crushing him.

When I scramble to my feet, I realize he isn't yelling because I knocked the wind out of him, and he can't suck in a breath. Not waiting for him to recover enough to be able to yell at me, I hurry off to grip the rope for round two.

Dominic recovers his breath enough to join our team. He looks like he wants to say something, probably not anything nice or flattering, but before he can say whatever is on his mind, all the people who won round one begin squaring off for round two. We repeat this process until only one team is victorious. Fortunately, I manage to refrain from causing further injury to Dominic. Also, we win.

Next up is the wheelbarrow race. Frank and Eve are lined up with several other pairs. We might lose this one. Eve is only two and unlikely to be a good wheelbarrow. It might be nice to let somebody else win one, I muse. When the whistle blows to start the race, Eve moves her tiny arms like a windmill. She is practically a blur as Frank races behind her, holding her ankles firmly. My mouth drops open in shock. How could somebody so tiny contain such strength? She's never been a typical child; maybe this is just another example of her being abnormal. I've often wondered if we should be more concerned about her uniqueness. Have her tested or something. I don't have time to worry because, within seconds, Eve and Frank cross the finish line while the other teams struggle in behind them, or simply lie in the grass in defeat. So far, our family is having a clean sweep of events.

There's a brief pause in the competition as spoons and eggs are handed out. Once everybody is ready, the whistle blows, and a terrier mix holding a spoon in his mouth with an egg balanced on it streaks across the field. Wait, that's *my* terrier mix. I thought Jane was entering this one. I didn't even know dogs were allowed to compete in these events!

Not surprisingly, Benji crosses the line first. Surprisingly, he still has the egg balanced on his spoon. Which is more than I can say for several of the racers. Luckily, they're fake eggs, so we don't have any raw egg mess to worry about. We all learned our lesson the year the Jenkins twins got into a disagreement about which one of them would be racing. In their anger, they started throwing eggs at each other. The eggs not only hit the Jenkins twins but also several bystanders. By the time their mom got hold of them, there weren't any eggs left for the race. But there were several angry egg-covered people.

There's a brief break in the events, allowing everybody to get a drink and a snack. I head over to CC for my snack. She is such a good mom, always prepared. She hands out bananas, peanut butter crackers, string cheese, and juice boxes. Huh, not *my* idea of a snack. Once CC's kids get their snacks, she hands me a bag of chocolate-covered pretzels. Much better, I think, happily munching on my snack.

"I can't believe Nell is missing this," I say. "Why couldn't she come back? She's only an hour away. This is important. It's the

Family Sports Festival, and not all of our family is here." I get a little misty-eyed thinking of Nell so far from me. I know it's only been a couple of months and she's visited often, but it's not the same without her.

Dominic wraps his arms around me from behind and rests his chin on my head. "Don't worry, she'll be here next weekend for the Halloween party," he comforts me. How does he know so much about the kids? I wonder. First Kyle's murals, and now Nell's schedule. He's really inserting himself into our family. I frown as I contemplate my feelings on this. Deciding my feelings are too complex to contemplate in the middle of the Family Sports Festival, I finish my pretzels and accept the lemonade CC holds out to me.

Hearing the announcement for the three-legged race, I try to shrug out of Dominic's arms to head to the starting line. I'm unsuccessful, so we both head to the starting line. I get a little teary-eyed remembering all the years Nell and I won this race. Who will fill her place? When Dominic ties my left leg to his right leg, I realize he plans to fill her place, at least in the race. He once again wraps his arm around me. This time, I also wrap my arm around him.

"Okay," I say, "it's very important to synchronize our movements. I know we haven't known each other long, but you seem to be able to read my mind, so focus. These contests mean the world to Ann. Plus, she's mean when she doesn't win."

I prepare myself for the whistle. As soon as I hear it, I move my outside leg. Unfortunately, Dominic moves his inside leg. We almost go down, but he manages to catch us both. "Inside leg," he barks. Following his lead, I move my inside leg. "Outside. Inside. Outside. Inside," he chants as we move across the field, catching up to the other racers.

Within seconds, we are in the middle of the pack racing across the field. A few more seconds, and we have passed all but one pair. Closing in on them, Dominic starts chanting faster, and we move our legs faster to match the pace of his words. At the last second, we pull ahead and win!

"We did it!" I yell in victory. Dominic wraps his other arm around me and kisses me. He kisses me right there in front of the whole town. If they weren't talking about us before, they are now. I don't know how long we would have put on a show if Ann hadn't jumped onto us, nearly knocking us down. Fortunately, Dominic manages to keep us upright. I think we have given the town enough to talk about. I don't think the busybodies could survive us rolling around in the grass together.

"I thought you were going to lose for sure," Ann shouts, "but you managed it. We are undefeated!" She gives Dominic a quick hug before darting off.

"Huh, I guess I was just a sack of potatoes and Dominic did all the work," I grumble, frowning after Ann. She follows the crowd to the sack race track. I don't know that Jane will be able to keep up our winning streak. She's not very competitive and is easily distracted, especially by animals. I briefly worry for her if she lets Ann down, but realize she has survived this long … Besides, she has a couple of years and several inches on Ann. Also, CC will probably step in if it gets out of hand.

Dominic doesn't seem to be in any rush to join the crowd. Deciding on safety in numbers, I head to the sack race course. Sadly, I forget that I'm still tied to Dominic's leg, and I'm pulled up short. He's so solid it's like being tied to a tree.

"If I didn't know better, I'd think you were trying to get away from me," Dominic murmurs in my ear.

A cheer from the sack races kicks me into gear. Reaching down, I tug at the knot until it gives way. I casually saunter toward the crowd. Just kidding—I run away. If this had been a race, I would have won. Spotting CC, Jake, and their kids, I head that way. Since Ann is still smiling, I assume Jane won. Turning to congratulate her, I'm surprised to see her holding a young fox. I mean, if anybody was going to have a fox, it would be Jane, but I'm still surprised she found one in the middle of The Family Sports Festival, and apparently, while winning the sack race.

I don't have time to ask her about the fox before I'm swept along by the crowd to the obstacle course. Ann is already at the starting line. She is bouncing with barely contained excitement. The other competitors don't look nearly as excited. In fact, Ms. Fitzpatrick's oldest grandson looks like he might cry. I wonder how many times Ann has beaten him at whatever he thought he was good at. Ms. Fitzpatrick is trying to console him while also encouraging him, but we all know Ann is going to win. I can count on one hand the number of times she has lost at any athletic endeavor in her ten years of life.

Ann flies across the course. She takes the monkey bars two at a time, scales the climbing wall like most people climb stairs, crawls through the tunnel so fast that if I'd blinked, I would have missed it, crosses the balance beam as if she were an Olympic gymnast, clears the low jumps without even breaking stride, and runs through the agility ladder as if it's not even there.

I'm glad it's not me. I'm one hundred percent sure I would have slipped off the monkey bars, never been able to scale the climbing wall, gotten stuck in the tunnel, fallen off the balance beam, caught a foot on the low jumps, tangled my feet in the agility ladder, and gone down like a ton of bricks. Ann makes it look effortless. She finishes the race a full obstacle ahead of her closest competitor. Once more, she celebrates with a victory dance.

The crowd drifts toward the basketball court while she finishes her dance. Dean and several others are warming up with some dribbling. Dean's dribbling is uncoordinated, and he has to chase after his ball a couple of times before the competitors form a line starting at the free-throw line. One by one, everybody shoots the basketball at the hoop. Those who make a basket move to the back of the line. Those who miss are out.

After several rounds, it's down to Rick, the star of the high school basketball team, and Dean. Dean looks like he's running calculations in his head. He probably is. He's told me several times that it's all a matter of determining the force, trajectory, and some other math terms I can't remember.

After several more rounds where neither of them misses, Rick's ball bounces off the hoop. Ann rushes onto the court, hugging Dean. With only one more contest to go and our family having won all the others, we are assured first place again!

CC and Kyle are already standing at one end of the horseshoe pits. I'm not allowed to play horseshoes after the unfortunate incident involving Old Tom's squad car and a stray horseshoe. Hey, anyone could hurl a horseshoe thirty feet off course.

Deciding to forgo the excitement of watching horseshoes fly, I head to my folding chair and flop down. Folding chairs are not meant for flopping, and mine tips precariously. It's touch and go until I manage to regain my balance. Jane is seated near me with her new fox friend and Dominic's puppy, Meg, curled at her feet.

"Where's Benji?" I ask her. Jane gestures toward a group of young kids kneeling in a circle on the grass. In the middle of the circle is Benji. He alternates between performing tricks for the delighted children and shamelessly offering his belly for belly rubs.

"Claire, long time no see," Missy says as she stops in front of me. Her sharp gray eyes take in every detail. I panic. If Missy is talking to me, she's seeking more gossip. Before I can say or do something embarrassing, she continues, "It's nice to see the sheriff having fun and joining the community." I can tell she's fishing for gossip.

"Yeah," I answer, before realizing I don't know what to add. Deciding that saying nothing is for the best, I zip my lips. The silence drags on for approximately three seconds before I blurt out, "He seems to be enjoying himself."

"I am," Dominic says, seating himself in the chair next to me and lacing his fingers through mine.

Missy's delighted smile tells me she found the gossip she was looking for. "We were all so impressed with how you handled that incident at Mr. Johnson's a couple of months ago." She keeps fishing. "Claire was so lucky you were there to save her."

My mouth drops open in outrage. He didn't save me! I would have made a clean getaway if he hadn't blocked my exit. Remembering the door-to-his-temple incident that followed, I wince. I decide to keep my lips zipped, hoping he won't remember that part of the night.

"I'm just glad I was able to stop a dangerous individual," Dominic says. Foolish man, any response only whets her appetite. Wait, was the murderer and kidnapper the dangerous individual, or was I? I'm distracted by the feel of his thumb rubbing circles on my hand and almost don't hear Missy's next question.

"I heard you were in the city for a week. I hope everything's okay?" She's *still* fishing for information.

"Everything's fine. I was visiting an old friend and his wife to meet their new baby," he answers. It's like he doesn't even want to try to keep his private life private.

"Oh, that's wonderful! Catching up with friends is so important." Her eagle-eyed gaze scrutinizes him, cataloging and dissecting his response. It's as if she could determine exactly what happened during his visit. She probably could. She's very gifted at gossip. She's always accurate and usually the first to know everything.

"It was nice to catch up, but it also helped me put some things in perspective and make a decision," Dominic tells her with a private and heated look at me. Does he really have no idea who he's talking to? Missy is the queen of gossip, and he's just volunteering information.

I suddenly realize that this trip to visit an old friend and put things in perspective was probably about me, and that's why he's kissing me now. Huh, I don't know how I feel knowing he's talking to his friends about me. I'll have to talk to CC about it later.

Apparently satisfied that she's gotten all the good gossip on his personal life, Missy changes tactics. "We're all so shocked about that stolen painting at the museum. Have you found it yet?"

"I'm afraid I can't discuss an ongoing investigation," he tells her.

Before Missy can try to wheedle more information out of Dominic, his grandmother Rose walks up and stands right in front of me. Her long white hair is French braided and twisted into a coil at the back of her head. "You two can go get the other boxes from the van," she says, staring at me with her piercing brown eyes. I feel myself shrinking back from her. She purses her lips as she notices Dominic's and my joined hands.

Missy turns her attention to Rose. "Rose, how nice to see you. I was in Bake My Day a couple of weeks ago and tried your blackberry shortcake. It was delicious!"

"Thank you, I've been experimenting," Rose tells her, shifting the box in her hands. Dominic immediately stands to take it from her. He hands it to Jane and takes my hand once more. This time, he hauls me to my feet and leads me toward the parking lot, presumably to Rose's van. I miss the rest of Missy's interrogation, but I'm sure I'll hear all about it later through the grapevine.

We are silent while I contemplate what this public display of affection means to the gossip mill. What do people think of me dating the sheriff? Are we officially dating? Will the neighborhood kids start singing the "Sitting in a tree, K-I-S-S-I-N-G" song now?

"Kissing does sound like a good idea, but I think I'm too old for climbing trees," he says, backing me up against the van. I guess I wasn't silently contemplating after all. Then he kisses me, and I'm not contemplating anything.

A loud cheer from the horseshoe pits causes him to pull back. I remain leaning against the back of the van for support while Dominic opens the other door and hands me several boxes. He takes his own stack of boxes and slams the door without dropping any of them. I'm not sure I could have managed it. I can be a little klutzy.

As we head toward the tables already laden with chips, fruit, vegetables, buns, condiments, and every kind of salad known to man, I muse on the events of the weekend. A lot has happened in a short amount of time: Dominic has made his intentions toward me clear. Pierre's painting has been stolen. Pierre apparently has a crush on me. Kyle is painting murals for the city. Dominic has friends. His friends have babies. It's all a lot to take in.

Finding space for the boxes of cupcakes and cookies is a bit of a challenge, but we manage to squeeze them in. I also manage to snag a cupcake. Taking a huge bite, I moan in ecstasy. Rose is very good at baking. Dominic's gaze locks on my lips and darkens with what I'm coming to recognize as lust. Using his thumb, he brushes a bit of frosting off my mouth. He then sucks the frosting off his thumb. I've managed to swallow first, so I'm able to avoid another choking incident when my breathing becomes erratic.

A sudden cheer from the horseshoe pits signals the end of the final competition. What seems like the whole town descends on the food tables, loading plates and talking over and around each other, breaking the spell Dominic cast on me.

Joining the throng, I pile my plate to epic levels and beat a hasty retreat to my chair. CC, Jake, and their kids join me, settling into our group of chairs. Ann is busy recounting our winning moments so nobody else can get a word in.

"Will she ever stop?" A voice rudely interrupts Ann. Since everybody is looking at me, I guess it was my voice. Trying to backtrack, I continue, "I mean, how are people going to congratulate you if they have to interrupt you?" Not a great save in the grand scheme of things, but it seems to mollify Ann. She gazes around as if looking for fans. Spoiler alert, there aren't any.

The rest of our meal passes without incident, which, with me, is not always the case. A few people come to ask Dominic about the stolen painting and give him their two cents about what happened to it or who they think stole it. Mr. McIntyre suggests it was a shipping delay. He had a delay in his store's shipment of cereal recently. Mary thinks Pierre didn't paint it at all and was covering up his lie. A few more people have equally dumb ideas. Fortunately, I manage to keep my thoughts to myself this time, so I don't anger anybody.

As everybody finishes eating, the mayor announces that the kickball game will start in ten minutes. Most of the kids, and a few of the adults, head to the field. I join them. I love a good game of kickball. Rick is the captain of one team, and Frank is the captain of the other. Why don't I get to be captain? Nobody answers me, so I'm not sure if I kept my thoughts in or if they're just ignoring me.

Rick and Frank take turns picking teams from the assembled group. Rick chooses first and picks Ann. I frown at Frank when he chooses Dominic instead of me. After several more rounds where I'm still not picked, Rick finally selects me to join his team. Well, at least with Ann on my team, we're sure to win.

Our team does win, but it comes at the cost of Dominic's health. Let's just say one of us was the catcher and the other slid into home plate. The resulting collision caused a slight concussion. Luckily, the paramedics were at the Family Sports Festival, so Dominic got immediate medical attention. While Dominic was being treated, I managed to get CC and her family loaded into our cars and headed home. Some people might have called it fleeing, but I called it strategic retreating.

Chapter 8

The following day, as I stumble toward CC's kitchen and, more important, coffee, a stray thought permeates my caffeine-deprived brain.

"Why did Dominic have time to attend the Family Sports Festival?" I ask as I accept the mug of coffee CC holds out to me. "Pierre's painting is missing, presumably stolen, and he just spends the day at the park playing games. That doesn't seem very professional."

"It was Sunday, Claire. I think he's entitled to a day off," CC says, taking a drink of her coffee.

"When Mr. Johnson was killed, he didn't take a day off," I counter. "He dropped by my house or office, sometimes both, every day to ask questions."

"That was a murder investigation, versus a missing painting. I think there's a significant difference," CC counters right back. I ponder this as I snag the last breakfast burrito. CC's kids only left me one. They must have been hungry this morning. It still seems odd not to have to rush off to work on a school day, but I'm getting used to it.

"Do you really think Pierre's painting was stolen?" CC asks me. "I thought Mr. McIntyre made a good point yesterday. What if it's just a shipping mix-up?"

"I'm pretty sure the museum lady would have personally checked that the painting was hanging behind the curtain before she started the event. She doesn't seem like the kind of person to leave things to chance, or to others, for that matter. Maybe we should go ask her," I say, holding my mug out for a refill of coffee.

"I didn't think you would want to investigate. Last time you were very resistant," CC says, her expression wavering between confusion and judgment.

"I think I did a great job last time. I solved the murder, found Jamie, and rescued her. Maybe I should become a PI. I'd look great in a trench coat and fedora," I tell her. "But maybe we shouldn't tell Dominic we're investigating. I don't know if he'll appreciate our help. I recall a lot of yelling about staying out of his investigation the last time."

CC seems to be on the verge of telling me that we shouldn't investigate the missing painting. "I'm not sure we should investigate the missing painting," she says.

I knew it! This just goes to show I'd be a great PI. "Hurry up and get dressed," I say, finishing my coffee. CC looks unsure but heads upstairs without further comment. From past experience, I know it will take her hours to get ready. Well, not really hours, I concede, but I still have time for a third cup of coffee.

After draining my mug, I head home to get dressed. Blackbeard glares at me from my shower, so I turn it on a trickle for him. The weird cat loves to shower with me, but since I showered last night, I don't intend to shower this morning. He'll have to make do with the trickle.

Leaving him splashing about, I pull on worn jeans and another punny T-shirt. It has a picture of a turtle, and I MISS THE SHELL

OUT OF YOU is printed around it. I hope CC can appreciate this one. (It's perfect because the painting is missing, and the shirt says I MISS THE SHELL OUT OF YOU. I crack myself up.) CC usually ignores my epic shirts, though, so I doubt she'll appreciate it. Sometimes I wonder if she's really my best friend. Risking my health, I turn the shower off, leaving a disappointed Blackbeard licking himself dry.

Our trip to the museum is faster than the last time because we don't have to engage in small-town greeting etiquette. Most people are at work, so there are very few people out and about when we drive by. We also find a parking spot right up front because the parking lot is mostly empty. So far, it's a good Monday morning. I'm not sure what our plan should be, but I follow CC up the steps anyway.

She walks with confidence to the front desk and the little old lady manning it. "Ms. Clark, so nice to see you again. How's your grandson doing?" CC asks. Social niceties are a requirement in our town.

Ms. Clark smiles warmly at CC. "He's doing great! He scored three touchdowns in the last game," she says proudly.

"That's wonderful! He was always so talented," CC says as if the only reason we're here is to exchange chitchat with Ms. Clark. Oh, well, it will give me time to formulate a plan. "Did you hear about the stolen painting?" she asks, lowering her voice conspiratorially. Huh, I guess we aren't *just* here for chitchat.

"I did!" Ms. Clark says, also with a conspiratorially lowered voice. "It's just awful. Poor Pierre has been beside himself since it happened. It was his masterpiece. I heard he was supposed to sell it for a million dollars, but now it's gone. And so is his chance to get all that money. Can you imagine having a million dollars?"

This is news to me. I had no idea Pierre was so talented. Yikes— did I say that out loud? Glancing around, I realize Ms. Clark and CC are still chatting and ignoring me, so I guess not.

Silently congratulating myself, I almost miss what Ms. Clark says next. "Pierre is threatening to sue the museum for the theft."

"I guess that makes sense. I mean, the painting was in the museum's possession," I say. CC and Ms. Clark look at me with slightly accusatory expressions.

"A lawsuit would be terrible for the museum," Ms. Clark tells me, turning back to CC. "The museum doesn't have the budget for a big payout. It could ruin the museum. Ms. Swanson—that's the museum's executive director—," she adds to me before turning back to CC. (I don't know why I'm singled out for extra explanations. CC doesn't know the museum director either. Maybe old habits die hard, and she remembers all the times she's had to explain things to me like I'm simple-minded.), "has been worried sick. It took her months to get Pierre to agree to host a show here, and now this."

A commotion down the hall draws my attention. Pierre and the museum lady, who I now know is Ms. Swanson, are arguing. That's weird. The last time I saw them, they were speaking conspiratorially. At first, I can't hear what they're saying, but the argument progresses in intensity and volume until they are clearly audible.

"This is all your fault! I want my painting back now!" Pierre shouts at Ms. Swanson.

"This is *not* my fault." Ms. Swanson seems to realize they are drawing a lot of attention. "Can we discuss this privately?" she asks, looking around nervously.

"Why does she look so nervous?" I ask no one in particular.

"A painting was stolen from her museum, which was revealed in front of a crowd at the big opening, and she is facing a lawsuit that might shut down the museum. I think looking nervous makes sense," CC says in a tone that implies I'm simple-minded.

I shoot her a quick glare before transferring my attention back to Pierre and Ms. Swanson. Pierre storms away from her, toward us. I think he is going to walk right by, but he suddenly stops and turns. His expression morphs from angry to interested when his eyes meet mine. Normally, when I stand next to CC, I'm practically invisible to men, so I'm surprised to be the sole focus of his attention.

"You are a beacon of light on an otherwise gloomy day," he says as he raises my hand to his mouth to kiss my knuckles. I barely manage to prevent my nose from wrinkling at this unpleasant mannerism. I also manage not to wipe the back of my hand on my jeans, but it's close. Impulse control is not a strong suit of mine.

His eyes lose a bit of their heat when he takes in my shirt and jeans. I'm starting to think he only likes me in my princess dress. Boy, is he going to be disappointed. I very rarely wear princess dresses.

"Pierre, so nice to meet you. My son is a huge fan," CC says. "As am I," she adds hastily. Pierre spares her a glance before returning his attention to me.

"Have you come to accept my offer to join me for dinner?" he asks hopefully.

"No." I answer him a bit abruptly. Seeing something dark swirl in his eyes, I add, "Sorry, still busy. With my friend CC," I add, gesturing toward her, trying to deflect his focus.

It doesn't work; he's still focused on me. Normally, I appreciate attention, but there's something about Pierre that I find off-putting. Fearing I've spoken my thoughts out loud again, I take a quick glance at CC. Her still-friendly expression assures me I've kept my thoughts in. The silence is starting to drag on. Never a good thing. I tend to fill silences.

Thankfully, I'm saved by Ms. Swanson. She looks like she hasn't been sleeping well. She has dark circles under her eyes that her makeup doesn't hide, and her hair is coming out of what seems like a hastily constructed bun at the back of her head. Her clothes are also slightly wrinkled. She doesn't look as confident and put together as she did at the art show.

"Pierre, can we speak in my office?" she asks, joining our little group at the welcome desk.

"There is nothing further to discuss." He dismisses her without even looking at her. He's still focused on me. I start to fidget under his continued attention.

"Sweetheart, I brought you lunch," a good-looking man says, joining our group. I wonder who his sweetheart is. When he bends slightly to kiss Ms. Swanson's cheek, I decide she is probably his sweetheart.

Ms. Swanson smiles warmly at him before introducing him. "Darling, you remember Ms. Clark?" Not waiting for a response, she glances at CC and me, but apparently despite not even knowing us, decides we aren't important enough and don't warrant an introduction. Ignoring us, she turns to Pierre, and says with aplomb, "This is Pierre. Pierre, this is my husband, Ian. He's a huge fan of your work."

"Pierre, it is an honor to meet you. I saw your work in New York last year, and I was blown away. Your use of texture and color is incredible," Ian gushes. He reaches out to shake Pierre's hand. Pierre seems to struggle with whether to preen under the praise or be annoyed at the interruption to his flirting.

"I must have spent hours here admiring your work while Linda oversaw the exhibit's installation," Ian continues effusively. "Every time I looked at one of your paintings, I found something new to appreciate." This is turning into quite a Pierre love fest. "In fact, I convinced Linda to buy one of the paintings from the exhibit." Ian wraps an arm around Ms. Swanson while he speaks. "It's the one that looks like a field of flowers. I'd love to have more of them, but I don't want to be greedy. Right, dear?" He smiles congenially at Ms. Swanson and kisses her temple.

"Why did you agree to have your show here?" I interrupt. "I mean, it seems like Oak Creek is a huge step down from New York. I didn't even know our museum hosted shows like this." Five pairs of eyes land on me. The expressions range from shock to judgment to reproach.

Nobody seems to know what to say at first, but finally, Ms. Swanson recovers from her shock. "The museum is well known for the size and quality of its collection. Also, the building's historical significance adds to its prestige. We often use the large reception room to host fundraising events or highlight up-and-coming artists." Her expression implies she doesn't appreciate my criticism. "When I approached Pierre about hosting an exhibit, this museum was one of only a few museums I suggested, due to those factors."

"You're the executive director of multiple museums?" I ask in surprise. I guess that would explain why I didn't know her. In our small town, everybody knows everybody, and their kids, and their dog.

"Yes, I oversee three museums across two states," Ms. Swanson says, with more than a hint of pride.

Pierre, who seems to dislike being ignored for so long, joins the conversation. "Everybody should have the opportunity to view great art. If I allowed my art only to be exhibited in big cities like New York, it would be a travesty to the public." He looks at me as if expecting applause for his magnanimity. I refrain. "However, if I had known that my painting would be stolen, I never would have agreed. It was my masterpiece," he laments, in what I consider to be an exaggerated tone.

"What does it look like?" I ask, realizing I have no idea what the missing painting even looks like.

"It is incredible," Ian interjects. "It has every shade of green with vertical slashes of brown. It makes me think of hiking in the forest. When I look at it, I can almost hear the birds singing and the wind blowing through the leaves." Pierre puffs up with pride at hearing his work described with such reverence.

"I have a picture of it," Ms. Clark says, flipping through a brochure. "Here it is." She turns the brochure to face me. While the picture is small, I can see what Ian means. It does make me think of a peaceful day in the forest. It is both more and less realistic than Pierre's other paintings.

"It *is* incredible. All of your paintings are," I concede, causing Pierre to smile warmly at me. I manage to tuck my hands behind my back before he can clasp them again.

"How big is it?" I ask. Suddenly realizing he might take that inappropriately, I continue. "I mean, I know you paint a variety of sizes, so I was just trying to get an idea of scale."

"It is about eight feet by eight feet," he says.

"That seems pretty big to sneak out. Even if they removed it from the frame and rolled it up, it would be impossible to just walk out with it," I muse. "When was the last time the painting was seen?"

Ms. Swanson frowns at me. "Why are you asking? Who are you anyway?" she asks me in an accusing voice.

"She is a menace and a busybody who should stay out of police investigations," Dominic says, joining our group. I was right about him sporting a shiner today.

"Rude," I tell him, not even trying to keep my thoughts in. I glare at him, but when his gaze drops to my shirt and a slight smile twitches his lips, I forgive him. At least somebody appreciates my T-shirt; CC ignored it, just like I assumed she would.

"Excuse us," Dominic says, wrapping his long-fingered hand around my arm. He doesn't wait for a response; he just starts towing me away from the group. "Why are you butting into another one of my investigations?" he asks grumpily.

"I think I did a good job last time. In fact, without my help, you might not have solved the case or rescued Jamie," I defend myself, placing my hands on my hips. His jaw clenches as if he disagrees with my assessment.

"Now would be a good time to go home," he says with a glare, turning and walking back to the group still gathered around the information desk. I march after him, ready to give him a piece of my mind for his dismissive words.

"Pierre, Ms. Swanson, I have a few more questions for you both. Ms. Swanson, is there a more private area we can use?" Dominic asks.

"Wow, that sounds so professional. I'll have to remember that when I open my PI office." Once again, I find all eyes landing on me with expressions ranging from shock to judgment to reproach.

"I will arrest you," Dominic says, "if you even consider opening a PI office." He seems unsupportive of my new career choice.

When I don't reply, there's an awkward pause. I guess nobody knows what to say when a budding PI is threatened with arrest.

After several awkward seconds, Ms. Swanson seems to pull herself together and gestures down the hall. "Of course—right this way," she says. Dominic and Pierre follow her down the hall and disappear from view.

"Well, that could have gone better," I sigh. "I told you he probably wouldn't appreciate my help." CC wraps a supportive arm around me, but doesn't say anything.

"Do you think he will be able to recover the painting?" Ian asks us. I'm surprised he asked us. We've only just met. Plus, why isn't he asking if *I'll* recover the painting? I'm a crack PI after all. Well, an aspiring crack PI.

"I'm sure he will," CC reassures him, as if I weren't going to be the one solving the case. "He did a great job on his last investigation." For some reason, this doesn't elicit a relieved expression. Instead, I'd describe Ian's expression as concerned.

Mulling this over, I'm barely aware of CC steering me out of the museum. "Do you think Ms. Swanson had something to do with the theft?" I ask her as we settle into my car. "Her husband seemed concerned when you said Dominic would find the painting. Plus, rude that you didn't say I would find it." I glare at her to let her know I don't appreciate her lack of support. "And she's the one who convinced Pierre to have his exhibit at one of her museums. And she picked the museum. And she was the one in charge of setting up the exhibit. And she was the one who hired security. Who would question her moving about the museum?"

"Why would she risk her career for a painting from a new artist? If she was going to steal a painting from the museum, why not the Van Gogh that's on loan?" CC asks. These are excellent questions, I think, as I turn the ignition key. I smile when my baby rumbles to life, the engine vibrating the whole car. A few men nearby turn to stare at me admiringly. I smooth my messy brown hair back from my face, subtly preening. A thought that they might be admiring my car and not me intrudes, but I dismiss it. I take appreciation where I can get it.

I'm still musing over the little I know about the missing painting when I plunk myself down on a barstool in CC's kitchen. CC whips up a chicken wrap for each of us. I contemplate what I know while I eat my lunch.

"What do you think happened to the painting? Pierre seems to be acting suspiciously, but I don't see what he would gain from stealing his own painting. Ms. Swanson could have taken it, but you're right, other paintings would have been worth more. I suppose it could be a random art thief, but I'd think he would steal the Van Gogh. None of this makes sense."

I look to CC, hoping she has some insight. Not only does she not have any insight, she isn't even in sight. As in, she's no longer in the kitchen. How does she keep disappearing? How deeply was I contemplating? Maybe my observation skills aren't as great as I assume.

Deciding I've given enough thought to the painting theft for one day, I head home to finish reading my book. I spend the afternoon curled up with it. It makes me realize how much I've missed reading.

I love books. Books of all kinds. My built-in bookshelves are crammed with books from a variety of genres. Westerns, sci-fi, fantasy, young adult, and even some children's books fill the space. Classics are mixed with contemporary in a hodge-podge that brings me joy. I try to get some reading in every day, but I haven't made it much of a priority recently, and I'm now realizing how much I miss it. Another pro to not working is getting through my to-be-read pile. My to-be-read pile also includes some to-be-reread books. Hey, it's my pile and I can put whatever I want in it.

I must have lost myself in the story because before I know it, Eve bursts through my back door. She allows the door to slam backward into the wall. If I were the kind of person who was easily startled, I would have jumped a mile high. Luckily, I only jump a little bit.

"Benji," she calls, "time for dinner."

"What about me?" I ask from where I'm now sprawled on the floor. I might have jumped more than I'd like to admit. I might have jumped so much that I fell off the couch.

Eve seems unconcerned and is kneeling on the floor petting Benji's shamelessly offered belly. "I guess you can come too," she says, not even bothering to look at me. "Come on, Benji," she calls, jumping to her feet. Both Eve and Benji trot out the door without a backward glance.

Setting my book aside, I haul myself to my feet in outrage and storm after them. I can't believe she loves my dog more than she loves me. I am her favorite aunt. I do so much for her. (I can't actually think of anything I do for her off the top of my head, but I'm sure there are things.) What does Benji do for her?

Everybody is already seated when I storm into CC's kitchen. "I can't believe you invited my dog, but not me, to dinner," I accuse Eve.

She seems unconcerned about my ire. "You always come for dinner, but Benji sometimes gets left at your house. I wanted to see him," she explains as if I'm simple-minded.

Meatloaf, mashed potatoes, and green beans are being passed around the table, so I slide into my place and load my plate before they can pass me by, but I still glare at Eve. She ignores me and slips a green bean to Benji under the table.

The kids are talking over each other, but I catch snippets of conversations. The big topics of conversation are Halloween and the town party. I love Halloween. I get to dress up however I want, scaring people is socially acceptable, and they just hand out chocolate. It also happens to be the day after my birthday. The number of candles on my cake is rapidly approaching the denial stage, but I still love my birthday and Halloween.

In addition to trick-or-treating on Halloween, our town puts on a big party the Saturday before. There are carnival games, a straw bale maze, a costume contest, a lot of junk food, and a dance. It takes over all of Town Square Park and takes days to set up and tear down. I still have flashbacks to the year CC made me help. It was horrible.

Mitchell probably has flashbacks, too. There was an incident that involved a stack of straw bales waiting to be placed, Mitchell, and gravity. I may have had a slight hand in it as well, but I will swear to my dying day that the straw bale stack fell all on its own. I absolutely did not cause it to fall on Mitchell. The good news is that I am now banned from helping with setup or teardown. Also, Mitchell is fine.

Why our town schedules two festivals on back-to-back weekends, I'll never know, but I like both the Family Sports Festival and Halloween, so who am I to complain? Not that it would do me any good.

"What won't do you any good?" Jake asks me. Apparently, some of my thoughts became words again.

"Complaining," I answer. "That's why I never do it." CC's snort implies she thinks I do complain. I laser-death-glare at her, but she ignores me.

"Didn't you complain last week about the construction at your office?" Amelia, Frank's girlfriend, asks from her place beside Frank. Her wildly curling brown hair brushes Frank's chin as he wraps an arm around her shoulders and pulls her close to his side to whisper something in her ear. Her warm, golden-brown skin is a striking contrast to Frank's fair complexion. I'm never sure if she doesn't understand our joking or if she's a little slow. Frank seems to like her, though, so it's probably that she's just nicer than we are.

I continue the conversation as if Amelia didn't say anything. "I was just thinking about why we have two festivals on back-to-back weekends, and it would make more sense to spread them out a bit. That's all," I tell Jake.

"*That's* what you spend your time thinking about?" CC asks as she and Jake start clearing the table.

"What should I be thinking about? What do you think about?" I counter. "Wait, don't answer that. There are children present." There are only a couple of children present—most of them have already left after helping to clear the table—but I'm still worried her thoughts might be X-rated and possibly scar the children, or me.

"Is there any news on Pierre's painting?" Kyle asks. He's really focusing on this painting, I think. Surreptitiously looking around, I assure myself that I did just think it and not say it.

"I'm afraid not," I tell him, trying to sneak a peek at his sketchbook. I have to lean precariously over Eve to see what he's drawing, but I manage it. It's a colored-pencil drawing of me.

I almost don't recognize myself. It's from the night of the art opening. My emerald-green eyes are the focal point; they look impossibly green in my face, and I wonder if they really look that green or if Kyle has embellished them. They're so compelling that I almost don't notice I'm not alone in the drawing. Dominic is practically wrapped around me. While the drawing only shows part of me, it's obvious that his arms are encircling me. His face is pressed to my neck, and I get a little warm just remembering what his face had been doing to my neck.

I would feel worse about exposing Kyle to this kind of behavior, but Jake is currently wrapped around CC and nuzzling her neck in a very similar manner, so I don't think it's my fault. "Get a room," I tell them.

"I have a room," CC tells me. "In fact, I have all the rooms. It *is* my house." Properly chastised, I scoot out of the banquette and head home. Just kidding—I head to the refrigerator and open it, forcing Jake to release CC or get hit by the door. Grabbing a beer for myself, I close the door but maneuver to stand between them, thwarting their make-out session. I smile at my victory as I take a swig of my beer.

My smile dies when Jake simply crowds into me, smashing me against his chest to reach CC's lips. I sputter and flail until I break free. Jake flashes me a quick, satisfied smile, before resuming kissy-facing with CC. Admitting defeat, I take my beer and head home.

Chapter 9

The next morning, I slowly regain consciousness. First, I become aware of birds chirping, then of the sound of rain pattering against my window, and finally of the smell of coffee.

This last one causes my eyes to snap open. I see a mug of still-steaming coffee on my bedside table. Worried an intruder has broken in, I sit bolt upright, ready to use my self-defense skills. My sleep-fogged brain doesn't question why an intruder would bring me coffee. My impressive reflexes allow me to jump out of bed, grasp the intruder by the wrist, and execute an over-the-shoulder flip. Well, that's what I thought would happen. What actually happens is my feet get tangled in my sheets, causing me to fall off the far side of the mattress.

"Honestly, Claire, why do you always have to be so dramatic?" CC asks as she rummages in my closet. She doesn't even turn around to check if I'm injured. "I need a beret for Kyle's costume. Do you have one?" Picking myself up off the floor, I circle my bed to grab my coffee. I take a deep swallow.

"I think I have one on the top shelf in the back corner," I tell her, draining my cup.

"Found it!" CC calls triumphantly as she exits my closet, holding said beret. "Excellent, now I don't have to buy one. Come on, it's past time you got up. You can't spend all day in bed." Not waiting for me, she sweeps out of my room. I dutifully trail behind her. Mostly because there's more coffee and breakfast at her house.

We get a little damp from the rain as we cross our yards. I knew there weren't many beautiful fall days left. I just hope a few more sunny days remain. Trick-or-treating and the town Halloween party aren't as fun in the rain.

Since CC is busy gathering costume components for her many children, I have to refill my coffee mug myself. Looking around for breakfast, I'm shocked to find none.

"Where's breakfast?" I call loudly to CC, who is no longer in the kitchen.

"In the fridge. You slept in so late, I didn't want it to go bad," she yells back from the living room, where she is presumably assembling costumes. I grab a yogurt parfait out of the fridge, hop onto the counter, and start eating. Having finished my second cup of coffee and my parfait without CC reappearing, I refill my mug and debate going to check on her costume assembly or heading home to squeeze in some more reading.

"Claire, bring me the fruit basket, please," CC calls, deciding for me. I hop off the counter and grab the fruit basket. I carry it and my third cup of coffee into CC's living room.

CC accepts the basket from me with a frown. "Why didn't you take the fruit out first?" she asks in exasperation. I ignore her and plop down on one of her couches in the only free space left. Costume pieces are spread around in what looks like the mess left after a tornado, but I suspect it's organized in a way that makes sense to CC.

The next several hours pass with CC working hard to piece together over half a dozen costumes, while I offer unsolicited and unappreciated advice. She occasionally takes pieces of fabric to the sewing machine she's set up in one corner, or asks me to pass her miscellaneous items.

Slowly, the scattered pieces are grouped into costumes, and order emerges from the chaos. Placing a stethoscope on a set of scrubs, CC looks around, nodding her head with satisfaction. "There," she says, "everything is set for Saturday." Turning on her heel, she heads for the kitchen. I once more follow her, but realizing I'm still in my pajamas, I head home to change quickly.

Now wearing jeans and a T-shirt, I rejoin CC. She's not alone. I'm gobsmacked to see Dominic carrying three glasses to the table. He smirks when he sees my shirt. This one has a black cat and reads I DON'T BRING BAD LUCK. YOU JUST MAKE BAD CHOICES.

"How fitting," he says as he sets the glasses on the table and goes back to grab the pitcher of iced tea. CC has already assembled meatloaf sandwiches for all three of us. She somehow manages to guide first me and then Dominic to the table. She practically pushes him onto the bench she has already pushed me onto. I scoot over so he doesn't sit on me.

"I forgot to ask you yesterday. How's your head?" CC asks, joining us at the table. She doesn't comment on his black eye, so either it's not as noticeable as I think it is, or she's choosing not to mention it. She's probably choosing not to mention it. It's pretty noticeable.

"It's fine. It's just a mild concussion," Dominic answers, taking a bite of his sandwich. "This is delicious," he tells CC. She smiles happily. She loves feeding people.

I scoot a little farther down the bench so Dominic's leg isn't pressed against mine. He also scoots a little farther down the bench so his leg is pressed against mine. I frown at him and shift again. He wraps his arm around me and pulls me back against him. It's like he's ignoring what happened at the museum yesterday.

"If you'll excuse me, I have to go help set up for the town Halloween party," CC says as she stands. I'm surprised she hasn't choked from eating her lunch in record time. I can only watch as she callously leaves me without a backward glance. For once, I regret that I'm not allowed to help set up the party.

Dominic's soft laughter vibrates through me where I'm pressed against his side, making me think I'm thinking out loud again. "Scared to be alone with me?" he asks, popping the last bite of his sandwich in his mouth.

"Don't be ridiculous," I counter weakly. We both know he's correct. "But you did threaten to arrest me," I remind him. Perhaps reminding him was a bad idea. I'm not sure how to extract myself from his arm or this situation, so I silently formulate a plan. I could distract him by pretending Benji needs me. I could pretend my phone is ringing and somebody needs me to come to get them. Or I could use my self-defense skills to extract myself.

"Benji rarely needs you. I wouldn't fall for the fake phone call. Your self-defense skills might make my concussion worse. You wouldn't want that, would you?" He smiles boyishly at me.

I guess I wasn't silently formulating a plan after all. "What did you tell your friend about me? I mean, if you even talked about me when you visited him." I feel my face heating with embarrassment. I didn't mean to ask him about what he might have said about me. Mostly because I'm afraid the answer won't paint me in a flattering light.

He takes so long to answer that I think he isn't going to. "I did talk about you. You were a big topic of conversation." I'm not sure how I feel about this. On one hand, I'm flattered that he was talking about me with his friend. On the other hand, I'm embarrassed that he was talking about me. On the other other hand, I'm dying to know what he said about me.

Fortunately, he continues, so I'm spared the embarrassment of having to ask what he said about me. "I told him that you're a menace who butts into everything and that you inflict injury on me all the time." I wince, but don't even try to defend myself since it's true. "I also told him how beautiful, loyal, interesting, determined, and smart you are." I study his face to determine his sincerity. "He asked me if I would be happier without you butting into my life."

He pauses so long I don't think he's going to continue. "I wouldn't be," he finally says.

I'm completely overwhelmed by the significance of this. It explains the shift from the injury-and-yelling stage to the kissing-and-hand-holding stage in our relationship, although the injuries are still happening.

I need some time to process this, so I ask for a little space and time to think. Actually—I panic and blurt out the first thing that comes to my mind as a distraction. "Did you find the painting yet?" I ask, perhaps a little desperately.

He sighs as if disappointed in the abrupt change in topic, but answers me anyway. "Not that it's any of your business, but no."

He looks like he might try to turn the conversation back to the original topic, so I continue, ignoring his curt response. "Do you think it was Pierre? Or Ms. Swanson? I heard Pierre is threatening to sue the museum, but if he was going to sell his painting for a million dollars, it seems like stealing it would be a high risk for a minimal reward. And if Ms. Swanson was going to steal from her museum, I would think she would steal a more famous painting." I share my thoughts on the case with him despite his not asking.

"And just where did you get all this information from? Do not butt into another one of my investigations." He glares directly into my face from about three inches away.

Unable to scoot back, due to his arm still anchoring me to him, I try distraction again. "Ms. Clark, that's the little old lady at the information desk, said Pierre was getting a million dollars for his painting, but now that it's gone, he obviously won't. She also said he was threatening to sue the museum, but the museum doesn't have the money for a big payout."

"Not that it's any of your business," he repeats, "but I agree it seems unlikely Pierre or Ms. Swanson would steal the painting." His eyes drop to my lips. When I lick my lips nervously, his gaze goes a little unfocused. I'm not sure he's aware he's still talking. "I've looked into Ms. Swanson, and she's very well-off. She comes from old money. Her reputation is worth more to her than any stolen painting could be. I didn't find any official record of Pierre's existence prior to two years ago." He clenches his jaw as if suddenly realizing he's spilling information about the case. "I shouldn't have said that," he confesses. "I was thinking out loud. Maybe your inability to keep your thoughts in is contagious."

I'm not sure how to take this. On one hand, rude. On the other hand, I'm glad he's sharing his thoughts with me. On the other other hand, I don't know how I feel about the significance of his sharing his thoughts with me. On the other other other hand, I did like the kissing. Before I can run out of hands, my thoughts are cut off when Dominic closes the short distance between us and kisses me.

If I had any thoughts left in my head, I'm pretty sure they would all be about how this kissing is becoming quite the habit. I'm so caught up in the feel of his mouth on mine, I don't hear the telltale clicking of nails until it's too late. Trying to reach me, the danger floof pretending to be a Newfoundland rears back and slams his front paws into Dominic's back. Unfortunately, the laws of motion mean that instead of Dominic gently realigning our lips, he slams his face into mine.

"Ouch," we both say at the same time. I rub my chin while Dominic holds his hand to his nose. A trickle of blood oozes out from between his fingers. Bear, apparently realizing we don't appreciate his efforts to get affection, flops onto the floor dejectedly. His expression is so forlorn that if he wasn't such a pain in the rear—or in this case, pain in the face—I'd feel bad for him.

"You're bleeding," I exclaim, probably unnecessarily. Using my quick thinking, I jump up to grab some paper towels. Sadly, Dominic is blocking my escape. Even sadder, the momentum of my jumping up bodychecks him to the floor. He's sprawled on CC's black-and-white checkered kitchen floor with blood oozing from his nose. Remembering what happened the last time I approached him when he was stretched out on the floor, I carefully scoot past him to grab paper towels.

Clutching the roll, I debate the best way to give him the paper towels. He is spread-eagled, and I'm worried about getting too close in case a repeat of the scene in my kitchen occurs. When Dominic holds out his hand, the one not covering his bleeding nose, for the paper towels, I inch close enough to hand him a wad. I fight the urge to wring my hands in a useless gesture. He sighs as he holds the paper towel wad to his nose and then heaves himself back onto the bench seat.

"What happened to the sheriff?" Ann asks, walking into the kitchen ahead of her siblings.

"Nothing!" I yell. Six pairs of blue eyes land on me. The expressions range from incredulous to judgmental.

"It was Bear's fault. He jumped on Dominic—the sheriff," I correct, "and knocked him into me." Jane looks disappointed that I'm blaming her pet. Ann and Dean look like they have already lost interest in the conversation.

"Why was he so close to you?" Eve asks. Frank and Kyle look like they know exactly why I was so close to Dominic's face.

"Who wants a snack?" I ask somewhat desperately. I don't wait for a reply. I turn toward the pantry and start grabbing snacks at random and passing them out. While the other kids file out of the kitchen with bags and boxes of noodles, cereal, tea, and rice, Kyle joins Dominic at the banquette. Kyle ended up with a bag of croutons for his snack. Dominic removes the wad of paper towels from his nose and finds a clean section to test if the bleeding has stopped. I'm relieved to see that it has.

"Do you think you'll recover Pierre's painting?" Kyle asks Dominic. I notice a smear of what looks like shaving cream across his left arm.

"I'm doing my best to find it," Dominic answers. Kyle nods glumly, as if he knows the sheriff is doing his best, but he isn't convinced he'll find the painting. Kyle doesn't even ask me if *I* think *I'll* recover the painting. It's like he doesn't think I'm a great detective.

"Pierre isn't quite what I expected, but I still love his art," Kyle continues.

"What do you mean?" Dominic asks.

Kyle shrugs. "I don't know. I read an interview he gave. He talked about how he grew up in France but moved to the United States for college. About how he has no family and struggled for years before being discovered in L.A. last year. He just seems different from what I thought he would be." Kyle shrugs again, handing a page from his sketchbook to Dominic. Looking over Dominic's shoulder, I see that it's the sketch Kyle was working on the night before. The sketch of Dominic and me at the art show opening.

"Wow!" Dominic finally says. "This is amazing. Kyle, you have incredible talent." Dominic and I both raise our gaze to Kyle, only to discover he's gone. Huh, I guess he can teleport like his mom.

"Honey, I'm home," Jake calls, coming in the back door.

"Welcome home, darling," I say, moving to greet him. I wrap my arms around him and stretch up on my tiptoes to kiss him. Before my lips can make contact with his cheek or lips—I haven't decided what I'm aiming for—I'm pulled backward out of Jake's arms. Dominic wraps an arm under my rib cage and pulls me against him.

Jealous much? I think. Wait, I didn't think it, I said it. Shoot! Jake smiles widely at me. Then he transfers his gaze to Dominic, and an unspoken communication seems to pass between them.

"Where's CC?" Jake asks, apparently finishing the secret silent man talk with Dominic. Jake looks around as if he expects to spot her.

"She's still helping set up the town Halloween party," I tell him, subtly trying to ease out of Dominic's hold. He doesn't release me. Not one to give up, I try again. My next attempt isn't as subtle and causes me to wriggle around in a way that might be construed as arousing, or like a fish out of water. Either way, when I realize how I must look, I freeze in mortification. The only saving grace is that Jake has already left the kitchen, and nobody is around to see my embarrassment.

"We're off to the bowling alley. See you later," Jake calls as he and the children march through the kitchen and out the back door. Jake always takes the kids bowling on Tuesdays for a father-kid night.

"He didn't even slow down to make sure I was all right," I say in outrage.

"You're with the sheriff. How much safer can you be?" Dominic asks. I don't have an answer for him. Or for myself. All I have are confused feelings. The ringing of my phone finally allows me to wriggle free. I'm both relieved and disappointed, proving once again I am a complex person with complex emotions.

"I'm finishing up here," CC says when I answer. "I'll meet you at Bake My Day."

"On my way," I tell her, perhaps a bit desperately. "I have to go," I tell Dominic, practically running out the back door. Some might say my leaving resembles fleeing, but I leave so fast I wouldn't have been able to hear them say it. Reaching the safety of my car, I sigh in relief.

My relief is short-lived as Dominic joins me in my car. I gape at him in shock. What does he think he's doing?

"What do you think you're doing?" I ask him incredulously.

"I thought I'd join you," he says. I'm stymied. I need to leave, but I don't want him to come with me, but he's in my car. I open and close my mouth several times, but no words come out. Dominic smiles at me unrepentantly.

"I heard Grandma made peanut butter pie today," he says.

"Peanut butter pie? I love peanut butter pie." I decide I can't waste time arguing with him, so I'll allow him to join me after all. Without another word, I point my sweet ride to Bake My Day.

CC smiles warmly as we walk in together. "Sheriff, what a nice surprise."

"How did the setup go?" Dominic asks as we join CC at the counter. I try to subtly put some distance between Dominic and myself, while CC fills him in on the setup. Since his fingers are laced with mine, I only get as far as our outstretched arms allow. Rose eyes our joined hands inscrutably. I can never tell how she feels about Dominic's interest in me.

"Grandma, did you remember to have lunch today?" Dominic asks. Rose transfers her gaze to Dominic with a fierce scowl. Even though her eyes aren't on me, I shrink back from her glare.

"I can take care of myself. I'm not a child," she tells him defiantly.

Dominic is made of stern stuff, so he doesn't shrink from her wrath. "I know you had that wedding cake tasting today, and I was worried you wouldn't take time to eat. I care about you and want you to live a long and healthy life," he tells her, causing her to soften slightly. I still find her terrifying, but Dominic seems immune. I guess if you've known her your whole life, you might not be as easily intimidated. But I can't picture what spending Christmas and Sunday dinners with her would be like.

"Hmmph," is Rose's reply. "Well, are you going to stand here all night, or are you going to order?"

"Claire and I would like a slice of peanut butter pie. CC, what would you like?" Dominic asks.

"Peanut butter pie sounds delicious. I'll have a slice too." CC, apparently not scared of Rose, smiles warmly at her. Rose returns her smile with a slight smile of her own. When her eyes land on me again, her smile fades, and a thoughtful expression enters her eyes. I face her scrutiny calmly. Not really—I rush off to a table at the far side of the restaurant like the chicken I am. I take the time alone to calm myself. Well, I tried. I need significantly more time than I'm granted, as Dominic and CC join me shortly. Dominic places a large slice of peanut butter pie in front of me, and I happily dig in.

I ignore the polite idle chitchat between CC and Dominic and focus on my pie. All too soon, I lick the last morsel off my fork.

Feeling a large hand settle on my thigh under the table, my whole body tenses.

"Do you want another slice?" Dominic asks. His voice is rough with what I assume is desire. I have a lot of feelings about Dominic and our developing relationship. All of them are confusing, and many of them are conflicting.

"I don't know what I want," I tell him honestly. I think we both know I'm not talking about pie.

Chapter 10

I am more zombie-like than normal when I stagger into CC's kitchen the next morning. I've spent most of the night examining my feelings for and about Dominic. A significant portion of the examination was spent on why I'm so scared of having a relationship with him. I always assumed my lack of desire to date was due to knowing all the eligible bachelors in town since birth, but now I have to question that assumption. For the first time, I'm beginning to think I'm the problem. That would also explain why I never dated the guys our line-dancing friends tried to set me up with.

"Am I the problem?" I ask CC as I accept the mug of coffee she hands me.

As always, my friend is a source of comfort and sympathy, so she lovingly supports me. "Probably," she replies, taking a sip of her coffee. Wait, that wasn't loving, comforting, or supportive. I glare at her. "What are you the problem of this time?" she asks heartlessly.

"Dating," I tell her. "I always thought I just didn't want to date guys I've known my whole life or the random guys presented to me at line dancing, but now I'm not so sure."

CC's expression softens. It appears she's struggling with how to ask me something. "Do you think you choose the safe option instead of what makes you happy because of your fear of uncertainty?" It sounds like she's talking about more than just dating. I wilt under this insight. Even though CC gives me plenty of time to respond, I remain silent.

"Maybe it would help if you think of what makes you happy," she says, refilling my coffee cup and setting a cinnamon roll in front of me. Leaving me to my thoughts, she heads off to do whatever she does while the kids are at school. I pick at my cinnamon roll, but still manage to eat it all. (Hey, I'm confused, not stupid.)

Since CC still hasn't returned, I refill my coffee mug and head home. If I'm going to be introspective, I might as well do it in the privacy of my own home. Deciding that getting dressed might at least make me feel productive, I put on a cheerful pink T-shirt with a picture of a smiling cartoon dumpster on it. The dumpster is on fire with THIS LITTLE LIGHT OF MINE, I'M GOING TO LET IT SHINE printed around it. It feels appropriate somehow.

I spend the next several hours curled up on my overstuffed sofa, with Blackbeard doing his best to crush me to death. I alternate between overthinking every aspect of my personality and shortcomings and staring into the distance with no thoughts in my head. It's not a pleasant way to spend the morning.

At some point, CC appears, carrying two bowls. She hands me one before settling on the other end of my sofa. Blackbeard lets his disgruntlement at being disturbed be known by using my spleen as a springboard when he jumps off my lap. I just hope he hasn't caused any lasting damage or internal bleeding.

"Tough morning?" CC asks, taking a bite of her egg roll in a bowl. I love egg roll in a bowl, I think as I take a huge bite.

"I don't know what to think," I tell her. "I'm starting to question all my life's decisions. Maybe I've played it safe my whole life, and I was just pretending to live."

"That's pretty deep," CC says, sounding surprised. It's as if she doesn't think I can have deep thoughts. Rude! "Maybe you should start doing what makes you happy, and stop doing what doesn't. Maybe start with your job. How long have you hated working at Brown and Son Insurance? Yet you haven't even bothered to look for another job."

"I don't think I should work for Jake," I tell her. "Not that he isn't a great guy, or that he wouldn't be a great boss, but if I do change jobs, I think I need to do it on my own."

"That's fair, I suppose," she concedes. "What do you want to do? If you could have any job, what would it be?"

"Is a brownie taste tester an option?" I only half joke as I contemplate what I might want to do. "Maybe I could be a bartender at the bar," I muse. CC's snort of disbelief tells me she doubts my bartending skills. I silently agree with her assessment. I can be kind of clumsy, and there's a lot of glass involved in bartending. I sigh. "I thought about being a PI, but Dominic threatening to arrest me kind of put a damper on it." I try to think of what else I might enjoy doing. I wonder if I could become a PI without Dominic knowing about it. I did solve Mr. Johnson's murder, rescue Jamie, and catch the killer—well, kind of. I would look amazing in a cool trench coat and fedora.

"I hate to leave you during this time of deep introspection, but I have to go help set up for the town Halloween party," CC says. Standing up, she collects my now-empty bowl, leaving me alone once more. I might have spent all day contemplating my life, my shortcomings, and my decisions, but the doorbell precedes the ear-shattering baying of Agatha. She really hates the doorbell.

I jump to my feet and rush to distract her before I'm permanently deafened. I grab the picnic-basket-shaped cookie jar and wave a treat in front of Agatha's nose. Just before she can snatch it from my fingers, I throw it into the kitchen behind us. She immediately dashes after it, racing Benji to see who can get the treat first. To prevent any losers, I toss several more treats.

Opening the front door, I'm surprised to see Pierre standing on my front porch. His expression is twisted into what I can only describe as distaste.

"Why do you have such an aggravating sound?" he asks in his French accent. I hope the language barrier is what causes it to sound like he doesn't like my dog.

"Agatha doesn't like the doorbell," I tell him. Taking in my dumpster shirt, his expression of distaste increases.

Apparently realizing my annoyance, Pierre switches tactics. "I hear the town has a Halloween party this Saturday. While Halloween is a child's holiday, I thought you might like to go with me. Kevin's murals are supposed to be unveiled then." I frown as I try to remember who Kevin is.

"Who's Kevin?" I ask, giving up on figuring it out on my own.

"Kevin is your nephew," Pierre says as if I'm simple-minded.

"Kyle," I correct him. "My nephew's name is Kyle." I see a flash of something unpleasant in Pierre's eyes. He seems unhappy about being corrected. Not for the first time, I wonder why he's so interested in me, since basically everything about me and my life seems to displease him. I guess when I was all dolled up in my princess dress, it made sense, but ever since then, he seems to have an aversion to basically everything about me. So why does he keep showing up and trying to get a date with me? Afraid I've said my thoughts out loud again, I cast a panicked look at his face, but he is just staring at me expectantly.

"Will you join me at the Halloween party and mural unveiling?" Pierre asks again with a slightly irritated tone. It seems he doesn't like having to repeat himself.

"Who are you?" a voice asks from the region of my knee. We both look down to see Eve. Pierre frowns at her, then transfers his gaze back to me. Eve's question causes me to remember that Dominic couldn't find any official records for Pierre prior to two years ago. So, who is he?

"You have a daughter?" Pierre asks with annoyance, distracting me from my thoughts.

"Eve is my niece," I tell him. "Eve, this is Pierre. He's the artist whose art show opening your mom, dad, Kyle, and I attended on Friday." Eve eyes him up and down, pursing her lips. She appears unimpressed.

"Can I take Benji for a walk?" she asks me, completely dismissing Pierre.

"Only if somebody goes with you," I tell her, turning back to Pierre. "Who are you really?" I wince at the directness of my question. "I mean, the sheriff couldn't find any records for you prior to a couple of years ago. Why is that?"

He looks momentarily nonplussed, then scared, and finally angry.

"Okay, let's go," Eve says before he can respond. She grabs my hand and tries to drag me back inside the house.

"You never answered my question," Pierre interjects before Eve can close the door on him. "Will you join me at the Halloween party and mural unveiling?" He asks for the third time. Persistent, isn't he? Fortunately, I keep my inner thoughts in.

Unfortunately, Eve does not. "No, she's going with us and the sheriff," she tells him, closing the door in his face.

"That was rude," I tell her. She shrugs, unconcerned.

"I don't like him," she says, hooking Benji's leash to his collar. Not that he needs a leash, but Eve likes to hold it.

"Ready," she says. She grabs my hand and begins marching to my back door. Benji trots happily at her side. Our walk around the neighborhood is interrupted several times by neighbors trying to gather gossip, but Eve is not one to be thwarted, so she quickly dismisses each attempt before any information can be exchanged.

After our little jaunt around the neighborhood, we join the rest of the family in time for dinner. Tonight it's lasagna, salad, and French bread. Yum! I'm spoiled, I think—or say, who knows. Talk swirls around me as several different conversations take place at the same time. I don't really listen to any of them, but I enjoy the commotion.

After finishing dinner, the kids trickle out, leaving CC, Jake, and me alone in the kitchen. "Have you given my job offer any more thought?" Jake asks as he helps CC clear the table and put the food away.

"I can't work for you," I tell him, "but I appreciate the offer."

"Claire is going to make a career change," CC tells Jake. "She's going to think of what she would enjoy doing and then do that."

"Is a brownie taste tester a job?" Jake asks. He gets me, I think—not for the first time.

"That's what *I* said," I tell him. I accept the beer he brings me and take a deep swig. Alcohol and good ideas always go hand in hand, I think sarcastically. Sadly, alcohol lets me down, and I head to bed with no new career ideas.

Chapter 11

I am being crushed to death. The little bit of air left in my lungs is slowly being pressed out. A massive weight on my chest prevents me from drawing in oxygen. If my eyes had been open, my vision would have been tunneling. The end is near. In a last-ditch effort to live, I push Blackbeard off of me. His angry meow promises retribution.

Before he can do anything I will regret, I slide out of bed and rush to turn on the shower. He happily trots into the bathroom and jumps under the spray. I decide I might as well shower too, so I also jump under the spray. I'm careful not to step on Blackbeard while I quickly shower. In record time, I step out and turn off the water. Blackbeard glares at me from his one green eye and begins licking himself dry.

"Weird cat," I mutter. Drying off, I throw on a pair of jeans and another fabulous shirt. I carefully weighed my options, trying to decide which shirt is just right for the mood I'm in. The winner has a picture of a carrot and the words I DON'T CARROT ALL on it. It sums up how I feel about all the self-reflection I've been doing recently. I'm not typically one for deep thoughts.

Breezing into CC's kitchen, I'm shocked to find CC eating breakfast with her children. They appear surprised to see me as well.

"I'm surprised to see you so early," CC says. I glance at the large red-rimmed old-school style clock and realize it's only seven thirty. Shrugging off the time, I pour myself a cup of coffee and snag a breakfast sandwich from the pile on the table.

Their conversation centers on the various items the kids need for their class parties tomorrow. It sounds like CC is going to have a busy day. Eventually, they all grab their backpacks and head to the bus stop.

"Finish your coffee," CC says, refilling my mug. What a great friend. "Then we'll head out." Wait, what? Head out where? I think.

"Wait, what? Head out where?" I ask.

"To get the kids' stuff for tomorrow," she says, sweeping up the stairs, presumably to get dressed. Since I'm already dressed, I have time for a third cup of coffee and a second breakfast sandwich before CC reappears. She is now dressed in a pair of houndstooth pants with a red silk shirt. She always looks more put together than I do, by a lot. It's almost like she's prepared for an impromptu fashion photo shoot. It's a good thing I'm secure in myself and don't feel self-conscious, I think, a little self-consciously.

"Let's go," she says. "We have quite a list to get through." She doesn't wait for me; she just breezes out the back door. I obediently follow her.

"Will this torture never end?" I wail hours later.

"For Pete's sake, Claire," CC admonishes. "It's just a few errands."

"This is our fifth stop," I remind her, loading more bags into my already full trunk. We've been to Mr. McIntyre's store for candy. To Party People for plates, cups, napkins, and forks. To Bake My

Day for cupcakes. Unfortunately, the cupcakes were for the parties tomorrow and not for me. I did manage to buy a cookie before CC dragged me out. Then to the farm stand for ten dozen pumpkins. Luckily, they were the miniature ones. And finally, to The Toy Box, where we bought what seemed to be every Halloween and fall-themed party game available.

"That's it," CC says, closing my trunk after we load the last bag. Finally, we can head home.

We both grab bags and haul them into CC's kitchen. Unloading my trunk is going to take many trips. On my fourth trip, I realize I'm the only one unloading.

"Hey, how come I'm the only one unloading?" I accuse CC as I set down the third large box of miniature pumpkins.

"I was making lunch," CC says as if that excuses her slacking. She places a bowl of salad and a glass of lemonade in front of me.

"Salad?" I ask. "We're having *salad* for lunch?"

"It's good for you," she says. "And you know you're going to be eating a lot of junk food in the next several days. Try it. You might like it." CC takes a bite, unconcerned with my opinion on her lunch choice.

Picking at it for a few more seconds, I finally take a bite. "This isn't half bad," I admit. She's added apple, chicken, and some other things I'm not sure of. The dressing is sweet and tangy at the same time. "I guess salad is fine," I concede.

"Have you given any more thought to what you want to do?" CC asks.

"I feel like that's all I've been doing." I stab at my salad in an effort to release some frustration. It isn't enough. I'm still frustrated. "I'm starting to think I have no interests or skills," I whine. CC makes a sympathetic face but doesn't comment.

"Unless I really do become a PI." I stir my salad around to avoid eye contact. I don't think CC will be supportive of this idea, despite her dragging me into a murder investigation just a couple of months ago. She frowns at me, but doesn't say anything. I know this trick. She's using my need to fill silence against me.

Before I can blurt out anything, my phone rings. "Hello," I answer, perhaps a bit desperately, happy for the distraction.

"Claire?" It's my boss from the insurance company, Brandon Brown. I'm not sure why he says my name like a question. Who else would it be? He called my cell phone, but he's not the brightest crayon in the box. I maintain my professionalism by keeping these thoughts to myself.

"Yes, Bran—" I stop myself before I can call him by his first name. "I mean, Mr. Brown," I finish. "How can I help you?"

"I was just calling to update you on the remodel." He tries to sound professional, but to my ears, he sounds like a twelve-year-old boy. He graduated in June with Nell, so I'm not far off. There's a long pause as he apparently waits for a response from me.

"What is the update?" I ask, trying to move the conversation along.

"I'm afraid it will be two more weeks," he tells me. He drones on about construction delays, but I tune him out. No longer resisting the urge, I allow my eyes to roll. Brandon doesn't allow his lack of skills to prevent him from feeling important, so his droning continues for so long that CC finishes her salad and excuses herself to go help with more Halloween party setup.

"That's too bad," I interject at a pause in his monologue. "Thanks for letting me know. I'm sorry, but I have to go."

"Oh," he says, sounding disappointed. "Okay, well, I guess I'll keep you updated." I feel a little bad. Sort of like I kicked a puppy. Well, not that bad. I'd feel terrible if I kicked a puppy, and I only feel a little bad about Brandon.

I sigh again. It's becoming a habit, this sighing of mine. I guess at least two more weeks without pay. Oh, well. I contemplate my life while I finish my salad. I finish my salad long before I finish contemplating my life. Giving up on contemplating, I head home.

I feel fidgety, so I decide to harness my restlessness and clean my house. I blast my favorite songs and sing along as I clean. I scour the bathroom. I use my dusting wand to annihilate the dust. I conquer a mountain of laundry. I wield my vacuum to eradicate all the dust bunnies. Finally, I decontaminate the kitchen, which, since I don't use it, is a quick task. My house is spotless, but my mind is still muddy.

Turning off my music, I head next door for dinner. I inhale appreciatively as I step into the kitchen. I eagerly take a seat at the banquette and hold out my bowl so Jake can fill it with jambalaya. I may have pushed Frank's bowl out of the way so Jake would fill mine first, but I'll never admit to it. Jake ignores my bowl and fills Frank's first.

"Rude," I say.

"Don't be so hard on yourself," he tells me. "I'm sure you *accidentally* pushed Frank's bowl out of the way." The look he gives me conveys censure and a reprimand. When he fills Kyle's bowl next, I whimper. Finally taking pity on me, he fills my bowl before his own. I dig in with gusto. Jane passes me the basket of cornbread, and I snatch two pieces before Frank takes it from me and continues passing it around the table.

"When will Nell be here?" Eve asks, almost spilling her bowl. Ann catches it before it makes a mess.

"Not for a long, long time," I tell her sadly. I miss Nell. She's been gone for so long, and she's so far away. I know she had to go to college, but it feels like a part of myself is gone, too.

"She'll be home tomorrow by dinner," CC corrects. "Honestly, Claire, why do you have to be so dramatic? She's only an hour away, and she visited a couple of weeks ago."

She can't understand my pain. She doesn't know what it feels like to have your child grow up and leave home. (Her eye roll tells me that I might have said it aloud and also that she disagrees with me.)

"Nell is *her* child," Amelia corrects me. Her brow is furrowed in confusion. Poor girl. Frank leans down to whisper something to her. I hope he's setting her straight gently. To avoid embarrassing her further, I focus on finishing my jambalaya.

Mission accomplished, I hold my empty bowl out for Jake to refill. Jane chatters from beside me. Well, that's odd, I didn't know Jane could make that sound. When a squirrel peeks out of her hair, I realize it was probably the squirrel chattering. When the squirrel scurries down her arm and tries to grab my cornbread, I defend it with my life. Not really, but I do snatch the cornbread out of its reach. The squirrel sits back on its haunches and chatters angrily at me. I lean back, fearing it might attack. Before I'm mauled, Jane pulls a walnut out of thin air and hands it to the squirrel. The squirrel happily accepts the nut and scampers back into Jane's hair.

"Disaster averted," I sigh. Nobody else seems nearly as relieved as I am. It's like they didn't think the squirrel was a threat. While I scrape the last of the jambalaya out of my bowl, the rest of the family clears the table. The kids all drift away, and CC and Jake put the leftovers away, rejoining me at the table. They bring glasses and a pitcher of iced tea.

"Remember, I'll be at the kids' schools all day tomorrow helping with the Halloween parties," CC reminds me. "You can come and help too." I debate my options: be home alone all day with no responsibilities, or be surrounded by sugared-up kids. Tough decision.

"I think I'll pass," I tell her. "Besides, Mr. Russell banned me from the school."

"That was years ago. He's probably forgotten by now." CC waves her hand dismissively, trying to persuade me. I have to agree with her. He probably *has* forgotten, but I still don't want to go.

"I'd better not risk it," I tell her with feigned regret. I change the subject before CC can browbeat me into going to the school parties. "Why do you think Dominic can't find official records for Pierre prior to two years ago?"

Both CC and Jake look surprised. "He can't find official information for Pierre?" Jake asks. At the same time, CC asks, "The sheriff told you he can't find any information on Pierre?" They exchange looks and what seems to be a silent conversation.

"He mentioned it in passing," I try to deflect. "Don't you think it's odd? I mean, supposedly, Pierre came to the States for college and wasn't discovered for over a decade, so why are there no records of him? I don't think he even found a college transcript. It's weird, right?"

"It *is* strange," CC concedes, "but I'm sure there's an explanation." We all contemplate what this might mean and how it connects to the missing painting.

If Pierre isn't Pierre, who is he? Why did he lie about his name? What else might he have lied about? "Wouldn't there be paperwork for Pierre entering the country?" I ask. "If there isn't paperwork, does that mean he entered the country illegally, or that he was always here?"

CC and Jake's surprised expressions imply they wouldn't expect me to have such insightful questions. I'd be mad about that, but it kind of surprises me, too.

"How did Pierre explain it to the sheriff?" CC asks.

"Umm, Dominic didn't say. He, uh, changed the subject," I lie. Well, it isn't really a lie. Kissing me *did* change the subject. "I think it's time for bed," I say, and hurry home before she can question me further.

Chapter 12

Even before I open my eyes, I can feel that this is going to be a great day. This is not a feeling I usually associate with mornings, but hey, I'm adaptable. I decide to dress for success before heading to CC's for coffee and breakfast. I slip on a pair of comfortable well-worn jeans and another perfect T-shirt. This one has a balloon animal and the words ONE TWISTED PARTY ANIMAL on it. It's perfect because it's almost my birthday. It's also a beautiful green that matches my eyes. Taking a few extra minutes, I quickly French-braid my hair.

"Good morning!" I greet CC and her family as I sail into her kitchen. Everybody looks shocked to see me. It might be because it's so early. Or because I'm already dressed. But most likely, they're shocked because I'm cheerful and coherent.

I ignore their judgment and pour myself a cup of coffee. I sit at the counter and watch CC man four skillets with omelets with a variety of ingredients in varying levels of completion. One by one, she plates them and hands the plates to Frank, telling him which sibling each omelet is for before starting a new one in the empty pan. It's just like the fancy omelet bars in fancy hotels.

In no time at all, CC places my plate in front of me. I dig in, enjoying the combined flavors of eggs, cheese, bacon, sausage, ham, tomatoes, mushrooms, and peppers. The kids are talking over each other about their school Halloween parties, the town Halloween party, trick-or-treating, and Nell coming to visit. They are practically vibrating with excitement. I must admit I'm pretty excited too.

As everybody finishes breakfast, they gather their normal school stuff and the boxes and bags of party supplies and file out to CC's Mommobile. Since CC is helping at the kids' schools, she follows them out the door. I wave them off as I refill my coffee cup. Even though they're loaded down with boxes and bags of supplies, I don't offer to help. Partly because I already carried all of the stuff once, and partly because I'm afraid CC will make me go with them after all.

"I left you some leftover jambalaya in the fridge," CC calls on her way out the door. "The reheating instructions are on the lid." She takes such good care of me. I contemplate what my life would be like without her, and shiver. It's a terrible prospect.

With nothing to distract me, I spend the morning deciding on my dream job, updating my resume, and applying for said dream job. Just kidding—I spend the morning staring blankly at my China-blue walls. While the color is beautiful, it doesn't warrant the amount of time I stare at it. When my stomach grumbles, I head back to CC's kitchen and reheat my lunch.

It's strange to be alone in CC's house. Usually, it's filled with people and noise. Now it feels more like my house: still and quiet, and maybe a little empty. This feeling does nothing to lift my spirits.

To distract myself from my maudlin thoughts, I mull over what I know about the missing painting: It's too large to sneak out easily. Pierre was supposed to get a million dollars for it. Pierre might not be who he says he is. Ms. Swanson's reputation is in trouble. The museum can't afford the lawsuit. Nobody saw anything or anyone suspicious.

This is a tough one. Who would risk stealing Pierre's painting when other, more prestigious paintings were also on-site? Now that they have the painting, what do they plan to do with it? Will they try to sell it to the buyer? Find a new buyer? Wouldn't they get caught if they did? If they don't sell it, what's the point of stealing it?

If I were a PI, I'd have a database of criminals, confidential informants, and other helpful stuff. I might have been envisioning some high-tech spy gear like X-ray glasses, or a lipstick taser—oh, and a grappling-hook gun. In my imagination, my trench coat and fedora have been joined by a Batman-like utility belt that holds everything I might need.

I'm distracted from my imagining when the back door opens and Nell walks in. "Nell!" I yell happily, jumping up to hug her. I clutch her perhaps a little desperately. "I haven't seen you in forever! I've missed you so much!"

"Aunt Claire, I was home just a couple of weeks ago," she says, sounding slightly muffled, from where she is still clutched in my arms. I'll never let her go, I think, but before I know it, my arms are empty as CC and her other children come bursting in the back door and somehow extract Nell from my grasp. They pass her around, hugging her and exclaiming over her. I manage to snag her for more hugging, but every time I do, she is snatched from my arms. Scowling at the group, I realize Nell's friend Jamie and a stranger have joined us. Since I'm cool under pressure, I subtly let the family know.

"Stranger danger!" I yell, pointing at the stranger in what some might say is a dramatic manner. It works! All the children move to safety while CC, using her self-defense skills, flips the stranger to the ground and holds him immobile, and a SWAT team rushes in and arrests him. Not really—everybody turns to stare at me with varying degrees of shock, reproach, and exasperation.

"Everybody, this is Theo Ward, my boyfriend," Nell says as she links her arm with his. Theo is a few inches taller than Nell. He has light-brown hair, and hazel eyes that are highlighted by his browline glasses. I suppose he's good-looking, if you like attractive college boys who are trying to steal your precious baby from you. Theo, more like Thee-No, I think. The fact that everybody looks at me with shocked expressions makes me think I did more than just think it.

"Auntie Claire," Nell admonishes at the same time CC says, "Honestly, Claire," in a disapproving tone.

"Great shirt," Theo says.

"Thanks!" I gush, smiling warmly at him.

"He seems nice," I tell Nell happily. Nell and CC both roll their eyes at me and my flip-flopping feelings about Theo.

"Theo, tell me about yourself. Nell hasn't told us anything." I glare at Nell while guiding Theo to the banquette. Cupcakes, presumably left over from the Halloween parties, appear on the table. CC and Frank bring cups and a pitcher of lemonade to the table while the other children settle into places at the table. Nell tries to distract me from questioning Theo by offering me a cupcake, but I'm nothing if not focused. (Not really—I snatch the cupcake and take a bite, returning my attention to Theo.)

"So, how did you meet? How long have you been dating? What's your favorite thing about Nell? What are your intentions?" I ask Theo rapid-fire. If only I had a bright light I could shine in his eyes like I see all the detectives do in the old movies. Oh well, I guess my interrogation will have to make do without.

"We met at freshman orientation, but only started dating a couple of weeks ago. Nell has many great qualities, but my favorite is her kindness. Since we've only been dating a few weeks and haven't known each other for long, it's too soon to plan our future, but I know how special she is and will always treat her with respect," Theo says. Huh, I guess those were all good answers. I take another bite of my cupcake.

I turn my interrogation on Nell. "Why didn't you mention Theo? Are you keeping secrets? What else are you hiding?"

"I didn't tell you because I have a right to privacy. If I told you what secrets I was keeping, they wouldn't be secrets. Besides, I brought Theo home so you all could meet him," Nell tells me with a glint in her eye, hinting that she's just about run out of patience with my questioning.

Taking advantage of the lull in my interrogation, the children jump in to fill the silence. They recount their Halloween parties, the Family Sports Festival wins, and other random details of their lives that Nell's missed while at college.

"Honey, I'm home," Jake announces, coming through the back door laden with Chinese takeout boxes. "Nell, welcome home," he adds, setting his load down on the table.

"Dad, this is Theo. My boyfriend," Nell tells Jake. Like all dads, Jake is protective of his daughter and thinks no boy is good enough for his daughter. He glares at Theo, who quakes under the thunderous expression.

Just kidding—Jake smiles warmly at Theo. "Nice to meet you, Theo." Is nobody else shocked and upset by this shocking and upsetting news? "We knew he was coming, Claire," Jake tells me. "Nell wanted to be sure he had a place to stay." Well, that makes sense, but why didn't I know about it?

"Speaking of places to stay," CC says as she brings plates to the table. "Since you aren't using your guest room, we thought ..."

"Nell and Jamie can stay with me," I interrupt CC. "Of course, Nell and Jamie can stay with me. They're always welcome." I smile warmly at Nell and then Jamie. "It'll be great." Jake, CC, and Nell all exchange glances, but before they can say anything, I continue. "It makes sense. You're out of bedrooms. Kyle and Dean share a room. Frank's and Eve's rooms don't have space for a cot. It wouldn't make sense to kick Frank out of his room for his sister's boyfriend, so Theo can take Nell's room, and Nell and Jamie can stay with me. Great idea!"

"Sounds like a plan," Theo says, removing the chopstick Eve stuck into his cup. He seems unperturbed by her antics. I can't help but wonder if Jake, CC, and Nell had a slightly different plan, but since Nell will be staying with me, I don't dwell on it. I notice Theo's using chopsticks, not a fork, to eat his food, and my opinion of him rises slightly.

When everybody has eaten their fill, CC and Jake put the leftovers away, while the children clear the table. I scoot home to put on my cowboy boots for our standing Friday night line dancing trip.

On my way back to CC's, I notice somebody standing near my car. Instantly suspicious, I skulk that way. I keep low and to the shadows, advancing like a ninja toward the unknown figure. As I leap from the shadows to restrain the intruder, he turns and snatches me out of the air. He spins and presses me between my car and his body.

Before I can panic and scream or flail, a warm, sexy voice washes over me. "Gotcha!" Then warm, sexy lips settle on mine. I know those lips. It was Dominic the whole time.

What's turning out to be an intense makeout session is interrupted by the closing of CC's back door and footsteps coming toward us. By the time CC joins us, there's a respectable distance between us. It's come at the expense of Dominic's shin. I had to resort to a little gentle kick when he didn't release me immediately. The fact that he's rubbing his shin and wincing tells me it might not have been as gentle as I thought. However, when he spots my shirt with the balloon animal, he smiles widely.

Before he can comment, we're interrupted. "Sheriff, I didn't realize you were here already," CC says, smiling warmly at him. My brain is still muddled from the kissing, so it takes me a minute to process the fact that CC knew the sheriff was coming.

I'm still processing when CC slides into the back seat and Dominic slides into the front seat. "Claire, what's wrong with you? Are you going to stand there all night?" CC asks, with a shocking lack of concern for me.

Kicking myself into gear, I too slide into my baby and turn the key. The rumbling purr from her engine returns some semblance of normalcy, and I drive toward the bar on autopilot. While I drive, I wonder why the sheriff is sitting next to me in my car. He showed up at the bar for line dancing a couple of times months ago, but I haven't seen him there since.

Now he's coming with us. If I'm honest with myself, I have to admit he is coming with *me*. I doubt he cares if CC joins us or not. I wonder what the regulars will say about this.

I don't have to wonder for long. Having reached the bar, we are greeted by the other regulars. As we walk in, Dominic keeps a hand at the small of my back in what some would call a possessive manner. (It's me, I'm the one calling it possessive.)

Dana, who's still been a little huffy about my ditching her idea of my perfect guy a couple of months ago, seems to thaw when she sees Dominic with me. Gwen, on the other hand, gets chillier. CC always says Gwen has a thing for me, and I have to admit the evidence keeps stacking up to agree with her. Everybody else simply makes room for all three of us at the table they've snagged.

I can't help but notice there are two gifts on the table. "This is from all of us," Stacy says, pushing a brightly wrapped box toward me. I gleefully rip the paper off the box and peer inside.

"Oooh, chocolate," I croon, pulling out several gourmet chocolate bars. There is also a pair of socks with IF YOU CAN READ THIS and BRING ME COFFEE printed on the soles and a coffee cup with lines indicating fill levels. The top line says DON'T TALK TO ME, the next one down says SHHH, then NOT YET, and the last one, at the very bottom of the mug, says OKAY, *NOW*.

"Thanks, everybody," I say, smiling at them all. "I can't believe you remembered!" I exchange a few hugs with those closest to me.

"You reminded them every week starting in September," CC rudely tells me. I ignore her.

"This is from me," Gwen says shyly, handing me the other wrapped box. I excitedly tear off the paper and open the box to reveal a framed linen square beautifully embroidered with a bouquet of wildflowers in a rainbow of colors.

"Wow," I breathe in awe. "Gwen, it's beautiful." Gwen smiles happily, and her cheeks glow with a soft pink hue. Her gray eyes sparkle in her heart-shaped face.

"Thanks, it's just a hobby I started to relieve the stress from work. I thought you might like this one because I know you can't keep real houseplants alive." She shrugs a little self-consciously.

"I love it," I tell her honestly. The thank-you hug I give her lasts a little longer than it should, and I think she's smelling my hair. CC might be right, I concede. Gwen wants me for herself.

"I heard your office is closed for remodeling," Stacy says. "How long will it be closed?"

"Who knows? Brandon hired an outside contractor, and they were behind schedule before they even started. At this rate, I may never go back to work," I tell her.

"Wow, you must be enjoying the time off," Gwen says. "I know you don't love your job." Gwen loves her job. She's a neonatal nurse.

"I've tried to convince her to use this time to look for a different job, but she's being stubborn," CC says.

"I'm not being stubborn," I defend myself. The looks being exchanged imply that nobody believes me. "I'm not passionate about anything. Well, except coffee and brownies," I clarify, "but I don't think anybody will hire me to be a brownie- or coffee-taste-tester. I'm just not passionate about a career like Gwen is. I just don't know what I want to do."

"What about working at a nonprofit?" Dana asks. "I know it would be the same kind of work, but it is so rewarding." Dana works for a nonprofit and loves it.

"My hospital is hiring," Gwen says. Why do all my friends have jobs they like?

"I don't think I want to do office work," I tell everybody. "I'm just not sure what I want to do instead. I thought about being a PI," I say quietly. Apparently, not quietly enough because everybody looks at me incredulously. It's like they have no faith in me and my abilities. "Hey, I solved Mr. Johnson's murder and saved Jamie," I defend myself. This seems to stymie everybody since I did, in fact, solve the murder and save Jamie, but it was a bit of a comedy of errors getting there.

The band starts warming up, saving the silence from becoming awkward. I put my gifts back in the boxes as everybody except Dominic prepares to head to the dance floor.

"I'll stay here and watch your stuff," he volunteers. His expression tells me that he's not happy that I'm considering being a PI, and that he thinks *he* solved Mr. Johnson's murder and saved Jamie. His expression is conveying a lot.

Before I can say anything, Gwen grabs my arm and leads me to the floor. I immerse myself in the music and familiar movements, completely ignoring Dominic's intense stare that never seems to leave my person. Actually—I hyper-focus on the fact that he can't take his eyes off me. When the band takes a break, I don't return to the table; instead, I flee to the bar. I don't feel up to facing Dominic and what his joining us at line-dancing night means.

"Hey, birthday girl," the attractive, dark-complexioned bartender greets me. I may have mentioned my upcoming birthday to him as well. His hazel-green eyes sparkle, even in the dim light of the bar. "How about Sex on the Beach?" he asks me in his deep, sexy voice. I feel my knees weaken under the onslaught of his sexuality.

"That sounds wonderful, Erick," I purr, leaning against the bar, mostly to support my weak knees.

"I've always wanted to try Sex on the Beach," Gwen says, joining me.

"Sex on the Beach for two coming right up," Erick says with a wink. Between the arm touching and smiling from Gwen and the oozing sex appeal of Erick, I'm feeling very popular tonight.

Feeling somebody on my other side, I'm not surprised to see Dominic. When Erick returns with our drinks, Dominic orders a beer. I take a sip of my Sex on the Beach, mostly to give myself something to do. I'm still not sure if I like the drink, but I loved ordering it, so I'm stuck with it. Gwen also takes a sip. Her face says she isn't sure if she likes it either.

"Are you ready for Halloween? I bought about twenty pounds of candy. I don't want to run out. I love seeing all the kids in their costumes." Gwen seems intent on holding my attention. Silly woman—my attention is slippery and fleeting, but I try my best. I'm half turned toward her, but I can feel that Dominic has adjusted his body to match my body's angle and is all but pressed against my back. I expected him to be angrier about me considering becoming a PI, especially after his reaction at the museum, but he hasn't said anything yet.

"Yeah, I have a ton of candy ready, and of course, my costume is all set for the town Halloween party tomorrow," I tell her, ignoring Dominic. At least I'm pretending to ignore him. When he reaches his arm past me to snag a few pretzels from the bowl, he comes in full-body contact with me. His breath stirs the hair near my ear. He offers me a pretzel. Without thinking, I open my mouth and let him feed me one. Gwen's shocked and slightly hurt expression suddenly causes my common sense to return. I handle the complex situation like the mature adult I am—I run back to the table and CC like the scared child I am.

The rest of the night passes in a blur as I fluctuate between desperately trying to ignore my rioting thoughts and feelings and obsessing on my rioting thoughts and feelings. I am at least smart enough not to add more alcohol to the mix. When the band finally calls it a night, I gather my gifts and join everybody heading toward the parking lot. There's a flurry of goodbyes, "Happy birthdays," "Happy Halloweens," and some hugs, as everybody prepares to leave. Gwen's hug is a little more intense than the others. She also glares at Dominic when she thinks I'm not looking.

Jealous much? I think. CC's choked laugh tells me I did more than just think it. Luckily, I seem to have said it softly enough that nobody else heard.

"Do you want me to drive?" Dominic offers hopefully.

I shoot him a disbelieving look. "Why would I want you to drive?" I ask, confused. "I only had one drink hours ago."

"Just thought I'd offer," Dominic shrugs nonchalantly.

"You just want to drive my baby," I accuse.

"Of course I do. This car is amazing," he says, but slides into the passenger seat. CC is already in the back seat. The drive home is uneventful, except for when Dominic casually puts his hand on my leg and I almost swerve off the road from the shock.

Since I didn't actually go off the road, I don't think it needs to be mentioned. Apparently Dominic disagrees, because he spends the rest of the drive home lecturing me on safe driving and accusing me of being a menace. Then, when we get home, he storms off. I concede he might have some remembered trauma from when I hit him with my car, or when I ran over his foot. I sigh after his retreating back. I take the time to appreciate how his backside looks in his jeans as he walks away before I take my presents and head inside.

I drop my gifts on the kitchen counter to worry about tomorrow, and then head upstairs to shower. Blackbeard is already waiting in my shower and meows at me to hurry up and turn on the water. Just once, I'd like to shower without my cat.

When I turn off the shower, I hear what sounds like footsteps. I almost call out, but then I remember every horror movie ever and decide stealth is the better choice.

Wrapped in a bath towel, I silently move into my bedroom. Agatha is snoring on my bed. She's no help against an intruder, unless they ring the doorbell. Benji hops excitedly to his feet when he sees me inching toward my door.

I hear another noise—this one is definitely coming from my kitchen. I slowly descend the stairs, clutching my weapon. (Some might say a scented candle isn't a great weapon, but it's what I have.)

Hearing the footsteps approaching the stairs, I time it carefully and jump out at the perfect moment. I immediately incapacitate the intruder. Or—I slip on the last step and almost land on my face at the intruder's feet.

"Auntie Claire, did you forget I was staying with you this weekend?" Nell asks as I regain my footing and dignity. (The dignity might not have been regained.)

"What? Of course not," I say, hiding the candle behind my back. "I was just coming to get a drink." She looks skeptical, but I keep up the pretense and continue to the kitchen for a glass of water.

"Okay, good night," Nell says with a hint of laughter in her voice.

"See you in the morning," I tell her, trying to fake nonchalance while I take another sip of my unwanted water.

Chapter 13

I wake up slowly, enjoying a slow stretch, the feeling of the sun on my face, and the knowledge that today is my birthday. I wish that's how I woke up. Instead, I'm startled awake when a cannonball lands on my stomach, accompanied by the whole family singing "Happy Birthday." The cannonball ends up being Eve. The family brought a full coffee cup and a brownie with a candle in it for me, so despite the possible internal bleeding caused by the human cannonball, it isn't the worst way to wake up. Having regained the breath Eve knocked out of me, I'm able to blow out my candle to a round of applause.

"Why don't you finish your brownie and coffee, then get dressed and come over for breakfast?" CC asks in a way that implies it isn't a question. Assuming I'll follow her dictates, she shoos her children out of my bedroom ahead of her.

I finish eating my birthday brownie and then pull on a pair of jeans and an orange shirt with a picture of a pumpkin and the pi symbol. While getting dressed, I contemplate why CC is so comfortable letting her whole family into my room while I'm sleeping. What if I hadn't been alone?

"Why are you so comfortable letting your whole family into my room while I'm sleeping? What if I hadn't been alone?" I ask CC when I join her in her kitchen.

"Please—you only share your bed with Agatha and Blackbeard. Besides, the sheriff was pretty mad when he left last night. I felt it was safe."

I take the mature way out and give her a pithy setdown that puts her in her place. Except I can't think of a pithy setdown, so I stick out my tongue at her instead. She ignores me while continuing to monitor the two waffle makers. With the size of her family, she might need to add a third waffle maker.

"Here, take one to Kyle, please," she says, handing me two plates with a waffle on each. I dutifully head to the table where the syrup, butter, peanut butter, bananas, mixed berries, and whipped cream are.

"Where are the chocolate chips and powdered sugar?" I ask.

"You already had a brownie and will eat nothing but junk food all day. You don't need chocolate chips and powdered sugar," she tells me with no trace of care or concern. She doesn't even care that it's my birthday. I mull over her point, decide she's right, and settle for peanut butter and bananas on my waffle.

Everybody is excitedly talking about the Halloween party and their costumes. Not a single birthday wish to be heard.

"Happy Birthday," Theo says, sitting across from me with his waffle.

"Thanks." I smile happily at him.

"Kyle was telling me about the missing painting. That's crazy. How do you think the thief got the painting out of the museum? It sounds like the sheriff shut down the museum quickly, so if they hadn't already removed it, it would still have been there, and they would have found it, right?" I'm shocked, both by Theo's intelligent questions and by the fact that Kyle told him so much. Sometimes I've gone days without hearing Kyle's voice, but he's Chatty Cathy with newcomer Theo.

"That's a great point," I say, ignoring my feelings about Kyle being so friendly with a near stranger. "I don't know how long it was between the last sighting of the painting and its being discovered missing. It's a big canvas, so it would be hard to sneak out, regardless of whether it was removed before or after it was discovered missing."

I ponder where the painting could be hidden in the museum. Not knowing much about museums, I can't come up with any good ideas. "Where could somebody hide an eight-foot-by-eight-foot painting in the museum?" I ask nobody in particular.

Theo answers my question. "If it had been removed from the frame, it could have been rolled into a tube. That would make it easier to hide, but it'd still be eight feet long. The museum's storage room in the basement would be the best place to hide it, but I don't know how that would help anybody get it out of the museum. And it would be risky, since people are often in the basement in the art restoration and study area, or the offices." He seems to know a lot about the museum.

"You seem to know a lot about the museum," I say, eyeing him suspiciously.

He smiles warmly at me. "My brother's girlfriend interns there. Sometimes when we all hang out together, she talks about the museum. I also got a tour last month." His answers seem to make sense, but I continue to eye him suspiciously.

"What has she said about the missing painting?" I ask.

Before Theo can answer, Jake interrupts. "Dominic, glad you could make it. Do you want a waffle?" Jake lets him in the back door.

Dominic is holding a present. "No, thanks. I already ate," he tells Jake. There's something in his gaze that I can't name. It might be uncertainty, but I'm distracted by the gift he's holding, so I dismiss whatever might be in his gaze. Dominic adds his present to a pile of brightly wrapped gifts on the table. I briefly wonder when the presents appeared, but I'm so excited about them that I don't give their sudden appearance much thought.

"Presents!" I exclaim happily. I love my birthday.

"Open mine first," Eve demands, shoving a box into my hands. I can tell she wrapped it herself. The wrapping paper is wrinkled, has some torn sections, and has enough tape to temporarily thwart my attempts to open it. Finally, I manage to get a finger hold so I can rip the wrapping paper off and open the box. Inside is a blue plaid dog collar with an attached bow tie and matching leash.

"It's for Benji. Won't he look so handsome?" Eve asks excitedly, pulling it out of the box to show it off. "I'll go put it on him," she says, and without waiting for a reply, she rushes out the back door.

"I feel like that gift is more for her than for me," I say, staring after her.

"Here, open mine," Ann says, pulling a box from the pile. I tear off the paper and reveal a holey ball and two paddles. "It's a pickleball set," she tells me. "It's super fun. Now we can play at the park." She seems very excited about my present.

"Thanks, Ann. I can't wait to give it a try," I tell her. It's a slight lie. I'm usually more of a cheer-from-the-sidelines than a go-sweat-it-out kind of girl, but I do love a good game of kickball, so maybe I'll like pickleball too.

"Mine next," Jane says, pushing a large box toward me.

"Ohhh, it's big," I say, eyeing the box. A few snorted chuckles tell me some people have dirty minds and have read innuendo into my innocent comment. When I rip off the paper and open the box, I reveal a goldfish bowl already filled with gravel and a plant. It's just missing water and a goldfish.

"If you win a goldfish at the Halloween party, you have a place to put it, but if not, we can get one from the pet store next week." Jane smiles serenely at me. Jane is always serene.

"Thanks, Jane. I do love the carnival games and winning. So fingers crossed I win a goldfish." I'm starting to think all my gifts are things the gift giver would like.

"Here, Auntie Claire, open mine," Dean says, unearthing his gift from the dwindling stack. I carefully unwrap the box. Dean's gifts have been known to activate upon unwrapping, and unwitting aunts have been known to be injured by this activation. I can't help but duck a little as I lift the lid off the box.

Even though I can clearly see what's in there, I don't know what it is. Not to worry, though. Dean is happy to tell me all about it. "It's an automatic goldfish feeder, so you won't have to remember to feed your fish every day," he says. He goes on to explain, in excruciating detail, how it works, how he made it, what materials he used, and on and on and on until my next birthday. (It isn't really that long, it just feels like it.)

Nell takes pity on me by interrupting Dean when he pauses for breath. "That's amazing, Dean. Aunt Claire, open mine." She pulls a flat box out of the stack and passes it to me. Opening the box, I see it's another set of cute pajamas. I'm starting to think she doesn't like my old yoga pants and T-shirts. This set has a cartoon cookie and glass of milk in an all-over print on the pants. The same cookie and milk are on the shirt with "BFFs" printed in big bubble letters above them. BFF, of course, stands for "best friends forever." I might be getting a little teary-eyed. Even though Nell's at college, I'm still her best friend forever.

Kyle interrupts what could become an embarrassing scene of me sobbing and clutching Nell desperately by handing me another present. Tearing off the paper, I see a framed oil pastel drawing of Benji. It's so realistic, I half expect the picture to bark. Under that picture is another one, an oil pastel of Agatha. She is, of course, sleeping. Her droopy ears and jowls are spread like a puddle across my floor. The last one is an oil pastel of Blackbeard. He's sitting with his tail wrapped around his feet. Kyle has captured his expression of superiority perfectly.

"Wow! Kyle, these are incredible. They're so lifelike. Thank you. I can't wait for your dad to hang them up in my house." I subtly slip Jake's implied help into my thank-you. Not that anybody would trust me with a hammer. Not after the unfortunate incident we will not name.

Frank passes me another box, and I eagerly rip it open. Inside is a coffee mug that has A DAY WITHOUT COFFEE IS LIKE … JUST KIDDING, I HAVE NO IDEA printed on it.

"Thanks, Frank. I love it. Maybe now your mom won't limit my coffee intake." CC rolls her eyes at me as if she disagrees with my comment, but she refrains from saying anything.

Trying to decide between the last two, I finally pick the bigger one. It's from Dominic. Opening it, I see a soft blue T-shirt with I AM printed above a picture of a koala and a tea bag. Under that shirt is another shirt. This one has a carrot poking at a pile of peas, with the words DISTURBING THE PEAS printed under it. A third shirt is a pastel green and has an old typewriter and the words JUST MY TYPE printed above it. The shirts seem to be communicating Dominic's feelings about me. They're surprisingly perfect gifts, but there's more: two books with old-fashioned-style covers. One is *Emma* by Jane Austen and the other is *Anne of Green Gables*.

I'm shocked speechless. Not a typical occurrence for me; I normally struggle with the opposite of being quiet. I open and close my mouth a few times, but no sounds come out. I finally raise my eyes to Dominic's. He looks apprehensive, as if he isn't sure I like his gifts.

"I love them," I blurt out.

His expression relaxes, and he smiles. "I know how much you love punny T-shirts. I haven't seen you wear these, but if you already have them, I can return them. Same for the books. I noticed your bookshelves are full of books, but I didn't see these two. I thought you would like them," he says in a rush.

"I love them," I repeat. I might be stroking the gifts lovingly as I say it. We could have gone on staring at each other all day, or we might have started kissing, but we'll never know because CC interrupts us.

"Last one," she says, pushing it toward me. I'm still feeling flustered by the incredibly thoughtful and insightful gifts Dominic picked out for me. How does he know me so well in such a short amount of time?

When I open CC and Jake's gift, I forget all about my confusing thoughts. Inside are a lei, retro-style sunglasses, sunscreen, a wide-brimmed sun hat, and a sundress. I pull out the items one by one, slightly confused. While I like everything, I don't know what I'm going to do with so much summer stuff as we head into winter. At the very bottom of the box is a printed itinerary, a hotel brochure, and a first-class airplane ticket to Hawaii.

"Hawaii!" I exclaim. "I'm going to Hawaii?"

"*We're* going to Hawaii," CC corrects.

"We are?! This is amazing!" I jump up and hug CC, then Jake, and then CC again. The kids are also jumping up and hugging. Different voices exclaim their excitement.

"We're going over the Thanksgiving break. I already talked to Brandon about your time off in case your office reopens before then," CC says. She's thought of everything. "Sheriff, could you please help Claire take her gifts home? I don't think she can carry them by herself." CC smiles warmly at him with an expression that is too innocent to be innocent.

"That's okay," I say, "I'll just make two trips."

"Don't be silly, the sheriff is happy to help—aren't you?" CC says with just a touch of steel in her voice.

"He's a guest. He shouldn't be expected to be my sherpa." My voice also has a touch of steel.

"I don't mind," Dominic says, already starting to gather my gifts. I admit defeat silently and also start gathering my gifts. Dominic has significantly more gifts gathered than I do; his arms are full while I only have Kyle's framed drawings. We're silent as we cross the yards toward my house.

Eve surprises me by opening my door as we approach. I forgot she went to my house. Benji is proudly wearing his new bow-tie collar. "Doesn't he look handsome?" Eve smiles happily. She doesn't wait for an answer. "Come on, Benji. Let's show everybody." Benji happily trots at Eve's heels as she heads home.

Dominic and I put my gifts on the counter next to the gifts from last night. I somehow manage to keep my thoughts to myself, probably because my thoughts are so muddled I couldn't even begin to put them into words.

"I think you should open a bookstore," he says as he places the last gift in the pile. My mouth falls open in shock. When I continue standing there, gaping at him, he continues. "You have office management skills, you love books, and you can have a little coffee area. It would be perfect for you. You could even wear your T-shirts." These are all convincing arguments. "Plus, you'd be too busy to butt into investigations that are none of your business." Well, that took a turn.

"I can't open a bookstore. I don't know the first thing about business," I tell him. Wait, that's not right. I have a business degree. I consider his suggestion. On the one hand, I love books. On the other hand, responsibility isn't my strong suit. On the other other hand, I'm an amazing office manager, so I guess I can be responsible. On the other other other hand, I don't know anything about owning a bookstore. On the other other other other hand, I did have a business degree. I was running out of hands, but not out of things to consider.

"Just think about it," Dominic says, as if I weren't already thinking about it. I do stop thinking about it when he wraps his arms around me and pulls me against his body. "Did you really like the shirts and books?" he asks, with a vulnerability I didn't think he was capable of. He's usually so self-assured and confident.

"I love them," I tell him honestly. He carefully studies my face before his expression relaxes. "They're perfect. I couldn't have picked anything better."

He smiles just before his lips meet mine.

"Aunt Claire, lunch is ready," Nell says, from my open back door. She doesn't wait for a response, just gives me a big smirk and turns to leave.

My face flames as I realize I'm now sitting on my counter with Dominic between my legs. Those legs might have been wrapped around him, but I'll never admit to that. I don't even remember how I got here, or how long we've been kissing. It's probably been quite a while, since lunch is ready. And Nell saw it all. The only thing that could be more embarrassing would be if CC had seen it.

I hop off the counter in a panic. Unfortunately for Dominic, he's still standing in front of me, so he gets body-checked to the floor. Again. For a big man, he doesn't seem to take a hit well. I've knocked him down several times now. Not seeing any blood, I decide he's probably fine and hustle to CC's. The grumbling behind me tells me Dominic is able to follow me, proving he's okay.

"What's for lunch?" I ask casually. When everybody stops what they're doing and looks at me, I realize Nell tattled. "It's not what you think. I had something in my eye. We absolutely were not making out in my kitchen. And for sure, my legs were not wrapped around him."

Nell's peal of laughter, normally a sound that brings joy and peace to all, now mocks me. Also, it tells me she might not have tattled after all. Jake snorts, trying not to laugh. CC rolls her eyes at my bald-faced lie and tries to hide her delighted smile. The children seem shocked. Jamie avoids eye contact, and Theo smiles in a good-natured way. I close my eyes in mortification.

Before I can recover, Dominic walks in the door behind me. Since I'm frozen in the doorway, he uses full-body contact to guide me inside. I jump away from him like I've been burned and rush to the banquette to put some distance between us. He slides in right behind me, forcing me to scoot over or be crushed. I scoot far enough away that no part of me is touching him, but when Ann complains I'm squishing her, I have to inch closer to Dominic.

He rests his hand on my leg under the table. My breathing hitches, and I start to feel lightheaded. "Breathe," he whispers in my ear. I suck in a breath, and my vision clears.

CC and Jake each bring two flatbread-pizza-sandwich things to the table, apparently unconcerned with my panic. I take a piece and eat it without tasting it.

I ignore the conversation swirling around me as I think deep thoughts. How did Dominic pick such perfect gifts? Why did he even get me gifts? How did he know to show up for the present opening time? Why is he suddenly always kissing me? He didn't even kiss me after our one date. (Although that might have been due to the paramedics and ambulance ride.) Is it just a coincidence that Theo has a connection to the museum and is dating Nell? Could I open a bookstore?

"You're opening a bookstore?" CC asks. Her surprised expression turns thoughtful. "Yes, I can see that. I think that's a great idea!" She beams at me. She wasn't this excited about my idea to be a PI.

"I don't know that I'm opening a bookstore," I try to deflect. "Dominic just suggested it." CC's sharp gaze lands on Dominic. I'm glad it isn't focused on me. Her gaze seems to reach into him, seeing his every thought and feeling. A small smile tugs at her lips as she turns to Jake. I can tell they're silently communicating, but I have no idea *what* they are communicating. How come everybody else can be silent, but I can't?

"Ms. Downing might be interested in selling her old antique shop. It's been empty since she retired last year," Jake says.

"Oh, that's such a nice space," CC says. "It has those big front windows, and it's in a perfect location. You could call it Books and Crannies."

"Or Book Bound. Or Cover to Cover," Nell suggests.

"What about Fairytale Endings or Once Upon a Time?" Ann says. Apparently, at ten, she still likes fairy tales.

"I like Novel Idea or Novel Experience," Frank says. Evidently, everybody's decided I'm opening a bookstore, and they're very quick to think of names. Dean suggests Bound to Please, Reader's Retreat, and Tome Raiders. Kyle suggests Plot Twist and As the Page Turns. Jane likes On the Same Page, Chapter and Verse, and

Literary Lane. Theo proposes An Open Book and What the Book? Jake comes up with Booked.

"What about Between the Covers?" CC says with a pointed look at Dominic and me.

"I like Buy the Book. With 'by' spelled B-U-Y," Dominic says, casually dropping his arm around my shoulder and pulling me closer to him.

"I haven't even decided if I'm opening a bookstore. I think picking a name is a little premature." I feel ganged up on, but I can't help thinking about it. I do love books. If I worked for myself, my boss wouldn't be an idiot. At least I hope I wouldn't be an idiot. But it sounds like a lot of work, and what if I'm not good at it? What if I fail?

"Well, enough talking about it for now. We need to get ready for the Halloween party," CC says briskly, but the look she gives me is speculative and promises we aren't done talking about this.

Everybody files out to change into their costumes. I'm pretty excited about my costume, so I patiently wait for Dominic to stand up so I can head home and change. I poke him in the ribs to get him to move faster. (I guess I'm not very patient.) He catches my finger and holds my hand to prevent more poking as he scoots out of banquette. When his thumb starts rubbing my palm, I start to think he isn't planning to release it anytime soon. Snatching my hand back, I hurry home, but my convoluted thoughts follow me.

Chapter 14

It takes me a while to get into my Halloween costume, so by the time I'm ready, everybody else is already in the driveway. Everybody looks great. Amelia has joined us, and she and Frank are dressed as zombies, complete with makeup. Jamie, Nell, and Theo are dressed as pirates. Nell looks amazing in her off-the-shoulder blouse, black vest, and asymmetrical red skirt. Based on the way Theo is checking her out, he agrees.

Jamie's costume is similar to Nell's, but her blouse is not off the shoulder, and her skirt is longer. For once, her hair isn't completely obscuring her face. Maybe Nell's friendship has given her more confidence. Just a couple of months ago, I couldn't have even pictured her dressing up in a costume.

Theo looks very dashing in his blousy shirt and large hat. The way he looks at Nell when she isn't looking tells me this might be a more serious relationship than I originally thought. I don't know how I feel about this. I want Nell to be happy, and Theo seems like a nice guy, but he's her first real boyfriend.

I'm distracted from my thoughts by CC's costume. She looks wonderful in her champagne-colored flapper dress. The sequins catch the light, and the tassels swirl around her shins with her every movement.

"Wow, you look incredible," I tell her honestly.

"Doesn't she?" Jake says, wrapping her in his arms for a kiss that is a little more passionate than a family gathering should allow. Jake also looks incredible in a zoot suit. The pinstripes accentuate his muscular frame.

I'm starting to feel like a voyeur, so I avert my gaze from them to check out the rest of the group. Ann is dressed as an Olympian, complete with several gold medals around her neck. Jane is wearing scrubs, and has a stuffed cat in her arms. I'm surprised it isn't a real cat, but the town Halloween party probably isn't the best place to bring a cat. Dean is dressed like a mad scientist, complete with a lab coat, safety goggles, and messy hair. Kyle is wearing my beret and a striped shirt, and holding a painting palette. Eve is dressed as Dorothy from *The Wizard of Oz* in a blue gingham dress, holding the fruit basket, with Benji at her side.

Finally, my gaze lands on Dominic. He's wearing snug black pants, knee-high boots, a white shirt that is open at the neck, a bottle-green vest, a duster-style coat, a top hat with goggles resting on the brim, and a belt with a pouch and thigh strap. I'm shocked. Not just because he looks so sexy, but also because he is dressed in steampunk style. My costume is also steampunk. How did he know what my costume was?

His heated gaze takes in every part of my costume from my lace-up shin-high boots to the mini top hat perched at an angle on my head. He spends a long time on my legs, which are exposed to mid-thigh by the front-gathered skirt, and on my chest, which is emphasized by my off-the-shoulder white shirt and leather-and-brocade corset. I feel warm all over.

When Dominic takes a step toward me, I panic and rush to jump in my car. His rueful chuckle tells me he knows exactly what I'm avoiding. His getting into my passenger seat tells me I won't be successful at avoiding it. Theo, Nell, and Jamie climb into my back seat, so I back out and head to Town Square Park and the Halloween party.

It's a very popular event, so the closest parking spaces we can find are several blocks away. We join the stream of people heading to Town Square Park.

Before I can avoid it, Dominic laces his fingers with mine. My subtle efforts to remove my hand escalate into what probably looks like a tug of war. CC's frown tells me she's noticed and thinks I should stop.

I spend the walk to the park trying to come up with a new idea to extract my hand, but I'm unsuccessful, so my hand is still enfolded in his when we arrive at the park. They did a good job setting up for the party. Scarecrows, witches, carved pumpkins, ghosts, oversized spiderwebs complete with oversized spiders, skeletons, black cats, and bats are placed throughout the park. The straw bale maze and carnival games are on the large grassy field just past the playground equipment. Tall spotlights are set up to illuminate the straw bale maze, but if I remember correctly, there will be plenty of dark corners once the sun goes down.

The carnival games have lights inside the booths that illuminate both the games and the prizes you can win. String lights, not yet switched on, are stretched between the carnival game booths and also between the food stands. The smell of apple cider and fried foods makes my stomach growl in anticipation. The picnic shelters have paper lanterns that look like jack-o'-lanterns and ghosts. The parking lot has been left open, but with small areas of chairs and straw bales set at intervals around the perimeter. Twinkle lights, also not yet turned on, crisscross the area above the improvised dance floor. The bandstand at the edge of the parking lot already has the DJ equipment set up for the dance later.

"Ghouls and goblins," the mayor addresses the crowd through a megaphone, "Kyle Moore has generously donated his time and talent to paint murals on the park bathroom building. The murals honor our town's history and highlight our community. . ."

I try to focus on the mayor's speech honoring Kyle, but he's droning on and on. Also, Dominic has wrapped his arms around me from behind and is nibbling on my neck.

". . . we'll be unveiling Kyle's murals in five minutes." The mayor finishes to a round of applause.

CC, Jake, and their children make their way to the front of the crowd gathering around the bathroom building. Wanting to be supportive and not wanting to be left out, I follow them. Dominic allows me to slip out of his arms, but once again grabs my hand as he follows me.

"There you are, Claire. I was afraid you'd miss it," CC says, as if I haven't been standing five feet away from her since we got to the park.

"I wouldn't miss it for anything," I tell her, smiling encouragingly at Kyle, who's standing near the sheet-covered building. "I'm feeling a bit of déjà vu," I murmur. Just a week ago, we were waiting for a different artist to unveil a different art piece. At least this one can't go missing. Unless David Copperfield puts in an appearance.

"And now, the moment we've all been waiting for," the mayor announces, beginning to count down from ten. The crowd joins in, and when we reach "One!" Kyle pulls the sheet off the side of the building we're facing. (Other people pull the sheets off the other sides of the building.)

The side we're facing has a scene of a small farmstead. A little girl is standing on the porch, clutching a rag doll. Her mom is in the yard hanging laundry on a clothesline. I swear I can see the clothes flapping in the breeze. On the other side of the yard, a man plants a field with a horse and plow. Chickens are scratching in the dirt, while a dog lies nearby.

It's incredibly realistic. I almost feel like I could step into the painting and into the past. The longer I look at it, the more details I see. Like the boy with the pitchfork in the barn's hayloft. Or the fox sneaking toward the chickens.

I can feel the crowd moving around me as they circle the building to see all the murals, but I remain where I am, still taking in the image in front of me. I almost gasp out loud when I catch a glimpse of two Native Americans in the background. One is peeking out from behind a tree. Another can be seen crouching behind a large bush. I wonder what else Kyle has carefully included that I just haven't discovered yet.

"Wow," I say. I'm at a loss for what to say next. Kyle is so talented. He's never even tried to create an art piece of this size before. "It's the most amazing thing I've ever seen!"

"It is very good," Pierre says from my left side. Surprised, I snap my head around to look at him. I hadn't expected him to come after I had turned his invite down. "In time, he may be a great artist like myself," he continues with a self-importance I don't like. He looks away from the mural to glare at Dominic. I'd forgotten Dominic was holding my hand, but now he wraps an arm around my waist in what I can only describe as a proprietorial manner.

Before I can defend Kyle, he appears. "Pierre, you came. What do you think of it? There are more on the other walls." Kyle seems to be seeking Pierre's approval, and I frown. Kyle is usually self-assured. He knows who he is and is comfortable with himself. I don't like that he is seeking validation from Pierre. He seems too self-absorbed to be a role model.

"Kyle, it is the most amazing thing I've ever seen," I interject honestly. "You're going to be a famous artist before you know it." He shoots me a quick smile before turning his hopeful face to Pierre.

"It is very good," Pierre says again. I know what's coming next, and it is not encouraging. To prevent Pierre from saying any unkind words, I discreetly kick him in the shin. He yelps in pain and clutches his leg. (I may not have been very discreet after all.)

"Oh, goodness, I'm so sorry," I lie. "Let me take you to get some ice." I'm somehow able to extract myself from Dominic's normally implacable hold, probably because he's trying not to laugh. I take advantage of this to grab Pierre's arm and steer him away from Kyle.

"Listen here, you," I hiss, guiding him a safe distance away. "You will say kind and encouraging things to Kyle, or else ..." I pause, since I don't know what a good threat would be.

"I would only offer encouragement to a young artist beginning their journey. I remember my early days in the art world. There I was, fresh from art school, filled with knowledge and passion, beginning to create my great works. A word of encouragement would have gone a long way to support my dreams."

I interrupt what is becoming a monologue of his early years. "Saying 'in time he may become a great artist' doesn't sound very encouraging to me." This reminds me that Dominic couldn't verify his early years. "Why can't the Sheriff find any official record of you before you were discovered in L.A.?"

The change of subject seems to take him off guard. "Maybe he is not thorough in his search," Pierre says with a lack of conviction, but a wealth of bluster.

"He is a very thorough person," I counter. I feel my face flame with thoughts of Dominic's thoroughness in kissing me, but I don't let that stop me from glaring at Pierre.

"I cannot be responsible for what the sheriff does or does not uncover in his investigation." Pierre tries to dismiss my question and then changes the subject. "You look exquisite in your costume." His gaze takes me in, and like Dominic's gaze, it lingers on my exposed legs and chest. Unlike Dominic's gaze, which made me feel warm, Pierre's gaze makes me feel annoyed.

"Just be honest. Why was there no history of Pierre until two years ago?" I push.

"There has always been Pierre. It's not my fault he did not find my history," he counters. I'm so frustrated by his lies that I stomp my foot. Sadly, for Pierre, I stomp on *his* foot.

"Ouch! You did that on purpose," he yells, without a French accent.

My eyes widen in surprise. "You aren't French?" I ask incredulously. "Who are you?"

"I have to go," he says, in his French accent again, and hurries off before I can say anything else.

"Are you okay?" Theo asks, joining me where I'm still standing, gobsmacked. "He seemed pretty upset." I'm surprised Theo noticed Pierre and me. Shouldn't he be focused on Nell? Was he watching Pierre? Was he watching me? Luckily, I don't say any of my thoughts out loud.

"Yeah, just a little misunderstanding. Do you know Pierre?" I ask.

"That was Pierre? The guy whose painting was stolen?" He whips his head around searching for him in the crowd, but Pierre has disappeared from view. "No, I've never met him, but I've heard about him and his art," Theo says, giving up his search.

"There you are. The costume contest is starting soon. Come on," Nell says, dragging Theo off. "Hurry up, Auntie Claire," she calls over her shoulder.

I obediently follow her toward the crowd gathering to either watch or participate in the costume contest. It starts with the youngest contestants, those under one year old. Only a few babies were entered, and it's quickly judged. I miss the winner because I'm making silly faces, trying to get an adorable baby wearing a monkey costume to laugh.

Then the one-to-four-year-olds are up. Eve has some stiff competition, but Benji steals the show with his begging pose, and soon Eve is pinning their winning ribbon onto Benji's new collar.

The contest judging continues with the other children's age groups. Dean wins his group, but Ann, Jane, and Kyle don't. They're good sports about it and congratulate their friends who did win.

Frank and Amelia and Nell and Theo enter the couples' category against several other couples, including CC and Jake. I'm ready to cheer for all three couples when I'm suddenly guided up the steps to join them. Turning my head, I confirm that Dominic is the one propelling me.

"Entering the couples' costume contest? Seriously? We'll be the talk of the town," I whisper out of the side of my mouth.

"You seem to be under the impression that I care if we're the talk of the town. I couldn't care less if people talk about us. Do you care?" he asks, his tone half taunting, half curious. I don't respond because I'm not sure if I care. It wouldn't be the first time the town talked about me, but it would be the first time it involved a relationship and not some horrible or embarrassing incident.

Unsurprisingly, CC and Jake win. Not only are they a gorgeous couple with top-quality costumes, but they're well-liked, too.

I slip away from Dominic in the bustle of congratulations and the spectators dispersing. I decide an elephant ear will help me untangle my thoughts, or at least make me feel better about my tangled thoughts. I take my cinnamon-sugar-coated deep-fried dough and find an empty table.

Even though my elephant ear is delicious, it's not enough to stop my thoughts from intruding. Do I care that the town is talking about Dominic and me? How did Dominic know about my costume? And Nell's visiting schedule? And Kyle's murals? Why does Kyle like Pierre so much? Why is Pierre faking an accent?

"Pierre is faking his accent?" Dominic asks as he joins me at my table. I'm not surprised he's joined me. He seems to always know where I'm at and shows up whenever it suits him. He has two soft pretzels and hands one to me. Well, at least he brought me food.

"Yeah, when I stomped on his foot—by accident," I clarify, "he yelled at me, but he didn't have an accent. When I asked him about it, he said he had to go, in his French accent, as if he hadn't just spoken without it. What do you think it means?" I pull off a chunk of pretzel and pop it in my mouth.

"It would help explain why I couldn't find any background on Pierre," Dominic says. "I've still been looking into it, but if he changed his name, especially if he didn't legally change it, it will be harder to find anything. Maybe I should have another talk with Pierre." I'm pretty good at this investigating stuff, I think, but luckily don't say. No point in making Dominic angry again.

"Auntie Claire, look what I won," Dean says, sitting down on the bench next to me. He proudly shows me a ping pong ball shooter. "I won it at the ring toss. It's easy to win. All you have to do is calculate …" I tune out the rest of his story, as it contains academic terms I didn't pay attention to even when I was being graded on them.

"Look what I won," Ann says, settling next to Dominic. She proudly displays a stuffed animal almost as tall as she is. "When you win, you can trade in your previous prize for a larger one. It only took me twenty tickets."

"Did you win a goldfish?" Jane asks me as she joins us. She's holding a young raccoon like a baby. I don't bother asking her where she found a raccoon, or why she's holding it like a baby.

"Not yet. I haven't played any games yet," I tell her, finishing the last of my pretzel.

"You can have my extra tickets," Jane offers. "I only played a few games." I accept the tickets from her and stand up.

"All right, time for some prizes," I say with a completely misplaced air of confidence. I rarely win at anything. I head toward the carnival game booths, searching for the goldfish one. There is the ring toss, dart throw to pop balloons, baseball throw to knock down milk bottles, Plinko, spin the wheel, rubber duckie pond, and basketball toss. Finally spotting the goldfish bowls, I head that way, since I'm apparently expected to win a goldfish for my birthday.

I hand over my ticket to Mary, who's running the booth, and get two ping pong balls. I eye the many small bowls filled with water, trying to choose the perfect target. Carefully taking aim, I toss my first ball. It bounces wildly between the bowls but doesn't land in any of them. This happens again with the other ball.

Not one to give up, I hand over another ticket. Once again, I manage to miss landing a ball in a bowl.

This pattern is repeated until I only have one ticket left.

I carefully practice my toss with the first ball. I visualize it going into the bowl. I confidently toss it, only to watch it bounce wildly off the table. Deflating, I haphazardly toss the last ball, knowing Jane will have to get my goldfish from the pet store.

"You won!" Ann yells.

"You did it!" Dean says as he high-fives me. I'm shocked. I can't believe I did it.

"I knew I could do it," I say. Mary fills a plastic bag with water and picks up a fish net as she turns to the tank with dozens of goldfish in it. I carefully examine my choices. Most of them are gold, but some have a bit of white or black. Finally, I spot the perfect choice.

"Can I have that one?" I ask, pointing to a black, white, and gold fish. Mary sighs as she releases the one she's already caught. She chases the one I had pointed out with the net for several minutes before she's finally able to scoop it up. She dumps it in the bag, adds air from a tube nearby, and then seals the bag shut by wrapping a rubber band around it about a million times.

"Thanks, Mary," I say, turning away and admiring my new pet. "I think I'll name him Jaws."

I wander through the carnival game booths, with Dominic once more at my side. I watch the hopeful participants trying their luck at the various games. I see Frank win Amelia a medium-sized stuffed bear when he knocks down all the milk bottles with his first throw. At the Plinko booth, Theo wins Nell a trick ice cream cone with a hidden trigger that shoots the ice cream part. Nell then wins comically oversized sunglasses for Theo at the same game.

I spot Jake and CC at the strength-measuring tower thing. I can never remember what it's called, but it's the game where you test your strength by using a huge mallet to hit a target, and then the little puck thingie shoots up the tower to reveal your level of strength. It has markings with THAT'S EMBARRASSING, WEAKLING, GETTING BETTER, NOT TOO BAD, HAVE YOU BEEN WORKING OUT?, HERCULES, and similar things.

I wince when I remember the year I tried my strength. I missed the target, but not Ralph, who was in charge of the game. I was banned from trying my strength ever again.

Jake swings the mallet and, of course, does not miss the target. The little puck flies up the track to the very top to ring the bell. CC looks over the prize choices in the winning category and happily chooses the manicure gift card.

"Ohh, a manicure gift card," I croon. "I want one." Dominic hands over a ticket and accepts the mallet from Jake. Dominic swings the mallet; he also does not miss the target. I'm starting to think it's just a me thing. The puck once again rings the bell. I happily snatch the last manicure gift card from the prizes.

"Thanks!" I beam at Dominic, and then, standing on my toes, I press a quick kiss on his lips. I realize it's the first time I've kissed him. He's always been the one to initiate kissing. His eyes tell me he also realizes it's the first time I've kissed him, and he likes it.

Deciding a strategic escape is prudent, I turn to the nearest booth and hand Mitchell the ticket I just snatched from Jake's hand. Only after I'm handed the darts do I realize which booth I'm at. Mitchell steps far off to the side, half hiding behind the booth's support pole. It's as if he's afraid my aim will be so bad that I might hit him instead of popping the balloons. His fear might be justified, but that doesn't stop me from squinty-eyed glaring at him before turning back to the targets. My first four darts pop a balloon each. My last dart, however, somehow ricochets off the board the balloons are attached to and embeds itself in Dominic's arm.

Everybody freezes as we stare at the dart sticking out of his arm.

"Oh my gosh, I'm so sorry!" I say, rushing to pull it out. He sucks in a breath as the dart slides free. "Are you bleeding? CC, get a bandage." I start tugging his coat off his shoulders. Once I get it off, I hand it to Jake. Then I grab Dominic's wrist and start unbuttoning his shirt cuff so I can push the sleeve up and assess the wound. There's a small spot of blood welling from where the dart pierced his skin.

CC hands me a bandage, and I rip open the wrapping and stick it on the wound. Only after it's adhered to his skin do I realize it's a Superman band-aid. The design probably has some hidden meaning that a therapist would have a field day with, but I don't want to think about it. Dominic chuckles when he sees the design. I guess he isn't mad at me.

"You aren't mad at me?" I ask softly.

"In the grand scheme of injuries you have inflicted on me, this one barely counts," he tells me, rolling his sleeve down and rebuttoning his cuff. I droop with the truth of his words. I've inflicted a lot of injuries on him in a short amount of time, some of them requiring care from medical professionals.

Mitchell interrupts the moment by handing me my prize. It's a pair of socks that look like cowboy boots.

"I won these for you," I say as I offer the socks to Dominic. He smiles, and even in the dim light, I can see his eyes heat.

"Thank you," he says seriously. There's something in his tone. I'm not sure what it is, or what it means, but I kind of like it.

"I'm hungry," Eve says as she and Benji run up to join us. Kyle trails behind her. Obviously, he's having a difficult time keeping up with her. As if some secret signal is transmitted to them, soon all of CC's kids—and Amelia, Jamie, and Theo—join us as well. We all head over to get dinner from the food stands.

With our dinners in hand, we manage to find two empty tables next to each other, so there's space for all of us. I sit at a table with Dominic on one side, Kyle on the other, and Jaws' bag propped in front of me. He seems content with his placement, slowly swimming around in his bag. I got a corn dog and a basket of fries with cheese sauce. CC's been feeding me healthy food all week, and I'm allowed some junk food. I eat all of my food and also manage to steal several of Dominic's onion rings.

A group of costumed kids run up to the table. "We're going to the maze. Want to come?" they ask.

"Oh, no thanks. I think I'm going to look at Kyle's murals some more," I tell them. They turn to look at me, then look back at the other side of the table. It's possible they were inviting Jane, Ann, and Dean instead of me.

"Sure," Ann says as they jump up to join them.

"I want to go to the maze!" Eve declares from where she's standing on the picnic table. Jake catches her midair as she jumps off the picnic table, and then carries her off toward the maze. Benji follows them without even looking back at me. I'm starting to think he can be bought, and that he loves my birthday gift from Eve.

At least Jaws hasn't abandoned me. It's probably because he's trapped in a bag of water, but that's not important. Carefully picking up his bag, I head back to the bathroom building to see Kyle's other murals. He painted the three sides of the building that didn't have doors, and I've only seen one side.

I expect all the murals to be similar to the first one of the founding farmers—maybe even a continuous scene wrapping around the building—but it's not.

"It's just a bunch of squares. It's not at all what I was expecting," I say, moving even closer to see if I missed something.

"Step back here and take another look," Dominic says from several feet behind me. I move to join him, not sure how distance is going to make a difference.

"Oh, wow!" I breathe. From up close, it was just a bunch of small colored squares, but from a distance, the squares blend together to make a phoenix rising from flames. "Even though I know he's so incredibly talented, I'm still shocked by how incredibly talented he is."

We stand in silence, taking in this mural for a few more minutes before I move to the last side of the building to see his third mural. This one is made up of a bunch of colors that don't seem to have edges. The colors change from one to another, but it's hard to pinpoint when it happens. They all kind of resemble clouds in that way. When I stop trying to force the image into focus, it becomes clear. It's a tree-lined street with a sunrise at the end of the road.

"He is going to be one of the great artists that everybody studies," Dominic says, his voice full of the same awe I'm feeling. I just nod, because for once I can't think of anything to say.

"Do you like them?" Kyle asks as he joins us. He adjusts his gold wire-rimmed glasses in what other people might consider a nervous gesture, but I know it isn't. Kyle is quiet, not self-conscious.

"Kyle, they are amazing!" I tell him, wrapping him in a hug. "I'm so proud of you. When you get crazy famous, don't forget your

Auntie Claire always believed in you." He hugs me back for a minute before he starts struggling. When Dominic helps him escape my embrace, he sucks in several deep breaths as if I've been suffocating him. I might have been hugging him a little too tightly.

"You have a real gift," Dominic says, still holding me off of Kyle. Probably for the best, since I'm contemplating snatching him back into my arms. When Kyle smiles happily, I see a smudge of something blue across his right cheek. I don't even try to figure out what it is. That kid can't stay clean for anything.

"Did you know Pierre isn't French?" I ask him.

Kyle cocks his head as if thinking deeply. "That makes sense," he finally says. "It explains why there's only very general information on him before his discovery. He never even names the college he attended. Or anything specific about his time living in France. But why would he pretend to be French? What's the benefit of it?"

These are good questions. I silently ponder his points. Is it hard to keep up a fake accent, or does it become second nature? If he isn't Pierre, who is he? If I made up a fake persona, what would my name be? What about my backstory? What would that be?

"What about an orphaned princess who had to flee her country? Or maybe a spy sent to uncover national secrets. I know! A witness to a crime whose testimony will put a kingpin away for life." Dominic's chuckle tells me I switched from silent pondering to out-loud pondering.

"I like you just the way you are," he tells me. Somehow, he followed my convoluted thought process. He pulls me into his arms. Luckily, he takes Jaws' bag out of my hand before pressing my body full length to his, so Jaws isn't squished between us. Dominic takes full advantage of the scant privacy afforded by being on the far side of the bathrooms.

Only when the DJ starts the music for the dance does Dominic pull back. It takes me longer than I'd like to admit to regain any thoughts. My first thought is, *Wow!* He's a good kisser! My second thought is, did we just make out in front of Kyle? A quick glance tells me he left, hopefully before we started making out. My third thought is, Does Dominic really like me just the way I am? Most people have a list of things they would change about me. Some of the lists are very long.

"Next up is a Halloween favorite, 'Thriller.' I'd like to invite all those 'Thriller' fans to join me on the dance floor," the DJ announces, interrupting my thoughts.

"I love the 'Thriller' dance!" I say. I'm in such a rush to join the dancers already gathering on the dance floor that I don't think twice about abandoning Jaws with Dominic. I find CC, Jake, Nell, Frank, Theo, Jamie, and Ann in the crowd on the makeshift dance floor and join them just as the music starts. CC and I spent a whole month learning the dance moves one year in middle school. We passed on our knowledge to all of her children, but apparently, not all of them want to show off their moves.

"You were scared to join us?" I half taunt Jane, Dean, Kyle, and Eve when the song ends and we rejoin them.

"You guys were really good," Amelia says. "I don't think I could remember all the moves." She's so nice, but she really shouldn't leave herself open for an attack on her mental abilities.

"I'm sure you can," Frank assures her. "I'll teach you. It'll be fun." She smiles warmly at him. When he returns her smile, his dimples accentuate his boy-next-door good looks. He looks just like his dad did when he was that age. I notice several teenage girls are staring at Frank longingly, even though he's taken.

"I might have tried to join in, but I was holding Jaws." Dominic holds up the fish as proof. "Maybe you could teach me later so I'll be ready for next year." The promise in his eyes and voice makes me swallow hard.

When a slow song comes on, Dominic hands my fish to Jane. "Will you watch Jaws for us?" he asks her. The implied "us" is not lost on me, or—based on her expression—on CC either. Jane accepts Jaws in his bag from Dominic, and he leads me onto the dance floor.

Once again, I'm wrapped in his arms. This time we are swaying to music. At first, I'm tense and self-conscious, but as Dominic guides me around the floor with the other couples, I relax. In no time, I find myself cheek to cheek with him. When he dips me and gives me a quick but thorough kiss, I panic again.

As soon as the song ends, I slip from his arms and articulate my boundaries clearly. Just kidding—I run away. I don't pay attention to where I'm going, and I end up in the straw bale maze. I stop just inside the entrance to catch my breath and calm my thoughts.

While I'm able to catch my breath, I'm not able to calm my thoughts. Hearing footsteps approaching, I dash deeper into the maze. I'm not ready to face Dominic.

I pass a few people, but the maze seems mostly empty. After several minutes, I'm far enough in that I haven't passed anybody recently and feel safe. But no sooner do I think this than Dominic comes around the corner.

Shoot, I'm not safe after all, I think. Wait, no, I said it. Not taking the time to be embarrassed, I turn to run, only to face a wall of straw bales. I've trapped myself in a corner.

"Why aren't you safe?" Dominic asks, advancing toward me and cutting off any hope of dashing around him to escape.

"No reason," I lie desperately. He stares at me silently. The silence stretches, and I fidget against the need to fill it. (How does he know I can't stand silences?) I can resist. I am strong-willed. I won't break. "I don't know what to think about our relationship. I don't even know if it *is* a relationship. Why do you even want to be near me? I've caused you bodily harm over and over again. What happens when you get tired of me?" I did not resist. I was not strong-willed. I did break.

"I can't help you with how you feel, but this *is* a relationship. I like being near you because even though you're a menace to society, you're a hard worker and fiercely loyal to those you love. You're responsible enough to keep a job you hate, but you're enough of a dreamer that you're considering opening a bookstore. You have a soft spot for the underdog and misfits, and you're more intelligent than most people realize. Also, you're the most beautiful woman I've ever seen. How could you possibly think I could get tired of you?"

His words sound familiar. I think back and realize they're very similar to the ones he yelled at me one night in my driveway. It sounds nicer when he isn't bellowing it.

"Is there anything I can say or do to help you feel better?" he asks in a supportive way. "*Anything at all* to make you feel better?" He wiggles his eyebrows suggestively.

"Is kissing all you can think about?" I ask with a frown.

"Kissing isn't the only thing I'm thinking about. But we can start there." Then he suits actions to words.

Hearing footsteps approaching, I pull us both into the darker corner behind me, hoping Dominic's dark clothing will help us blend into the shadows so I won't be caught necking in the straw bale maze like a high school student. Not that I was ever caught necking in the maze as a high school student. Nope, not me. I'll deny it until my dying day.

I wait for the footsteps to pass, but they don't pass. They stop on the other side of the straw bale wall. After several long seconds, they're joined by another set of footsteps. A hushed argument ensues, but since it's hushed, I can't hear what it's about. Luckily, the argument increases in volume. I recognize Pierre's voice, without his French accent.

"That's Pierre!" I whisper in Dominic's ear. His swift intake of breath tells me he's shocked by my detective skills, or he finds my whispering sexy and distracting—possibly all of the above.

"How did you find me here?" Pierre says. "I don't want to see you. That's why I left L.A."

"Please, Lester, can't we work this out? I love you," a woman's slightly nasal voice begs. Before Pierre—or should I say Lester—can reply, Dominic rounds the bales separating us. I follow him, hoping he won't notice and yell at me to butt out of his investigation.

"I think we need to talk," he says to Pierre—I mean Lester, "and if you aren't completely honest with me this time, our talk will be down at the station." Ohh, he sounds serious, I think, and thankfully don't say.

"Sheriff," Lester says in a surprised tone. "I guess I knew this would come out eventually." Now his tone is resigned. He sighs. "My name is really Lester Jones. I made up Pierre and the whole French persona. I wasn't having any success as Lester. I thought changing my name and inventing a different history would help my career. And it did! All of a sudden, galleries were interested in my work. I started making some sales, and then I was 'discovered' and all of my dreams were coming true." It's like once he starts talking, he can't stop, and his whole story comes rushing out.

"That's when he dumped me and ran away. He wouldn't even take my calls," the woman cuts in. She's short and painfully thin. Her hair shows significant damage from bleaching, making it frizzy. "I gave him everything, and then he just packs up and leaves. Like I'm nothing." She glares at Pierre. (Wait, his name is Lester.)

"You followed your ex-boyfriend across the country?" I ask her, shocked. "Didn't his leaving you and not taking your calls tell you he wasn't interested?" Everybody turns to look at me: Lester with an appreciative expression, his ex-girlfriend with a hostile expression, and Dominic with a resigned expression.

"I know I should have told you my legal name, but I was afraid it would get out and ruin my life. My painting being stolen is bad enough, but I couldn't bear losing my reputation," Lester tells Dominic, apparently deciding to ignore my interjection.

"When did you get to town?" I ask the ex-girlfriend with a suspicious glare. "Stealing your ex-boyfriend's painting before it is unveiled would be quite the payback."

"How dare you!" she counters. "I love Lester. I would never do anything to hurt him."

"Ms. ..." Dominic starts, and then seems to realize he doesn't know her name.

"Walker, Beatrice Walker."

"Ms. Walker, do you have proof you weren't involved?" Dominic asks.

"I have my airplane ticket," she digs through what is possibly the biggest and ugliest brown purse in the world. She pulls out a paper boarding pass and hands it to Dominic. "I flew in two days ago. When was the painting stolen?"

"You didn't hear about the stolen painting?" I ask her. "It's been all over the news for a week. How did you not hear about it?"

"I've been busy," she counters.

"You fly across the country to stalk your ex, and you're too busy to see the news stories about him?" I ask incredulously. "I don't believe you."

"I don't care what you believe, homewrecker," she says.

"Homewrecker? What are you talking about?" I ask her, confused.

"You were trying to steal Lester from me," she accuses, placing her hands on her hips.

"What are you *talking* about? I wasn't trying to steal Pierre—Lester—whoever he is. Why would you think that?" I'm more confused than ever.

"Don't try and deny it, I saw you with him," she accuses, leaning forward menacingly. "You can't have him. He's mine."

"Were you stalking him? Did you notice it was always him initiating contact?" I ask, turning to Lester. "In fact, why *were* you initiating contact?"

His face reddens—whether in embarrassment or anger, I'm not sure. "I thought you might have information on my painting. I saw how the sheriff looked at you. I thought he might have told you something that would help me get my painting back," he admits.

"You were trying to use me?" I ask, outraged.

"Enough, all of you," Dominic interrupts, handing Beatrice back her boarding pass. "Mr. Jones, is there anyone who wants to hurt you?"

"Not that I can think of. Of course, other artists might be jealous of my success, but I don't think any of them would steal my painting. In fact, the publicity is doing great things for my career. I've had offers on all the other pieces in the exhibit."

"So, the stolen painting isn't a tragedy; it's actually a blessing," I say. Dominic's glare tells me he doesn't appreciate my interjection.

Lester's expression changes from surprise to anger. "That painting was my masterpiece. It being stolen is a devastating loss."

"You were going to sell it. So what's the difference?" I ask. "One could say that the sale of all your other works, the lawsuit against the museum, and the publicity are worth more than you would have gotten for that one painting. One might think you stole it yourself."

Lester clenches his jaw and his fists. Suddenly, I'm very glad Dominic is standing next to me. I might have shifted slightly, so Dominic is between Lester and me. A shield from Lester's anger seems like a prudent choice.

"I didn't steal it. Ms. Swanson and I were together when we did the final walk-through at two. After that, I had an interview panel for the local schools until four. I used the car service provided by the museum to go back to my hotel and change before returning to the museum for the opening. The only time I was alone was while I was changing into my tuxedo at the hotel. I'm sure there are security cameras that can confirm my whereabouts," Lester says. He seems upset.

"I *have* checked the security cameras to confirm your alibi," Dominic says with a pointed look at me. "That's why I asked if anybody was interested in hurting you."

His look seems to be telling me I should butt out of his investigation. At least this time he isn't *yelling* at me to butt out of his investigation. Maybe being in a relationship with him comes with more benefits than just kissing. Fearing I said that part out loud, I glance around. I'm relieved to see nobody's looking at me, so I assume I kept silent. Yay me!

"I can't think of anyone," Lester answers. "It isn't like anybody could just walk in and take it off the wall." He has a point. The exhibit room was probably locked until the reception. There were security guards on-site, both before and during the event. It was an eight-foot-wide painting, for crying out loud. Not exactly easy to sneak out.

"Who would have had access to the reception hall between you leaving and the painting being discovered as missing?" I ask, earning another glare from Dominic.

"How would I know? I wasn't there," Lester answers, exasperated, before Dominic can yell at me.

"If everything was set up, wouldn't the room be locked until the opening? Who had a key?" I ask, ignoring Dominic's glare.

"I wasn't in charge of the museum side of things," Lester says. "Maybe you should ask Ms. Swanson." His tone is getting decidedly more hostile with my continued questioning. It's like he isn't supporting me in my new PI career.

"Can I talk to you for a second?" Dominic asks me. Without waiting for an answer, he pulls me several feet away. "Go back to the carnival." I huff an annoyed breath at his bossiness. It's like he isn't supporting me in my new career either, but before I can unload my ire on him, he asks, "Why don't you get a caramel apple?"

I do like caramel apples. "Great idea!" I say. "See you later." I head out of the maze and straight to the caramel apple stand. Finding my way out is easy. In seconds, I'm back at the food booths accepting my caramel apple from Mr. McIntyre. (Not really—I take wrong turn after wrong turn and end up in another dead end.)

Oddly enough, I don't pass a single other person. Where are all the high school kids looking for a dark corner for a little kissy-face smooching? I sigh as I turn around and try another path. Several more minutes and dead ends later, I've resigned myself to never escaping the labyrinth. I will die here. CC and her family will mourn my loss deeply. My ghost will haunt the town's Halloween party for all eternity.

Turning another corner, I slam into a wall. The wall turns out to be Dominic's muscular chest. "I thought you were going to get a caramel apple," he says.

"I was trying to," I defend myself. "I got lost. There is no way out of this thing. It is impossible."

Dominic laces his fingers with mine and guides me out of the maze in seconds with nary a wrong turn. He obviously has mystical powers. Or maybe he was a Boy Scout and has great navigational skills. I imagine Dominic in khaki shorts, a khaki button-down shirt, a sash full of badges, a pith helmet, knee-high socks, and hiking boots. It makes quite a picture.

On the way to the caramel apple booth, I notice he seems distracted. His brow has a slight furrow, and he isn't saying anything. Maybe he's comfortable with silence. I can respect that. I'll just wait until he is ready to talk.

"What are you thinking about?" I blurt. Oops, I didn't wait until he was ready to talk. My discomfort with silence won out again.

"The theft just doesn't make sense," he says. "There were much more valuable paintings at the museum. Even if the thief was only interested in one of Pierre's paintings, stealing a smaller one would have been significantly easier. They won't be able to display it openly due to the publicity. I know he had an offer on it, but a buyer can't buy a stolen painting. It just doesn't make sense."

I have to agree with him, but I don't have anything helpful to add. I accept a caramel apple from Mr. McIntyre and take a big bite while I mull over what I know about the theft. It isn't a lot.

I notice Dominic didn't get an apple. "You don't want a caramel apple?"

He shakes his head. "I'm still full from dinner." That seems crazy. He didn't even eat all of his onion rings. Mostly because I ate several, but that's not the point.

I hold out my apple. "Do you want a bite?" His heated gaze is on me and not the apple. He leans forward slowly and takes a bite. My breathing hitches, and I almost drop my apple when my fingers go lax. Luckily, I have crack reflexes and tighten my grip before I drop it. I turn away from his gaze and see Pierre, I mean Lester, talking to Theo.

"That's weird," I muse.

"What is?" Dominic asks, licking a stray bit of caramel off his lips.

"What?" I'm distracted. He smiles at me.

"What is weird?" he repeats.

I manage to snap out of my carnal thoughts. "Oh, Pierre, I mean Lester, is talking to Theo, Nell's boyfriend. Theo said he didn't know him. What do you think they're talking about?" Dominic follows my gaze to where Lester and Theo are standing in the shadows, half hidden by a scarecrow decoration.

"They could be talking about anything. It doesn't make it suspicious," he says, but he doesn't look convinced. "I'll be right back. Stay here," he commands, moving toward them. Always one to obey authority, I wait for him to return. (Just kidding—I follow him immediately.)

"Theo, Pierre," Dominic greets the two men. "I didn't realize you two knew each other." Although it's a statement, the implied question hangs heavy in the air.

"We don't," Theo says. "Kyle pointed Pierre out to me earlier, and I was just telling him how sorry I was about his painting being stolen. My brother's girlfriend interns at the museum, and she mentioned how upset Pierre has been." This sounds reasonable, but I eye Theo suspiciously. This is a tricky situation. Theo's dating Nell, and accusing him might make Nell mad, but there are too many coincidences to ignore. I carefully consider the best way to subtly ask if Theo has any involvement in the theft.

"Did you steal the painting?" I blurt out. I guess I should have considered longer. That wasn't subtle at all.

Theo's expression changes from shock to amusement. "You are exactly as Nell described you." He smiles at me. It's a warm, open, and highly amused smile. "No. I did not have anything to do with the painting being stolen. And"—he answers my unspoken question—"neither did my brother or his girlfriend. I haven't even been to the museum in weeks. My brother and his girlfriend were out of town visiting my parents the weekend it was stolen. They left on Friday before lunch. I can provide contact information for witnesses if needed."

I bite my lip in embarrassment. "Sorry for accusing you," I tell him. "Sometimes I speak before I think."

"Sometimes?" Dominic mutters under his breath, but not far enough under his breath that I don't hear him. I glare at him, even though I know he's right.

"There you are," Nell says as she and Jamie join us. "What's going on?" She looks between all of us, but her gaze comes back to me with an accusatory hint.

"Nothing," Theo tells her, wrapping an arm around her and pulling her close. "I was just telling Pierre how sorry I was about his painting." He refrains from telling Nell that I accused him of being involved in the theft. I might like him after all.

"Then your aunt asked if I"—I glare at him. I can't believe he's going to tattle on me to Nell. I'm preparing what to tell Nell in my defense when he finishes speaking—"am enjoying the party." He shoots me a quick wink and a mischievous smile. I sigh in relief. I wasn't able to come up with a good defense.

"Lester, we need to talk," Beatrice says, joining us.

Lester closes his eyes as if he can erase the last several seconds by sheer force of will. "Beatrice, I've told you we have nothing left to discuss," he says in his fake French accent. Apparently, he wants to keep the Pierre persona. He takes her arm and steers her away from us. Probably to avoid more damage to his fake identity.

"Lester?" Theo says incredulously. "His name is Lester?" His tone is full of suppressed laughter.

"I'd appreciate it if you would keep that quiet," Dominic tells all three teens, and then turns his gimlet eye on me.

"Sure."

"Of course."

"Absolutely," they all assure him.

He never looks away from me, as if I'm the one he's worried about.

"I can keep a secret," I tell him defensively. "I mean, I haven't kept one yet, but I'm sure I could." He gives me one more pointed glare but doesn't say anything else.

"All right, monsters and mummies, this will be the last song of the night. So grab that special someone and hit the dance floor. I hope everybody had a great time, and Happy Halloween!" the DJ announces. Nell and Theo, with their arms wrapped around each other, head to the dance floor. I see Frank and Amelia and CC and Jake already on the floor.

Dominic plucks the stick with the apple core from my hand and tosses it into a nearby garbage can as he guides me to the floor as well. Most of the dancers have only rudimentary swing dance moves: a few underarm turns and twirl-outs, but nothing special. Angelica and Luis have some fancy steps that I envy.

"They look so cool," I say wistfully. Dominic follows my line of sight and smiles. He does some complicated hand movements that guide me through a twist and turn I didn't know I was capable of. I'm still in shock when he grabs my waist, lifts me, and swings me first to his right side and then to his left before setting me down in front of him and spinning me out again. He gently tugs on my outstretched arm and spins me back into his arms.

"You know how to swing dance?" I ask, perhaps stupidly, since he has been proving he does.

"I know some," he admits modestly before once again executing some fancy moves. I'm shocked that somehow my body knows how to follow his lead, and I can perform the steps gracefully. "Graceful" has never been a word people use to describe me.

Before I know it, the song is over and everybody applauds. Amidst the goodbyes and "Happy Halloween" wishes everybody is exchanging, I slip away from Dominic. At least, as far as our outstretched arms allow. He's once more laced our fingers together, preventing my escape. His unrepentant smile tells me he finds my attempted escape entertaining.

"All right, everybody, time to go home," CC says, appearing at my side with Jake. She casts a look at my still-outstretched arm, but doesn't comment. We all troop toward the cars. Jake is carrying Eve, who is conked out on his shoulder. She looks so peaceful and angelic when she's sleeping. Completely the opposite of her demonic side when she's awake.

The drive home is slow and uneventful. We manage to avoid pedestrians and other cars, all of which are trying to get home. Most people quickly move out of my way when they see me coming. People need to stop living in the past. I haven't hit anybody with my car in years. Unless you count when I hit Dominic a couple of months ago, but it was just a little tap, and he was fine, so I don't think it should count.

We all pile out of the cars in the driveway. Jake carries a sleeping Dean, and CC carries a sleeping Eve, into their house. They are trailed by Kyle, Ann, and Jane with the raccoon. Jamie silently heads into my house, while Nell and Theo move into some shadows to say good night. (Let's just say they were using their mouths, but not talking.) Frank left with Amelia, probably to walk her home, leaving me effectively alone with Dominic. I don't think Nell or Theo would notice if I started dancing a can-can.

"Well, good night," I tell Dominic somewhat awkwardly.

"I should help you get Jaws settled," Dominic says over his shoulder, already walking toward my door.

I scurry after him. "That's not necessary. I can handle it. It's just a quick pour, and he's all set." I try to intervene, but he's already entering my kitchen with Benji trotting at his heels.

"Traitor," I accuse Benji, but if he hears me, he doesn't let on. When I join them in my kitchen, Dominic has already removed the rubber band holding the bag closed.

"Welcome home, Jaws," he says, carefully pouring the water and Jaws into his new bowl.

"Okay, well, thanks. I'll see you later." I try to hint that he should go.

He leans back against my counter and cocks his head at me, not leaving. I search my brain for a subtle way to tell him it's time for him to leave.

"It's time for you to leave." Shoot, that wasn't subtle.

He smiles widely at me, obviously amused by my inability to keep my thoughts in. He pushes off from the counter and walks toward me. Even though he can keep his thoughts in, I know what he's thinking, and I back up. He keeps stalking me until my back comes up against the wall. He places both hands flat on the wall on either side of my head. I briefly wonder if it's to avoid a repeat of face-planting into the wall, but then he kisses me, and all my thoughts disappear.

"Don't mind me. I'm just going up to bed. With earplugs. I won't be able to hear anything at all," Nell says, with laughter in her voice, as she walks through the kitchen and up the stairs.

Dominic waits a couple more seconds before he pulls back. "Sweet dreams," he says, and then is gone. I take a few minutes to stiffen my legs before trying to navigate the stairs. This has been one heck of a birthday.

Chapter 15

I wake up to a paw smacking me in the face. Opening my eyes, I see Blackbeard sitting on my pillow. Seeing I'm awake, he smacks me again, this time adding a meow to let me know he's really upset with me.

I lever myself into a sitting position and look at the clock. It's after ten. I'm surprised CC, or one of her family members, hasn't come to check on me. Usually, sleeping this late results in a wellness check. Sometimes it involves standing outside my shower curtain while I shower to give me a heart attack.

Speaking of showers, I decide I might as well take a quick one since it's already so late. Blackbeard approves of my decision and races me to the tub. While shampooing my hair, I think about the events of yesterday. So much happened that I get distracted thinking of it all and end up with eyes full of shampoo, effectively ending my reminiscing.

"Jumping Jehoshaphat," I sputter, rinsing the suds out of my eyes. I turn off the water, quickly towel myself dry, and twist my wet hair into a bun. I pull on jeans and a white T-shirt with the words WITCH BETTER HAVE MY CANDY printed on it. The words are wearing a witch hat and have witch legs covered in striped tights and curvy pointy witch shoes as if the words were the witch's body. There's also a broom running through the words as if they are flying on it. It's a great shirt.

Speaking of great shirts, I spy the shirts Dominic got me. I run my fingers gently over them as if they were precious jewels. Shaking my head at my fanciful thoughts, I close the drawer and turn to go.

I'm only slightly surprised to see the family still at the table having breakfast. It's late, but we all had a busy day and a late night. Two empty pie dishes and one dish still half full of quiche sit in the middle of the table. I slide into the banquette, and CC places a slice of quiche on my plate. Jake brings me a cup of coffee.

"This place has great service," I tell them. "And the waiter is easy on the eyes," I add with a saucy wink at Jake.

He shoots me a quick, but still devastatingly sexy, smile and sits next to CC. "I hope you will take that into consideration when you tip your server," he says with another sexy smile. I'm starting to feel a little warm.

Deciding I'm not in the right mind space to engage in flirtatious banter with Jake, I turn my attention to my quiche. It has mushrooms, peppers, broccoli, cheese, and ham. It's like CC is trying to sneak healthy food into our diets since this weekend is full of candy and junk food. But it's delicious, so I don't complain about it.

The kids alternate between excited chatter about last night's Halloween party and tonight's trick-or-treating and spaced-out, sleep-deprived stares into space. I'm betting there will be some naps today.

"We're going to meet up with some friends," Nell says as she stands up. "We should be back around three."

Theo trails behind Nell and Jamie, who are excitedly discussing the plans for the day. It's nice that he can respect the friendship bond and not be jealous. That's an important quality in a potential partner, I think. CC and Jake exchange a look that tells me I probably said it. Oh, well, it wasn't exactly national security.

"Speaking about potential partners, tell me everything about you and the sheriff," CC says with a look that says she means *everything*. Jake ushers the children out of the kitchen to give us privacy for our girl talk.

I take a minute to gather my thoughts so I can articulate everything clearly. "He's a great kisser. He seems to be fine with the bodily harm I keep causing him. He got me the perfect gifts for my birthday. He doesn't care that the town is gossiping about us. He seems to know everything about me and still likes me. How does he know everything about me? Why does he still like me? He talked to his friend about me, and now suddenly he starts kissing me? It's like a switch was flipped, and now we're dating? I don't know anything about anything." I finish at a wail, dropping my head on my folded arms resting on the table. (I haven't articulated anything clearly.)

"There, there," CC says, patting my head in what feels like a very patronizing manner. "I think for once in your life, you're overthinking things. He likes you, you like him. What more do you need to know?" She makes a good point. Maybe I *am* overthinking things. "Besides, I think he's good for you." I mull this over. She might have a point. He saved me from a killer, kind of. And he gave me his brownie once. And even though I hit him with a door, which required stitches, he still stayed with me to make sure I was okay. He gets along with CC and her family. Maybe this could work.

I finally raise my head. "Okay, maybe it could work," I say.

"Atta girl." CC pats my hand encouragingly. "All I'm saying is don't overthink it and give him a chance. Now, about your bookstore."

I drop my head again. "Geez, can't I tackle one life-altering decision at a time?" I ask the table where my face is currently resting.

CC's silence is heavy with judgment.

"Fine," I say, raising my head. "What about the *possible* bookstore?" I want her to know I won't be bullied into anything.

"I set up an appointment for tomorrow at ten to view Ms. Downing's old storefront," CC informs me. I guess I will be bullied into viewing a storefront. I sigh. My life feels out of my control. Deciding to take control of my life, I stand with purpose and confidently cross the kitchen. To the coffee pot, to refill my coffee cup.

I consider my future. What if I do open a bookstore? What if I don't go back to work for Brandon? What if I was my own boss? The head honcho, the top dog, the big cheese. Why do we say cheese for a picture? Why is a picture worth a thousand words? (I may have strayed from the topic when I was considering things.) When I yawn hugely, I decide to head home and take a quick nap myself.

Since it's still daytime, Agatha is melted across my floor, not my mattress. I get the whole bed to myself. That is, until Blackbeard joins me. He lies across my pillow but allows me to keep a small corner to rest my face on. Benji also decides to join us and curls up behind my knees. I find his small, warm body comforting.

When I wake up, I'm disoriented. Daytime naps have a tendency to do that to me. What time is it? What day is it? Did I miss dinner? (I ask the important questions first.) Forcing my eyes to focus on my alarm clock, I see that it's almost three. I guess I needed a long nap.

Despite having slept for hours, I feel bleary and uncoordinated. It takes me two tries to untangle my feet from the sheets and blankets. Finally freeing myself, I stagger upright, but then sway slightly. Taking a moment to pull myself together helps slightly. At least I don't trip down the stairs.

The fresh air helps to wake me up as I cross my backyard. By the time I cross CC's yard and enter her kitchen, I'm mostly back to normal. Some people would say my normal is still an uncoordinated and bleary mess, but I try not to focus on the negatives.

CC is working on an early dinner. We always eat early on Halloween so the kids have time to put their costumes on before trick-or-treating time starts. I consider offering to help, but then decide the most help I can offer is to stay out of her way.

Ann is setting the table while talking a mile a minute about her trick-or-treating route. She's mapped out the houses that give out full-sized candy bars, so she can hit them first, and the houses that give out raisins or toothbrushes, to avoid.

Nell, Jamie, and Theo come through the kitchen door talking and laughing. Frank and Amelia aren't far behind them, and soon everybody's gathered around the table. Since I was at the table first, when everybody else arrived, they sat around me, so there isn't a spot next to me when Jake and Dominic come through the back door. I don't know how I feel about this. Dominic's look tells me he would prefer a different seating arrangement, but he sits next to Eve without comment.

CC brings two large platters with hot dogs wrapped in strips of dough to look like mummies. Jake grabs the plates holding peppers carved to look like jack-o'-lanterns, and peeled mandarin oranges with small pieces of green pepper as stems, making them look like mini pumpkins. It's like CC is trying to sneak in healthy food by making it cute. That won't work, I think. I grab the coolest-looking carved pepper before anybody else can. I also snag a mandarin pumpkin. Maybe it's working, I think, as I eat my fruits and vegetables.

The kids appear to have gotten their second wind because they're all chattering about their trick-or-treating plans for tonight. Their animated jabbering allows me to avoid conversation. Which is probably for the best. I don't think I would be very coherent. Have CC and Jake adopted Dominic into the family? Why wasn't I consulted? Aren't we a big enough family already? Is it really cheaper by the dozen? Why is it a "cheap thrill"? Who would want to be thrilled to death? Why is "Death by Chocolate" the name for something really chocolatey? My thoughts are very jumbled.

Everybody seems to be in a hurry to eat, probably so they have time to get into their costumes. I keep a close eye on the clock so I can run home in time to avoid any unfortunate trick-or-treating-related doorbell incidents. Everybody knows how much Agatha hates the doorbell, but sometimes they forget, or they like to hear the baying of a thousand hellhounds.

All the kids seem to finish about the same time, and it looks like a mass exodus as we all leave the kitchen: the kids to get changed, CC and Jake to help the kids get changed, and me to get home before the official start of trick-or-treating. Yes, our town has official trick-or-treating times. I want to be mad about how controlling the rule is, but it's actually really nice, so I let it go.

It isn't until I swing the door shut behind me that I realize Dominic has followed me.

Unfortunately, the door doesn't slam shut. It slams into Dominic. His long-suffering sigh indicates he thinks I might have meant to slam the door on him.

"Oh my gosh, not again!" I say, having flashbacks to the other times I hit him with a door. Luckily, this time the door seems to have caught him on his shoulder and not his face. His aggravated yet resigned expression speaks volumes.

"Maybe you should be more careful around me and doors," I tell him. "You seem to get hit a lot." This does not seem to pacify him.

"And I was going to give you the chocolate mousse my grandma made."

"You *were* going to? But now you're not?" I question desperately. "Is there any way I could change your mind?"

His eyes darken. Feeling bold, I step closer to him, crowding into his space. He doesn't seem to mind. I place one hand on his nicely muscled chest. I remember how great his abs looked the first time I saw him. I allow my fingers to do a little exploration. I can feel his heart rate increase with my exploration. I shift even closer to him and then stretch up on my tiptoes. Just as my lips touch his, I snatch the bakery bag from his lax fingers and dance backward out of his reach. He tries to catch me, but his reflexes are slowed, probably by lust.

"Tease," he says without heat, as he watches me open the bag and pull out the containers of chocolate mousse. He seems more entertained than annoyed by my antics. He also seems to have either forgiven me for hitting him with the door or to have forgotten I hit him with the door in the first place. Either way, it's a win for me.

I grab a spoon and dig in to the first chocolate mousse container. It is so good: rich chocolate flavor with just a hint of mint. I may have moaned. I definitely lick the spoon clean. He seems more interested in watching me eat my mousse than in eating his mousse.

His intense gaze is a little distracting, but I don't let it stop me from enjoying the rich chocolate treat. He's the opposite of distracted. He is laser-focused on me. I may be licking the spoon and my lips more than strictly necessary just to torment him. I also eat his chocolate mousse.

As if realizing I've eaten his share, he presses me between the counter and his body. "I just want a little taste," he murmurs sexily. I'm not sure if he's talking about the chocolate mousse or me. Too bad for him—a knock on the front door interrupts his plans. He allows me to slip from his embrace.

When I open the front door, I'm greeted by a chorus of "Trick-or-treat!" from a trio of princesses. I coo appreciatively over them and their costumes while I hold out a big bowl of candy for them to choose from. Before I close the door, I wave to their parents standing at the curb.

Before Dominic can try to kiss me again, another knock sounds. The next several hours are filled with knocks, cute costumed kids, and handing out candy. I think Dominic will be annoyed at the constant interruptions of his seduction, but instead, he smiles warmly and engages with the kids as he helps me hand out candy. Why is he handing out candy at my house? I wonder.

"Why are you handing out candy at my house?" I ask him in a lull between trick-or-treaters.

"I didn't think anyone would come to my house. Between the long driveway, being outside the town limits, and it being the sheriff's house," he shrugs, "I just figured nobody would come."

I realize three things. One, Dominic wants to be included in our small-town community. Two, he likes kids. And three, I have no idea where he lives.

"I have no idea where you live."

"I'll have you over sometime," he tells me with a promise in his eyes. I don't have time to overthink what-all might be included in his having me over sometime before there's another knock at the door.

When nine o'clock finally hits—the official end of trick-or-treating—I'm exhausted. It seems every kid in town came to my house. They probably did. I followed Ann's advice and got regular-sized candy bars. It was weird, all I did was open the door, tell kids their costumes were amazing, and give them candy, but I feel like I've run a marathon. Well, I don't know what running a marathon feels like, since I'm not a runner, but it seems like an appropriate comparison.

Dropping down on my couch, a thought occurs to me. "Why aren't you out maintaining law and order? Preventing house-egging evildoers and catching toilet-papering perpetrators," I ask. He smiles at me. He has a great smile. When I first met him, I didn't think he even knew how to smile, but now he smiles regularly. I knew I brought joy to all.

"I was here with you, so one egging evildoer was under surveillance." I gasp at his accusation. The alleged egging he is speaking of happened long before he became sheriff. Isn't there a statute of limitations on egging? Besides, when I may have admitted to the egging, it was under duress, so it shouldn't count anyway.

"I have my deputy on it," he continues. "One of the perks of being the boss is delegating." He joins me on the sofa. All of a sudden, I don't feel so tired. He leans in. I lean back. He leans in closer. The overstuffed arm of the couch prevents me from leaning back any farther. He takes advantage of this and closes in. My last thought is, I guess he finally got a taste.

"Aunt Claire, I'm home," Nell announces, coming through my back door with Jamie some unknown time later. Her announcement might be an attempt to prevent a repeat of catching me making out with Dominic. It works. By the time she and Jamie can see into the living room, I'm sitting casually on my cushion, and Dominic is sitting on his cushion. He's holding his rib, where I may or may not have elbowed him when I flailed into an upright position. Nell's expression tells me my casual pose isn't as believable as I hoped.

I jump into action before she can say anything. "Well, thanks for helping me hand out candy. Good night," I tell Dominic in a rush while I pull him up off the couch and practically push him out the door. Closing the door behind him, I lean against it for support. The door does not offer the level of support I need. The level of support I need may require a licensed professional.

Chapter 16

The sound of voices pulls me from sleep. I spent most of the night tossing and turning—well, as much as I could, since I was trapped between Agatha and Blackbeard. I feel like I just closed my eyes. I'm too tired to even panic at the thought of strangers in my house. I try to ignore the voices and slip back into sleep, but it's too late. I'm awake now.

Gathering the little bit of energy I have, I roll out of bed. Luckily, my feet hit the floor first, and I'm able to stagger upright instead of falling. I may be ricocheting off the walls as I try to get through my doorway. On the third try, I make it out the door without bouncing off the doorframe.

I do, however, slip down the last several steps. Surprisingly, strong hands manage to catch me before I can seriously harm myself. Even more surprisingly, the hands do not belong to Dominic. I'm getting used to him showing up unannounced. Instead, Theo's the one who keeps me from falling.

"What? Why? When?" I ask Theo with a complete lack of intelligence. Theo smiles at me. I seem to be entertaining him.

"Nell, Jamie, and I have to leave after breakfast so Nell can make her afternoon class. I'm helping carry their suitcases. I'm sorry if we woke you." He has an answer for everything, I think. His delighted smile widens, making me think I said it out loud. "I've enjoyed meeting you. Now when Nell tells stories about you, I'll be able to picture you more clearly."

I bask in the knowledge that Nell talks about me, but then a niggling thought makes me think the stories might not paint me in the best light. In fact, the stories might be downright embarrassing.

"Auntie Claire, I hope we didn't wake you," Nell says as she and Jamie come downstairs. I notice neither of them slips on the steps. I'm starting to think it's just me who has difficulty with the stairs.

"Thanks for letting me stay here this weekend," Jamie says softly. Jamie's a little shy, and I have a tendency to overwhelm people, so I'm surprised that she makes eye contact when she talks to me. I'm also surprised her hair is brushed back from her face. When I first met her, her long brown hair obscured most of her face, but now it's pulled back in a loose braid. She seems to be more confident in herself. Good for her, I think. When her brow furrows in a questioning way, I suspect I'm still thinking out loud.

"Come on, Aunt Claire, let's get you some coffee. It might help," Nell says, wrapping her arm around my shoulders and guiding me toward CC's kitchen and coffee. I can't help but think her actions resemble Frank's with Amelia when we confuse and overwhelm her.

"Rude," I tell her, not even trying to keep my thoughts in. Nell just laughs, probably at me. Jamie and Theo, who's carrying two rolling suitcases, follow us.

CC is standing at the stove, stirring two large skillets of scrambled eggs. Jake is next to her, manning the toaster. Eve is spinning in a circle in the middle of the kitchen. I don't even pause to think about why Eve is spinning in a circle. I head straight to my best friend, Mr. Coffee. Pouring myself a mug, I take a deep drink.

Only after finishing my cup and refilling it do I ask "What's up with Eve?" as I watch her short blond curls fly around her head while she twirls like a top.

"She got into her candy this morning. She's on a sugar rush," Jake tells me. CC just tightens her lips.

"Oh, somebody isn't happy," I say. Shoot! I meant to think that, not say it. I take another big drink of coffee, trying to hide behind my mug.

CC shoots me a glance that is communicating something, but it's too early in the morning for me to figure out what. It probably isn't anything I want to hear anyway. I refill my mug again and sit at the banquette. CC and Jake's kids trickle in, joining Nell, Theo, Jamie, and me at the table. CC and Jake bring the scrambled eggs, toast, and a big platter of sliced melons, apples, and pears to the table. The kids, except Eve, eat quickly and then disappear up the stairs, only to reappear minutes later with backpacks slung over their shoulders. Meanwhile, CC has to wrangle a sugar-hyped Eve into eating several bites of egg. Then she resorts to carrying a resisting Eve up the stairs. Eve fluctuates between wild flailing and being completely limp. I pity her preschool teacher more than usual. Eve isn't an easy child at the best of times, and today is not her best of times.

When CC and Eve reappear several minutes later, Eve is dressed, but it's come at a cost to CC. She looks like she's been through the wringer. Her carefully styled hair has fallen on one side, and her clothes, normally pressed, are now wrinkled.

She hands Eve to Jake. "You can take her to the bus stop," she tells him with a look that dares him to argue.

"Come on, guys, tell Jamie, Theo, and Nell goodbye, and let's go." Jake wisely does not argue with CC. Smart *and* handsome, I think. His quick wink at me tells me I said it. At least it was something nice this time.

Everybody hugs Nell and says goodbye to Jamie and Theo. I notice Kyle hands both Theo and Jamie a drawing. I shamelessly peek to see what he drew them.

Jamie's is a drawing of her and Nell in their pirate costumes. Their heads are close together as if they were sharing secrets. They both have wide smiles and dancing eyes. I can almost hear their giggles.

Theo's drawing is of Nell and Theo holding hands. Kyle has chosen to draw them from behind as if he was watching them walk away together. Their heads are tilted toward each other as if they're the only people in the world. Even though their faces are not in the picture, it's easy to tell that it's them. Kyle is so talented, I think, for probably the millionth time.

"I can't believe you're leaving already!" I say, a bit teary-eyed as I clutch Nell to me. Her response is muffled since I am clutching her so tightly. I assume it's an assurance of how much she loves me and how she misses me desperately. That college is full of sadness because I'm not there.

When Theo manages to extract Nell from my clutches, she sucks in a deep breath as if she narrowly escaped being smothered to death. Her expression tells me she thinks I'm being overdramatic.

"Auntie Claire, you're being overdramatic," Nell says. (It isn't just her expression that tells me.)

"I just love you so much, and it's so hard that I can't see you every day like I have for your whole life. You can't possibly understand how it feels to have your child ripped away from you," I tell her, trying to help her understand. Her expression softens, and she declares she will never leave me again. She's dropping out of college immediately and will spend all of her free time with me. (She doesn't really say that. It was just wishful thinking on my part. She just rolls her eyes at me.)

"I'll see you in a couple of weeks," she tells me with a shocking lack of emotion. Theo smiles warmly at me. The sparkle in his eyes makes me think I am vastly amusing him. Before I can do anything else embarrassing, they file out the door, leaving me all alone. Well, CC's still here, but she seems to be recovering from the morning with Eve and isn't emotionally supporting me.

"More coffee?" she asks. Without waiting for a response, she refills both our mugs. I guess she is sort of supporting me emotionally. We sit in silence, enjoying our coffee and thinking deep thoughts. Why couldn't Nell stay here forever? Is she serious about Theo? What do we even know about Theo? I mean, he's good-looking and supports Nell and Jamie's friendship without being jealous, and he seems to like all of us, but is that enough?

"I'm not sure he's good enough for Nell," I tell CC.

Her surprised expression implies she wasn't thinking deep thoughts about Nell's dating life. "He seems very nice, and Nell likes him. That's all that matters."

Well, if she wants to be a reasonable and supportive mother, I guess I can't stop her.

She finishes her coffee and stands up. "I'm going to get ready for the showing," she says. "You should, too."

I sigh. I can't believe she's forcing me into touring a storefront for a bookstore I might not even be opening. I decide I have time for another cup of coffee before I get dressed.

After my fifth cup of coffee, I feel ready to face the day. Also, my heart rate feels like a hummingbird's, and my muscles are a little twitchy.

I choose the shirt Benji presented to Dominic when Pierre showed up on my porch. It's the one with the seal saying BOOOOOO! and SEAL OF DISAPPROVAL printed around it. It feels like the right message to send to CC and her bossy ways.

Since I'm hyped up on coffee, I change in record time and end up waiting for CC in her kitchen. I think about drinking another cup of coffee while I wait, but decide my heart probably can't take it.

When CC joins me, her hair is piled on top of her head in an intricate yet casual style. She's changed out of her wrinkled clothes and now wears a pair of robin's-egg-blue twill pants and a white eyelet shirt. As usual, she looks ready for a fashion photo shoot, and I feel sadly lacking in comparison. I self-consciously smooth my T-shirt as if that would magically make me more fashionable.

Why does my best friend have to be so gorgeous? I wonder, not for the first time. My over-caffeinated brain doesn't allow me to focus on that thought for long. CC casts a glance at my shirt but refrains from commenting. She's probably picking her battles, and since she's already battled Eve this morning, she might be running low on energy.

"Let's go," she says.

"We could always reschedule if you aren't feeling up to it today. It wouldn't be any bother at all," I offer. She doesn't even respond, just walks out the door, assuming I'll follow her. I do follow her, but I resent the fact that she just assumes I would.

The short ride to Ms. Downing's storefront is uneventful. My muscle twitches cause me to swerve out of my lane a few times, but I don't hit anybody or anything, so I think CC is being overdramatic when she keeps screaming, "We're going to die!"

"You are being overdramatic," I tell her calmly, parking in front of the storefront. It has one of those doorways inset between huge display windows that always make me think the store holds treasures. The large plate glass windows, with TIMELESS TREASURES still painted on them, allow me to see into the empty store.

Well, it isn't completely empty. Mary is standing inside. She looks very professional in her red skirt suit with matching red heels. Her brown hair is pulled into a chignon, and she's holding a leather portfolio. When she sees us, she smiles a professionally distant smile. I guess she's taking her new job as a real estate agent very seriously.

The old-fashioned bell above the door jingles as we step into the store. "CC, Claire, so nice to see you. Come in. As you can see, the original wood floors are in amazing shape. As is the crown molding and brickwork." Mary continues listing all the original, historic, and beautiful features of the space, but I'm not listening. My eyes bounce around the huge empty room, picturing where I would put bookcases, the coffee counter, small seating areas, and even a children's section. I can see it so clearly. People browsing, the smell of coffee mingling with the scent of books, quiet conversations, and most important, the ringing of lots of sales on the antique cash register.

"I'll take it," I say, interrupting Mary's sales pitch. I guess I won't be a PI after all. I'll be a bookseller, a novel merchant, a story peddler. CC and Mary both look at me with surprised expressions. Mary's expression quickly morphs into a smile.

"I think what Claire means is she will take a look at the inspection report and price comparisons of comparable retail spaces," CC says, shooting me a look that says I should remain silent. Probably for the best—I might be making decisions while emotionally invested. And also while high on caffeine.

In no time at all, Mary has documents spread out on the old oak counter next to the antique cash register. She and CC pore over the documents, haggling over points and concerns. I leave them to it and spend my time wandering the space. I ignore the creaky stairs as I make my way up them. The second floor is about two-thirds the size of the first floor, allowing me to overlook part of the downstairs area. The carved oak balustrade is smooth as I trail my hand over it. The sunlight streams through the fan-shaped windows to pool on the floor. I can picture my bookstore bustling with patrons. It is perfect and I want it.

"Come on, Claire, it's time to go. Mary, we'll look these over with our financial planner and lawyer and get back to you soon," CC says. I may be petting the railing lovingly as I descend the stairs.

A financial planner and a lawyer, aren't we fancy? I think. Wait, no, I say it. Luckily, I say it quietly, and the ringing of the old-fashioned bell above the door seems to drown out my words, so Mary and CC don't hear. CC is holding a folder that probably contains the pertinent papers for review.

"Thanks for taking the time to show us the space, Mary." CC smiles warmly at her and shakes her hand. Not wanting to be left out of this grown-up ritual, I also shake Mary's hand. She's still smiling her professional smile.

"Thanks, Mary, I will carefully review the escrow and earnest money and get back to you," I say with a serious expression to let her know I'm serious.

Her professional smile turns into a real smile, and it looks like she's stifling a laugh. "I look forward to hearing from you," she manages to get out with some difficulty, probably because she's trying not to laugh at me. I might not know much about real estate terms or real estate in general. Oh well—I have CC and Jake, and apparently a financial planner and a lawyer, to help me.

"Let's go get some lunch," CC says as we get in my car. I don't ask her where she wants to go because I want to go to Bake My Day and get a giant brownie, and since I'm driving, she can't stop me. Speaking of stopping. I notice that Ms. Keller and her yappy little dog, wearing matching purple velour tracksuits, stop and step back against the buildings instead of crossing the street when she sees me driving by.

"Rude," I say. "I haven't hit anybody in forever, and Ralph and Mitchell are fine. Why does she have to hold a grudge?" CC gives me a look that implies Ms. Keller has every right to be concerned for her safety and to hold a grudge.

"Rude," I say again, but this time to CC.

"You hit the sheriff just a couple of months ago."

"That was barely a tap. It doesn't count." I wave my head dismissively.

"You knocked him down and you also ran over his foot." I choose to ignore her hurtful, but true comments. It's a short drive to Bake My Day, so we get there in no time. In my rush to get a brownie, I don't waste any time and quickly open my door. Unfortunately, somebody is standing in the way and gets whacked by the door. The impact throws them off balance, causing them to trip over the curb and fall to the ground.

I know before I even look at their face that it's Dominic. He's sprawled on the ground with a look of consternation on his face. I debate whether running away would be better than facing him. Since I'm not much of a runner, and Dominic knows where I live, I decide to face him bravely.

"I didn't mean to," I tell him as I scurry behind CC. She doesn't make a great shield since the top of her head only reaches my chin, but she creates a barrier.

"Sheriff, are you okay? Claire, you really need to be more careful," CC says as she breaks free of my hold and assists Dominic to his feet. He's favoring his right leg, probably where the car door made contact. He ignores CC's motherly fussing as he looks at me over her head. His expression is hard to read, but if I had to guess, I would say he's exasperated.

"It's not like I *mean* to hurt you," I tell him, fidgeting under his gaze. He sighs deeply, possibly questioning the life choices that brought him here.

"I know," he finally says, somewhat grudgingly, as if he's trying to convince himself it was another accident. I fight the urge to wring my hands. It's a pointless and useless gesture. When he takes a slightly limping step toward me, I lose the battle and wring my hands anxiously. Another limping step brings him within arm's reach.

He reaches out and pulls me toward him. "You could kiss it and make it better," he offers. I feel like I'm drowning in his eyes. In an almost hypnotic state, I rise onto my tiptoes and gently press a kiss against the corner of his mouth.

Before it can turn X-rated, a voice calls out. "Dominic, are you going to stand in the parking lot all day, or are you coming inside?" Rose is standing with CC in the open doorway to the bakery. I jump away from him like a scared rabbit. He only lets me get as far as our now joined hands will allow. Being tethered to Dominic by our outstretched arms is becoming increasingly common.

"Coming, Grandma," he calls to her as if she didn't just catch us kissing in public in broad daylight.

"She just caught us kissing in public in broad daylight," I say, embarrassed.

"We are adults and are allowed to be kissing in public, and in broad daylight," he says in a quiet, sexy voice. "In fact," he continues, "we are allowed to kiss in darkness and in private." I shiver as his words form a picture in my mind of what kissing in the dark and in private might lead to. It's a good thing he's holding my hand, or I might not make it safely across the parking lot. I'm very preoccupied with the images his words form.

"Well, it's about time you made it inside. I was starting to think you had decided not to come in after all," Rose says from behind the counter, eyeing our joined hands. Her expression makes me feel like a kid caught with their hand in the cookie jar. When she transfers her gaze to my face, I feel the need to confess. Luckily, I'm strong-willed and can resist such tactics. I will not break. I will not reveal anything embarrassing.

"Your grandson is a really good kisser, and I like it when he kisses me." I was not strong-willed. I did not resist. I broke and revealed embarrassing information. I feel my face flame. Dominic smiles cockily. CC snorts out a laugh. Rose looks surprised, but then a grudging smile tugs at her lips.

"I just took a batch of brownies out of the oven. I'll get you one," she says, turning away from me. Is embarrassing myself the way to get brownies from Rose? Not my favorite way to get a brownie, but I regularly embarrass myself, so at least I'd get a brownie out of it. When Rose returns with our still-warm brownies, I excitedly accept the plate and head to a table outside to enjoy the beautiful day.

"How's your investigation going?" CC asks Dominic with polite interest. I don't bother with conversation. Instead, I take a big bite of my brownie. I think my eyes roll back in my head in pleasure. This may distract Dominic because he answers CC's question with actual information instead of his standard I-can't-discuss-an-ongoing-investigation response.

"Not well. Pierre and Ms. Swanson have been cleared, and I don't have any new suspects. I still have no idea how the painting could have been removed from the museum, and I haven't been able to find it *in* the museum. It's like it disappeared into thin air." As if suddenly remembering himself, he grimaces. "I'd appreciate it if you didn't repeat any of that. I shouldn't have discussed an ongoing investigation."

Ha, I knew that's what he would say, I think. (A quick glance tells me I did just think it.) I congratulate myself on my inside thoughts staying in. That deserves another brownie. I snatch a second one off the plate and take a big bite.

"Claire and I toured Ms. Downing's old storefront today. I think it might be perfect for her bookstore," CC casually mentions, as if she isn't planning my life for me. Although now that I think about it, Dominic is also planning my life for me. He's the one who suggested I open a bookstore.

"Perfect, huh?" he asks me with a warm smile. It's a good thing I'm sitting down because that smile could cause my knees to give out. "So, you're going for it? You're going to open a bookstore?"

"Uhhh," I respond intelligently. I'm having trouble forming any thoughts with his warm chocolate eyes staring into mine, and with that sexy smile still hovering on his very kissable lips.

His smile widens. "You think my smile is sexy and my lips are very kissable?" he asks. Apparently, my celebration of inner thoughts staying in was premature.

"Uhh," I respond again. He leans in so close I can smell his chocolate-scented breath. I bet his lips are chocolate-flavored, I think. Wait, no, I say it. I don't have time to be embarrassed because he proves his lips are chocolate-flavored by kissing me.

I'm not sure how long we're kissing before a car horn honking, accompanied by whooped laughter, pulls me back to reality, and I jerk away from him. When I scramble out of my chair, I somehow manage to crush his fingers between the arms of our chairs. His hissed in breath tells me it probably hurt.

"I have to go," I tell him desperately. "I have to get CC home." I reach to grab CC's arm to make a quick getaway, only to realize she's gone. I swivel my head around, looking for her. I probably resemble a deranged owl, but she's nowhere to be seen. I can't believe she abandoned me. Maybe she was kidnapped. I should call the police. Wait, the police are already here, and I'm trying to avoid him.

My indecision gives Dominic time to recover. He takes my hand in his uninjured hand to prevent my escape. I tug my hand, trying to reclaim it. He doesn't release it. With a frown, I tug harder. He puts the hand holding mine behind his back, forcing me closer to him. How is he so strong?

"I think every time you injure me, you should kiss it and make it better," he says in my ear. I may be tilting my head to allow him to nuzzle my neck.

Before we can get carried away, Ms. Blanche and Ms. Bianca toddle over to a nearby table with a plate of petits fours. Their thinning white hair is styled in matching bouffants. They also have matching shirtwaist dresses that may very well be as old as they are.

"Hello, dear," Ms. Bianca says, smiling at me. "How are you doing? We heard there was another construction delay at the insurance company. Any news on when it will be completed?" Her voice is soft from age, but her eyes are sharp where they rest on Dominic and me.

"No news, yet, Ms. Bianca," I answer, pretending a nonchalance I don't feel. "But I'm doing okay. Just enjoying some time off."

"Yes, we can see that," Ms. Blanche adds with a knowing look at Dominic, who is still holding me. "Sheriff," she greets him, "have you found that missing painting yet?" While her question could be considered a dig at his sheriffing skills, her tone is simply curious.

"Not yet," he tells her. I'd think he might feel compelled to defend his lack of progress, but he doesn't. It's like he doesn't need the approval of a couple of near-centenarians.

"We saw CC helping take down the Halloween party booths. You still aren't allowed to help?" Ms. Blanche asks me. I think we both know the answer.

"Well, I'm pretty busy, so …" I trail off. This is not a believable lie since I just confirmed that I have time off work. "It was lovely to see you both, but I have to go," I continue, bluffing my way out of my embarrassment. I once again try to tug my hand free from Dominic's grip, but when it doesn't work again, I simply turn and walk away, assuming he will follow me. Or he will stand still and I'll be pulled off my feet, or dislocate a shoulder, or something. Luckily, he follows me, so I avoid further issues and possible injuries.

When we reach my car, I think he will kiss me goodbye, and I vow to keep my wits about me. Instead, he releases my hand and gets into my passenger seat. I stare at him, gobsmacked. This is not what I was expecting. Why is he in my car? What am I supposed to do now? I open my mouth, but I don't know what to say, so I close it again. He just waits patiently while I try to figure out what to do. Realizing Ms. Blanche, Ms. Bianca, and Rose are all watching me, I get into my car and drive away.

"Where are we going?" I ask him once we're out of the parking lot and away from prying eyes. I worry my lip as I wait for his answer. Surely he isn't planning on going to my house. What if he's planning for us to go to *his* house? He said he would have me over sometime. What if he meant now? I can't help thinking back to him saying we could kiss in private. I might have started hyperventilating.

"Can you drop me off at the museum? My car had an unfortunate run-in with some egg-throwing evildoers when my deputy was patrolling last night," he says. I knew it! He's trying to get me alone. Wait, drop him off at the museum? That's not getting me alone. I guess I don't "know it." I have mixed feelings about his choice: I feel relieved, disappointed, confused, and embarrassed.

"This looks promising," he says, looking through the folder from the real estate agency. "It's a nice space, it seems to be in good condition, and it looks like it's at a fair price." It takes me a minute to drag my mind from imagining a dalliance to real estate. It's like he hasn't been imagining X-rated activities at all.

"It's like you haven't been imagining X-rated activities at all," I say, perhaps petulantly. He tries to smother his smile, but I see it before he can regain a straight face.

"Trust me, I have a very active imagination," he tells me in that sexy voice of his. I may have swerved slightly into the other lane and blown through a stop sign, but since I didn't hit anything or anyone, I won't admit to it.

"I should write you a ticket," Dominic says as he relaxes slightly from his braced-for-impact position. Luckily, since I've pulled into the museum parking lot, he just storms out of my car. (I didn't even realize you could storm out of a car, but Dominic manages it.) I decide to leave before he can reconsider his ticket writing, and motor toward the parking lot exit. Based on how fast Dominic jumps back from my car, he's afraid I'll run over his foot again. Rude! I ignore him and keep driving.

I'm almost out of the parking lot when I suddenly swerve into a parking spot. I bite my lip while I consider my plan. It isn't well thought out because I just thought of it, but now that I have, I can't let it go. What if the painting never left the museum? That means it's still there. I bite my lip harder. If it's still in the museum, Dominic should have found it, but what if he just hasn't looked in the right place?

Before I can stop myself, I open my car door and head toward the museum. I might be humming the *Mission: Impossible* theme song as I do so.

Ms. Clark is busy with a family of tourists and doesn't see me enter. I scoot toward the door marked employees only. Serendipitously, just as I approach the door, it swings open and a young woman strides out.

I manage to catch the door before it clicks closed and sneak through it. I silently congratulate myself on my stealth, but then promptly trip on my feet and almost fall down the stairs. Luckily, my reflexes don't let me down for once, and I grasp the handrail to save myself. Still holding the handrail, I carefully descend to the basement.

Just like Theo told me earlier, the basement is a huge space, probably the size of a football field. Most of it is for storage, but off to one side a wall of windows looks into a restoration and study area and several small offices. Luckily, the offices and restoration room are unoccupied. If they weren't empty, whoever was in there would be looking directly at where I'm standing, and I would be caught before I could put my plan into motion.

Slowly spinning to take in the storage area, I am overwhelmed by the amount of stuff that fills the space. Crates and storage racks litter the area with seemingly no rhyme or reason. I heave another sigh. Some people might call it overdramatic, but I would disagree. It feels just the right amount of dramatic.

Not even knowing what I'm looking for, I begin wandering the basement. Discounting anything that isn't at least eight feet long, I make pretty good time as I investigate the space. I'm methodical in my search. I utilize a grid pattern and quickly work through the whole space. Actually—I wander like a squirrel, darting here and there, sometimes looking at the same section multiple times.

A sudden motorized clunking sound startles me. When I hear voices, I duck behind a large crate. I peek around the crate to see Dominic and Ms. Swanson exiting the elevator. Why didn't *I* take the elevator?

Ms. Swanson looks even worse than the last time I saw her. One side of her hair has come loose from her messy chignon, and even from this distance, I can see wrinkles in her clothes. She's pale and looks like she's lost weight.

They move into one of the offices and close the door so I can't hear what they're saying, but I assume it's about the missing painting. I'm kind of stuck. If I move, I'll be clearly visible through that big window, but if they come out and start walking through the storage area, I'll be caught. I chew my lip again. I can't help but remember Dominic's threat to arrest me.

I debate my options. Stay where I am and get caught, or move and get caught. Not great options. I fidget as I try to come up with a third option.

When Ms. Swanson and Dominic both turn their backs to the window, I don't hesitate. I dash across the open aisle and move deeper into the storage area. I move between crates and shelving, possibly humming the *Charlie's Angels* theme. I almost forget that I'm supposed to be looking for something that could hide an eight-foot painting.

After a couple of hours of searching, I find nothing. Well, actually, I find a lot of things, spiders being the main ones, but no missing paintings. Giving up on the storage area, I stealthily make my way toward the office area. All the offices are dark again, and there's no sign of Dominic or Ms. Swanson.

I search all the offices. It doesn't take long because they're basically fancy cubicles, and there isn't anything an eight-foot painting would fit in. The restoration and study area has a wall of shelves that could easily hold the painting. Spoiler alert, they do not hold the painting. They have various art pieces that look like they're being restored, and some packages that look like they're waiting to be mailed.

I wilt under the disappointment of failing to find the painting. I know I shouldn't be surprised. I mean, I'm sure Dominic has searched the place, so it's unlikely I would find it just lying around, but I half expected to.

Giving up, I head toward the elevator. When I see a keypad requiring a key card, my shoulders slump. I turn to the stairs and start climbing. At the top, I push the door gently, planning to peek out to ensure nobody will notice me leaving the employee area. The door doesn't move. I push harder; still nothing. Starting to panic, I push the door with all my strength. It doesn't budge. I'm locked in the museum basement.

My mind spins, searching for possible solutions. I could take the elevator. I don't have a key card to access the elevator. I could wait until tomorrow when the museum opens and the basement is unlocked. I don't want to sleep on the crates, and CC would worry. I could call CC for help. I don't know how CC would unlock the door to get me out. I could call Dominic for help. He would probably arrest me. I could kick the door open. I don't think I'm strong enough to kick the door open. I could pick the lock. I don't actually know how to pick a lock, and I don't have lock-picking tools. I could use my PI-issued laser cutter from my PI utility belt to cut a hole in the door. I don't actually have a PI-issued laser cutter. I'm not liking any of my options.

In frustration, I drop my forehead against the door. When it suddenly opens, I almost fall on my face. Somehow, I manage to regain my balance and don't make a further fool of myself. My shocked gaze meets Ian's—Ms. Swanson's husband's—shocked gaze.

"Why were you in the basement?" he asks, recovering his wits first.

"What? Why were *you* in the basement?" I counter. Apparently, my wits are still missing since he's not in the basement. "I mean, I got lost looking for the bathroom, and then somehow the door got locked and I was stuck." I silently congratulate myself on a completely believable story.

His expression implies he doubts my story.

I crowd into his space, forcing him to step back and allow me to join him in the hallway while I frantically search for something to distract him. "How did you unlock the door? Do you have a key card?"

His eyes dart away from me and then back. "The door wasn't locked. It sometimes sticks," he says quickly. "Didn't you see the big employees-only sign?" Uh-oh, he still doesn't seem to believe my bathroom story.

I try distraction again. "Have they recovered Pierre's painting?" I ask, as if I don't already know the answer.

"No," Ian says, "and I'm starting to think they never will. Linda is beside herself. This whole thing has been terrible for her and the museum. She's having trouble sleeping, and she isn't eating. She's just so upset."

"That's terrible." I sympathize with him. "It's nice that she has you to support her."

"Ian, I didn't know you were stopping by today," Ms. Swanson says from behind me. Her voice sounds raspy, like she's been yelling or crying for a long time. When she sees me, her expression changes from happiness to confusion. "What's going on?" she asks.

I force an innocent look onto my face. It's a bit of a challenge, as innocence isn't really my normal look. I'm relieved to see Dominic isn't with her.

"Ms. Swanson, I was just telling your husband how nice it is that he's able to support you during this difficult time," I interject before Ian can tattle on me.

Her expression changes from confused to delighted. "Ian is a wonderful husband," she confirms, smiling warmly at him. "I'm still counting my lucky stars that we met at the museum fundraiser auction last year." Her adoration is a little nauseating.

"I'm the one who's lucky," Ian says, wrapping her in his arms and placing a kiss on the top of her head. I look away from their public display of affection. As my gaze runs over the walls, I spot the clock. Shoot, if I don't hurry, I'll be late for dinner and CC will call for a search party.

"Well, it was lovely to see you both again, but I must be going," I say as I walk away quickly. I hurry to my car, only to pull up short when I see Dominic leaning against the hood with his arms crossed. Uh-oh, I think. I bet he suspects I was snooping into his investigation.

"I *know* you were snooping into my investigation," he says. Shoot, I didn't think it, I said it. "How many times do I have to tell you to butt out of my investigations. I'm a trained professional, and you are a menace to society."

"Rude," I tell him, not even trying to keep my thoughts in. "I did a great job in your last investigation." When I see his face darken, I realize I'm not helping myself.

Deciding to retreat for my safety, I jump into my car and quickly back out of my parking spot. Unfortunately, Dominic has opened the passenger door and is trying to get in when I start backing up. The open door takes him down like a lumberjack takes down a tree.

"Oh, my gosh," I say.

"A menace," he grits out from where he is sprawled on the asphalt.

"Is my door okay?"

His expression darkens further. "You're concerned about your car?" he asks incredulously.

"My car can't heal like a person can, and it's really hard to find parts," I defend. He glares at me while he picks himself up from the asphalt. I consider driving away without him, but his glare intensifies, and he hasn't closed the door, so that would be problematic. He gets in before I can decide, so I guess it's decided for me.

"Why didn't you go home after dropping me off?" he asks testily.

"Ummm"—I stall, trying to come up with an excuse—"I had to use the restroom?" It definitely sounds like a question, probably undermining my credibility.

"You dropped me off a couple of hours ago," he points out.

"Ummm, I had food poisoning?" It still sounds like a question. I'm not projecting confidence. His silence indicates he doesn't believe me. My need to fill the silence is strong, but I am stronger.

"Okay, I might have accidentally been in the basement," I blurt out, filling the silence. Once again, I realize I am not strong.

"Accidentally?" he asks. "How did you 'accidentally' end up in the basement? You have to have a key card to access the basement. I was in the basement and I didn't see you. If you were 'accidentally' in the basement, why didn't I see you? Is it because you were hiding?"

"You ask a lot of questions," I counter. Before he can say anything, I pull into my driveway. "Well, I'll see you later," I say, bolting from my car and toward the safety of CC's kitchen.

Once through the door, I lean against it, preventing any unwanted and possibly angry guests from entering. CC and Jake look at me like I have three heads.

"Hi," I say casually, "how was your day? Did you get the Halloween party decorations all squared away?" They don't seem to be buying my casualness.

CC frowns at me. "Why are you acting so strange?" she asks. I'm pushed several inches into the room as the door opens behind me. Using all of my strength, I push back. A loud thud and a curse indicate Dominic might have been in the way of the slamming door. I wince but don't allow the door to open.

"Claire!" CC says in a shocked voice. "Did you just slam the door on the sheriff?"

"What? No!" I assure her. Out of the corner of my eye, I can see Dominic glaring at me through the glass in the door.

"Claire, open the door or else," he growls. He sounds angry. It's not really convincing me to open the door.

"You sound angry. It's not really convincing me to open the door," I tell him, still holding the door shut. He growls. He actually growls. Then he starts pushing the door open. Despite my best efforts to keep the door shut, I'm slowly pushed out of the way. Before the door can open all the way and trap me between it and the counter, I jump free and scurry to hide behind Jake.

After several seconds pass and nothing happens, I peek around Jake. Dominic is gone. Huh, I guess Jake is an excellent shield.

A strong hand wraps around my upper arm. I don't need to look to know it is Dominic. He didn't leave. He snuck around to catch me unawares.

"We need to talk," he says, dragging me outside.

"Help! Call the police! Wait, he is the police. Call the FBI!" I yell as Dominic drags me across the kitchen and down the back steps. CC and Jake don't look like they're going to be calling anybody. Traitors!

I notice the sleeve of Dominic's shirt is torn, and his elbow has some road rash and is a bit bloody. That's probably adding to his anger and frustration at me. I realize he isn't stopping in CC's backyard. He is continuing to mine, and then into my house. There won't be any witnesses, I think.

"Even if there were witnesses, nobody would blame me," He doesn't stop until he propels me onto my sofa. He stands over me, his mouth opening and closing several times, but no words come out. He seems to be struggling to put his thoughts into words. I don't have a lot of experience with that problem, as most of my thoughts become words without any effort on my part.

"On a scale of one to ten, with one being 'not mad at all' and ten being 'furious beyond words,' how mad are you?" I ask.

"Eleven," he grits out between his clenched teeth.

"I don't know why you're so mad. The museum is open to the public, and I might have gone into the employee-only area, but it's not like you hadn't already searched it. And I might have knocked you down with my car door, but I've caused more injury in the past. So why are you so mad?"

I can see by his expression that this is not helping. I stand up, despite his looming over me and making it a challenge. I have to crowd past him, but he allows me to walk past and up the stairs.

When I come back downstairs less than a minute later, he's walking out my back door. "Where are you going?" I ask, perplexed.

"I thought you wanted me to leave," he says without turning around. "You left the room without saying anything."

"To get my first aid kit," I say, holding it in the air to prove my point. He finally turns to face me. He scrutinizes me as if he isn't sure what to think. He looks less angry, so that's a plus.

His shoulders slump, and he closes the door. "I shouldn't have gotten so mad at you. You're right, you've done much worse than today." That doesn't really show me in the best light, but in all fairness, it's true. "I'm really frustrated I can't find the painting and the thief, but I shouldn't have taken it out on you. I thought you went upstairs because you didn't want to see me anymore, and I can't say I'd blame you." He rubs the back of his neck, which I know means he's embarrassed. For once, I don't know what to say.

Instead of saying anything, I set the first aid kit on the kitchen counter next to Jaws's bowl and open it up. Dominic is still standing by my back door, so I grab his hand to guide him to the first aid kit. I realize it will be impossible to roll the torn sleeve up far enough to be out of the way. I bite my lip while I consider my options.

There are no options. In order to treat his elbow, I'm going to have to take the shirt off.

He remains motionless while I start unbuttoning his shirt, but his breathing and accelerated heartbeat tell me he isn't as calm as he pretends. My breathing and heart rate might be proof I'm not as calm as I pretend, either. But I pretend anyway. When I push his shirt off his shoulders, he sucks in a quick breath, and his pupils dilate. My pupils might have dilated too. He has perhaps the most impressive six-pack abs I've ever seen.

Mentally shaking myself, I examine his elbow. Now I'm the one to suck in a quick breath. "It looks bad," I say.

"Not exactly a reassuring bedside manner," he says, trying to get a look at it. Since he can't see his elbow, he's unsuccessful. I carefully apply hydrogen peroxide to the area. This time, his sucked-in breath is from pain. Having carefully cleaned the area, being sure all the loose gravel pieces are removed, I smear a large gauze pad with antibiotic ointment and put it on the scraped area. Realizing the scraped area is bigger than the gauze pad, I add more gauze pads smeared with ointment until the area is covered. It takes both of us to hold the many pads in place as I wrap the whole thing with an elastic bandage.

"There. Good as new," I tell him, putting my first aid kit back in order. Jaws looks on, apparently impressed with my first aid skills.

"What about our deal? Remember, every time you injure me, you have to kiss it and make it better." I don't remember agreeing to that, but I press a gentle kiss to his wrapped elbow anyway.

"There, all better," I tell him.

"That's not quite what I had in mind," he says, sounding a little disappointed. But before he can do anything about it, Jake opens my back door and peeks inside.

"CC wanted me to check and make sure everything was okay. Dominic, I brought you a shirt since yours looked ruined. Also, dinner's ready." Jake seems to take in everything in a single glance and then has some silent communication with Dominic. I'm starting to get mad that I'm always left out of the silent conversations with everybody. I decide to have a silent conversation with

Jaws. Sadly, he doesn't seem to have anything to say. Since I'm not needed anyway, I sweep past Jake and head to CC's kitchen.

I slide into my place at the banquette, ignoring CC's questioning look. Since all the children are already present, she can't question me. Ha! While I fill my plate with Parmesan chicken, mashed potatoes, and broccoli with cheese sauce, Jake and Dominic join us. Jake and CC have yet another of those silent conversations I'm never a part of, and it seems to answer her questions. The children, oblivious to the events affecting the adults, chat about school, inventions, sports activities, and a litter of kittens.

Before I know it, the children have finished eating and leave to do whatever it is they do in the evenings. CC and Jake clear the table and then return with lemonade and the paperwork from Mary. The last time I saw it, it was in my car. How did they get it?

"That was in my car. How did you get that?" I ask in what some might say is an accusatory tone.

"I grabbed it when the sheriff was talking to you," CC says, completely unconcerned that the sheriff talking to me involved him dragging me forcibly from her house. "Anyway, I thought we could go over it before we visit the lawyer and financial planner tomorrow."

"We're visiting the lawyer and financial planner tomorrow?" I ask, starting to feel overwhelmed. My whole future flashes before my eyes. My heart is racing. I'm lightheaded and dizzy. My hands are tingling. I may be having a panic attack.

"Inhale—one, two, three, four, five. Exhale—one, two, three, four, five. Inhale—one, two, three, four, five." Dominic chants in my ear as he squeezes my hand. Slowly, I can feel myself returning to normal.

"Here, drink this," CC says, handing me a glass of lemonade. The sweet tart taste helps.

"I'm okay now. It just seemed so real, and was a bit much," I say. I'm embarrassed that I overreacted.

"It's a big decision, but you don't have to do anything you don't want to do," Dominic says, rubbing my hand between his like he's trying to warm it.

"Maybe we shouldn't discuss anything tonight," Jake offers. His eyes are full of concern. I'm starting to feel like a little kid who needs to be coddled and protected. While I like the caring attention, I don't like the sentiment that I'm weak.

"No, I'm okay now. I think it just all hit me at once," I assure Jake, taking another sip of lemonade. Dominic has not released my hand and is now drawing circles on my palm with his thumb. I find it very distracting, which probably helps with the panic.

I'm mostly quiet while the others look over the paperwork. Sticky notes appear as if by magic, and notes are added to the various pages. Before I know it, the last page has been reviewed.

"I think this is going to be so great." CC beams at me. I just nod my head without saying anything. I'm still not sure about this big change. I might not love my job at the insurance company, but it *is* familiar. Huh, maybe I'm afraid of uncertainty.

I mull that over most of the night instead of sleeping.

Chapter 17

Even though I'm wide awake, I remain immobile. I can't seem to find the energy to move, not even my pinkie. I stare at my ceiling for several minutes, trying to gather the energy to get up. When Blackbeard enters my field of view, glaring down at me, I begin to worry. When he growls at me, I find the energy and stagger upright.

Blackbeard's twitching tail tells me I'm still in jeopardy of being harmed. I rush to turn on the shower for him. It's still early, so I decide I might as well join him. I finish long before Blackbeard gets tired of showering, and it is to his deep disappointment that I turn off the water. I leave him licking himself dry while I blow-dry my hair.

When I open my shirt drawer, I am once again faced with the shirts Dominic got me. I pick the soft blue one with I AM printed above the pictures of a koala and a tea bag. Maybe it'll give me the boost I need today. I feel like I'm moving in slow motion, especially compared to Benji, who's jumping straight into the air as we head to CC's. I'm impressed that he can jump so high, and also that he can maintain his position at my side while doing so.

I collapse onto a barstool without even bothering to grab a cup of coffee first. Luckily, CC hands me a cup. I drain it and hold it out for a refill. I feel like I'm going to need a lot of coffee this morning.

As I drink my second cup, more slowly than the first, CC's children begin trickling in for breakfast. A plate of French toast appears in front of me between blinks. Perhaps my blinks are very long this morning. I begin eating more out of habit than conscious thought. There are so many thoughts swirling through my head that I can't pin down any of them.

"Claire? Earth to Claire," CC says, snapping her fingers in front of my face. Right in my face, like two inches from my nose. I slap at her hand halfheartedly. "Finally, I have your attention. I asked you three times if you were ready to go."

"What? Of course I am. Where are we going?" I might be overstating being ready. I have no idea what is going on. Trying to figure out what's happening, I look around the kitchen for clues. Since we're alone, I assume the children left for school. My crack observation skills seem to be missing this morning.

CC rolls her eyes at me. "To our meeting with the financial planner and the lawyer. Did you forget?" (She asks as if she already knows the answer and it is "Yes, I forgot.")

"No! Of course I didn't forget," I lie. She doesn't look like she believes me, but doesn't comment further.

"Good, then let's go." She loops her arm through mine and propels me toward my car. I'm not sure if it's a show of support or to keep me from backing out.

The drive to our appointment is uneventful. At least I assume it was, since CC seems fine when I park, but I don't actually remember driving there, so I can't be sure.

"Ms. Miller, Ms. Moore, it's so nice to see you both," Carol Jenkins greets us professionally.

"Carol, how are your kids?" CC asks.

"They're great. The twins started soccer and are loving it. Scarlet is trying out for the school play, and Kevin made the swim team. How are your kids?" Carol asks. Asking about one's family is expected. I don't have kids or family, so nobody asks me anything.

"They're great. Nell loves college and has a boyfriend now. Frank just got his driver's license and is still dating Amelia. Kyle painted the town murals. Jane's volunteering at the animal shelter. Ann just turned ten and is also playing soccer. Dean joined the robotics team, and Eve is enjoying preschool." CC loves talking about her kids. My attention wanders while she lists their accomplishments, so I take in the office space. It's tastefully decorated with sage-green walls, wood trim, and large landscape paintings. It hasn't changed in all the time I've been alive.

"I'll let Mr. Jenkins know you're here," Carol says, as if she isn't talking about her husband, somebody we went to high school with. Come to think about it, we also went to middle school and elementary school with Phil.

Carol picks up the phone and presses a button. "Ms. Moore and Ms. Miller are here for their appointment," she says into the phone. "It'll be just a minute," she tells us, setting the phone down. We've barely settled into chairs in the waiting area when Phil appears.

"Ms. Moore, Ms. Miller, it's good to see you. Please, come into my office." He sounds so professional, and not at all like we went to school together. I'm pretty sure he was involved in turning the sprinklers on during the girls' gym class, soaking us. Before I can ask him, Jake and Brad West, our financial planner (who we also went to school with), join us. Handshakes are exchanged while Carol brings in coffee, and we all sit around a large conference table.

The next hour is spent reviewing the real estate information, debating setting up an LLC, reviewing the pros and cons of taking out a loan versus self-funding, and going over a rudimentary business plan. It's a lot of information in a short amount of time. I mostly just listen, drink coffee, and nod my head when appropriate. More sticky notes, lists, and other paperwork are added to the point that the folder barely closes. Finally, everybody seems satisfied, and once more, handshakes are exchanged.

"Don't worry, Claire," Brian says, "it's not as scary as it seems." Obviously, I'm not doing a good job of hiding my panic.

I'm quiet all the way home, which is not a normal occurrence for me. My mind is spinning with all the things involved in opening a bookstore. A love of books is not enough.

"I don't know if I can do this," I tell CC once I park in my driveway. "A love of books is not enough."

She doesn't say anything, just lets the silence stretch. I fight not to fill it.

"What if I fail? What if I forget something important, like a business license? What if nobody buys a book?" I lose the fight.

She counters my questions with her own. "What if you succeed? What if you use your business degree? What if everybody buys books? Come on, you'll feel better after some lunch." I don't know if I believe her, but I'm willing to give it a try.

Spoiler alert, I do not feel better after lunch. When CC leaves to help finish taking down the decorations from the town Halloween party, I head home and seek the comfort of my sofa.

I spend the afternoon curled up on my sofa, looking through the paperwork. I have to admit a lot of it's confusing, but remembering my business degree, which I don't use often while managing the office of Brown and Son Insurance Agency, a lot of it makes sense. I'm getting pretty excited about my bookstore. (My possible bookstore, I correct myself.)

"I'm opening a bookstore," I whisper to Blackbeard, who's lying across the rest of my sofa. He seems unimpressed with me and my proclamation. He barely glances at me before turning away again, dismissing me as if I'm beneath his notice.

At least Benji is excited for me. Hearing my whisper, he jumps to a standing position and wags his tail excitedly before executing a backflip. Huh, I didn't know he could do a backflip. I reward his enthusiasm with a scratch on his ears.

Noticing the time, I set my papers aside carefully and head to CC's for dinner. I don't want CC to know I've decided to open the bookstore, so I act nonchalant.

"Claire, why are you acting so weird?" CC asks. I'm starting to think I don't know how to act nonchalant. She nudges me out of the way as she browns ground beef, washes and shreds lettuce, slices tomatoes, and grates cheese.

"Why are you cooking dinner? Isn't it Tuesday? Isn't everybody going bowling?" I try to distract her so she doesn't notice I'm acting weird.

"Bowling is canceled tonight. Missy and Ryan are celebrating their tenth wedding anniversary. Ryan closed the bowling alley so he could take Missy out for a nice dinner," CC reminds me. Ha! My distraction plan worked! Hoping to prevent CC from remembering that I'm acting weird, I get the tortilla chips out of the pantry. I might be snitching a couple as I pour them into a bowl.

CC pulls a stack of tortilla bowls out of the pantry and fills them with lettuce. She looks like she's about to comment that my helping with dinner is weird. Uh-oh. "What happened to Dean's lettuce-washing machine?" I ask her.

"Shhhh! It's still under the sink, but don't remind Dean. It almost broke the faucet the last time." She looks around as if Dean will spring out from hiding and demand she use his invention. Apparently deciding it's safe, she garnishes the lettuce with beans and tomatoes in between stirring the meat. She also grabs sour cream and salsa out of the refrigerator and places them on the table next to my carefully and lovingly prepared bowl of tortilla chips. And some people say I'm a disaster in the kitchen. I sure showed them.

When the meat is done, CC distributes it among the bowls and tops them all with cheese. Somehow, her family seems to know when dinner is ready, and they appear as if by magic. As everyone gets their taco salad bowl, I realize we have an extra bowl. It isn't for Amelia. She already has one. And then I know who it's for.

"Dominic," Jake greets him at the door as he lets him in.

"I knew it," I mutter.

"Miss me?" he asks quietly as he sits beside me. Very close beside me. I don't say anything because I did kind of miss him, but I don't want to admit it. "It's okay. You don't have to admit it."

How does he know what I'm thinking? I know I didn't say it out loud because my mouth was full of a huge bite of taco salad which I took to cover my unwillingness to answer him. Maybe he can read my mind. I think the question "Can you read my mind?" really hard. He just gives me a quick wink. Well, that's inconclusive.

"Nice shirt," he says, with a soft smile. I don't know what to say, but luckily he doesn't seem to expect a response. "How did the meeting go?"

Everybody seems to be waiting for me to answer, but when the silence stretches, Jake fills it. Ha! I knew I wasn't the only one who needed to fill silences.

"It was good. The storefront is priced competitively and is the right size for the bookstore. We have an outline for a business plan and a projected timeline of two to three months." My brain short-circuits at hearing the timeline. I could be the proud owner of my very own bookstore by the new year. I'm simultaneously terrified and ecstatic. I choose to focus on the ecstatic feeling.

"I can't believe I'm going to do it," I say quietly. "I'm going to open a bookstore." CC beams at me like a proud parent. Jake smiles encouragingly at me, and Dominic squeezes my hand where he's holding it under the table. For the first time, I actually feel like I can do this.

The rest of dinner passes without me noticing. I'm too busy thinking about everything I need to do to get my bookstore up and running. I only realize time has passed when Dominic pulls me out of the banquette. I look around the now-empty kitchen, confused about where everybody went.

"What? Where is everybody?" I ask, still confused.

"They went to bed," Dominic tells me, leading me toward my house. "And you should too." His words paint an X-rated picture in my mind that distracts me and causes me to stumble on the porch steps. Luckily, I don't fall.

Dominic gives me a quick kiss and then gently pushes me inside. "Good night," he says, closing the door behind me and disappearing into the night.

"Huh," I say to myself. I'm confused about Dominic's quick kiss before leaving, and I'm still confused about how I lost time. Instead of going upstairs to bed, I head back to my sofa and the paperwork.

By the time the sun comes up in the morning, I have a solid business plan. I decided on the LLC, a combination of self-funding and a business loan, made a list of tasks required to get everything ready, and set a timeline for task completion. It was a productive night.

Chapter 18

"Coffee," I croak to CC shortly after dawn. I'm still wearing the clothes from yesterday, having stayed up all night planning my future.

"Claire, are you okay? What happened?" CC asks, the concern in her voice and expression evident.

"I stayed up all night going over the paperwork and making plans," I tell her, still waiting patiently for coffee. "I need coffee," I remind her. I guess I'm not waiting patiently. She pours me a cup and waits for me to drain it so she can refill it before returning to sip her coffee. She seems to be waiting for something, but I'm not sure what.

After I finish my second cup, she pounces. Not literally—she's still leaning against the counter—but she starts peppering me with questions. "You're going to do it? You're opening a bookstore? When do you think it will open? What do you need me to help with? Did you make an offer on the storefront? Where are you getting the bookshelves and books from? What about the coffee area?"

"Shh," I say, holding up a hand to stop her questions. "I was up all night," I remind her pointedly. "I need sleep before you start the inquisition."

"Maybe drinking two cups of coffee isn't the best decision if you're planning to go to sleep," she tells me.

While she might be right, I would never admit that to her. "You're right," I say. "I'm going home to bed." (I guess I did admit it to her after all. Oh, well.)

I stagger zombie-like home to bed. Since Agatha is sleeping on my living room floor, I have the whole mattress to myself. I topple face-first, completely dressed, onto my bed and fall asleep almost immediately.

I wake up when Benji barks sharply in my ear. Not sure how much time has passed, I blink until my vision clears enough to read my clock. I blink several more times in disbelief. According to my clock, it's after five. My brain struggles to grasp the fact that I have slept all day.

Benji barks again and then runs to my bedroom door. He looks back at me expectantly. Sighing, I roll out of bed and follow him. He leads me to the front door. That's weird. I rarely use that door.

I open the door to find Beatrice trying to peek in my window. "What are you doing?" I ask, more surprised than angry.

She jumps and spins to face me. Apparently, she's surprised too. "Nothing!" she says, a little too loudly. I don't say anything to this obvious lie. Finally, she adds, "I was just looking for Lester."

"Why would you look here?" I ask, truly confused.

Her shoulders slump, and she climbs out of my planter bed to join me on the porch. "He isn't taking my calls, he checked out of his hotel, and I haven't seen him since the town Halloween party. I just want to be sure he's okay."

"I think you need to accept that the relationship is over. He's made it pretty obvious he isn't interested in you. Why are you so set on Pierre, I mean Lester? You flew across the country after he broke up with you and wouldn't take your calls. Why?"

"You wouldn't understand. You're beautiful and could get any guy you want. Not all of us are blessed with good looks. I supported Lester when he was struggling, and now he just throws me away. He owes me," she says, a militant expression on her face.

"First of all, thank you, but have you seen my best friend? She's a pinup model come to life. Guys barely realize I exist when I stand next to her. Secondly, if Lester can't appreciate you and respect you, then you don't need him."

"Will you tell me where he is or not?" she asks with a mix of desperation, resignation, petulance, and hope. It's a lot of emotions for one sentence, but apparently, she's a complex person with complex feelings, like me.

"I have no idea where he is. We are not dating. I haven't seen him since the Halloween party either. He only wanted to spend time with me because he was hoping I'd pass on information from the sheriff's investigation. Now that he knows I know that's the only reason he was hanging around, I doubt he would show up."

Her shoulders slump. "I don't know where else to look. He hasn't been back to the museum. Where would he go?" I hope this is a rhetorical question because I don't know him well enough to even guess where he would go.

She isn't making any moves to leave, so I start to think it's not a rhetorical question. "How do you know he didn't go back to the museum?" I ask, mostly to fill the silence.

"Some guy at the museum told me," she says distractedly, digging in her giant brown monstrosity of a purse. She pulls out her phone, quickly checks the screen, and then drops it back into her purse. "Lester still hasn't called me back. Ugh!" She stomps her foot and turns to go.

"Ian? Linda Swanson's husband? Ian was at the museum, and he knew Pierre—I mean Lester—hadn't been there?" I ask. That seems odd. Why was Ian there again, and why was he talking to Beatrice about Pierre?

Beatrice doesn't answer, probably because she is already halfway to the street. "Okay, well, thanks for stopping by, I guess," I call after her. She doesn't respond, so either she didn't hear me or she's choosing to ignore me.

Walking to CC's, I muse on why Ian seems to be at the museum all the time. Doesn't he have a job?

Eve interrupts my musing as soon as I enter the kitchen. "Why are you wearing the same clothes as yesterday?" I look down, surprised to see I'm still wearing the koala tea shirt Dominic gave me. Then I remember: I stayed up all night and slept all day, so I didn't change clothes. Not having a good response, I ignore her and sit at the banquette.

I don't have a chance to give Ian, Pierre, or Beatrice another thought because CC starts shooting questions at me rapid-fire, making me think she's been composing a list while I slept. "Did you make an offer on the storefront? Was it accepted? Have you started ordering books? Where are you putting the coffee area? Do you have bookshelves yet? Are you going to hire anybody to help run the bookshop? Who are you going to hire? Tessa would be a good choice, don't you think?"

Finally, she seems to run out of breath and pauses for half a second. "Well?" she prompts impatiently.

"I just decided last night and slept all day. No further decisions or actions have occurred," I tell her. Her frown tells me I've deeply disappointed her. Luckily for me, before she can pester me further, the timer dings, and she has to take two of the world's biggest casserole dishes out of her double ovens.

In a blink, her whole family is now seated at the table with me. I don't even remember Jake coming home. (It's possible my blinks are longer than normal and may, in fact, be better described as dozing off. I don't know how I can still be tired after sleeping all day, but I guess I'm an overachiever.) My poor muddled brain alternates between visualizing my bookstore, making to-do lists, fighting sleep, remembering to take bites of dinner, missing Dominic, considering where the missing painting could be, and wondering about Ian's continued presence at the museum.

"Why is Ian at the museum all the time?" I ask of nobody in particular.

"He is?" CC asks, sounding surprised. "Maybe he's trying to help his wife feel better. She must be very upset over the missing painting." I suppose that makes sense, but something feels off. I stab at a piece of broccoli in my cheesy potato and ham casserole while I try to determine why Ian being at the museum seems odd.

My poor brain apparently can't notice what's happening at the table and think all the thoughts, because the next thing I know, my plate has been replaced with a glass of tea. Maybe it's a good thing I'm opening a bookstore instead of becoming a PI. My observation skills could use a lot of work.

"Beatrice stopped by my house today," I tell CC. "She was looking for Pierre, and for some reason thought he might be at my house. She said he'd checked out of the hotel and hadn't been back to the museum. Do you think it's strange he just left?"

"You said he was avoiding Beatrice. Maybe he changed hotels and asked everybody at the museum to tell her he hadn't been there." CC has a good point. I mean, he did move to the other side of the country to avoid Beatrice. What's a hotel change in the grand scheme of things?

I can tell CC wants to talk more about my future bookstore, so I quickly drain my glass and stand up. "Well, I'm still feeling tired, so I'm going to head for bed," I tell her. Her expression shows the internal battle between wanting to press me for more information and wanting to mother me. I head home before I can find out which side wins.

However, once home, I can't let go of the question of why Ian was at the museum and was talking to Beatrice about Pierre. I do a quick internet search on Ian Swanson and don't get any hits. When I search for Linda Swanson, though, a lot of hits come up. It looks like she kept her maiden name, and I find several articles from her formative years as well. She graduated with honors from a good college. Her parents died several years ago, leaving her a substantial inheritance. She was named executive director of a museum the year after their deaths. She's become the executive director of two more museums since then.

There are several social media posts about her whirlwind romance with Ian. Strangely, he isn't tagged in any. Maybe he doesn't have social media. Is somebody not having social media even possible? They met at a museum fundraiser auction last year. Now that I'm reading about it, that sounds familiar. Thinking back, I remember that when I almost got caught in the basement, Ms. Swanson mentioned how they met. (I suppose technically I *did* get caught in the basement since Ian had to let me out, and she saw me—but I bluffed my way through it, so I don't think it counts.)

A year seems like a very short time to go from first meeting to already married, I think. There are several posts with pictures documenting their romance: intimate dinners at fancy restaurants, weekends at wineries, and strolls along streets lined with shops, just to name a few. They seem happy and smitten in all of them.

Continuing to scroll through the posts, I find one from six months ago covering their wedding, but very little information about Ian. It doesn't seem like he even existed until they started dating. In one photo, Ian is wearing a polo shirt with a small logo. I squint as if that will make the logo larger and easier to see. Despite the fact that my squinting does not make the logo bigger, I am able to recognize it as a college mascot.

I wish I had Dominic's database-searching abilities or Jake's programming skills to create an algorithm, or whatever it's called, to search for Ian-with-an-unknown-last-name in that college's alumni list. Sighing, perhaps overdramatically, I start scrolling through the list of names from the most likely graduation year. After what feels like years of scanning names printed beside professional head shots that are starting to blur together, I find him: Ian Newman.

Before I can do a search for Ian Newman, Benji barks sharply at me, reminding me I'm supposed to be going to bed. I consider ignoring him, but he stomps a foot and does a snorty growl that indicates that he will not be ignored. I sigh again and head for bed. (I'd like to say I organize the information I found and make sense of the situation, but I don't.) I fall asleep quickly, even though Agatha's snoring in my ear and Blackbeard's claimed my pillow.

Chapter 19

My weird sleep schedule catches up with me at about four in the morning, when I find myself wide awake. I try to go back to sleep, but after staring at my ceiling for fifteen minutes, I give up. Heaving a sigh, I get up to shower, much to Blackbeard's joy. He beats me to the shower and meows at me impatiently. It sounds suspiciously like the word "now."

I finish my washing much sooner than Blackbeard approves of, but I manage to avoid his wrath as I leave him chasing stray water drops. I dress quickly in my standard funny T-shirt and jeans, and French braid my wet hair. Only after I'm done with my hair do I realize Agatha is still in my bed. A glance at my clock confirms it's still early, and CC wouldn't have made coffee yet.

I don't know what to do with myself. I'm never awake this early. I head downstairs and then pause, still unsure what to do. Looking around for inspiration, I find none, but then I remember my research from last night. I decide now is as good a time as any to see what I can find on Ian Newman.

I don't find much. He graduated with a bachelor's in communications. He did not graduate with honors. I don't find any employment information.

I'm not sure what to make of what I've found (or not found), but when Agatha wanders into the living room and melts across my floor, I head to CC's for coffee.

"I'm surprised to see you this early."

"I think my sleep schedule is still messed up from staying up all night and then sleeping all day," I tell her, filling my coffee cup. "Did you know Linda and Ian have only known each other for a year?" (It feels weird to call Ms. Swanson by her first name, but it would also feel weird to use her last name and his first name.) "And they got married six months ago? Doesn't that seem fast?" I take a large swallow of coffee.

"Some people just know," she tells me, but she frowns slightly, as if unconvinced.

"Some people just know what?" Jake asks, joining us in the kitchen. The children trickle in behind him.

"When they've met the right person. Claire was telling me that Ms. Swanson, from the museum, and her husband only met a year ago, and got married after six months," CC tells him, apparently also finding the name thing an issue. She places a plate with several toasted bagel halves on the table, but the children snatch them all before I can get one. I watch enviously as they add the various toppings CC already set out.

"That seems fast," Jake says. "To go from strangers to spouses in six months seems crazy." I agree with Jake. I guess I could understand if they knew each other before dating and then got married after dating for only six months. Or got engaged after knowing each other for a year. Or even having friends in common—but this seems too fast.

"They seem happy, so I guess it worked for them," CC says, bringing another plate with several toasted bagel halves to the table. I grab a bagel half before they're all claimed by the children. I survey the topping choices, trying to decide what I want. There's butter, peanut butter, berries, cream cheese, bananas, jam, honey, and smoked salmon to choose from. While I smear some cream cheese on my bagel half and then top it with smoked salmon, I ponder why the speed of Linda and Ian's relationship bugs me.

As they finish eating, the kids gather their backpacks and other school necessities, then, as a group, the kids and Jake head out the door for school and work, leaving CC and me alone in the kitchen.

"Do you want to go to the museum with me?" I ask CC.

"Why do you want to go to the museum?" she asks, somewhat suspiciously. It's like she thinks I have an ulterior motive instead of an appreciation for the arts.

"Why do you think I have an ulterior motive instead of an appreciation for the arts?" I ask her as innocently as I can manage. Based on her expression, it's not as innocent-sounding as I hope. She refrains from commenting, which forces me to fill the silence. "I don't know why, but it's really bothering me how fast Linda and Ian got married. I don't even know what I think I'll find out, but what else do I have to do today?" I ignore my newly made to-do list of tasks required for opening my bookstore.

She looks like she's about to remind me of my to-do list, so I cut her off. "I'll wait for you by my car." Then I hurry out before she can say anything. While I wait, I admire the still-blooming roses lining my walkway. My mother planted them and tended them carefully. I'm trying desperately not to kill them.

A short while later, CC joins me. "Don't you have things to do to get your bookstore up and running?" she asks, getting into my passenger seat without waiting for me to answer. I slide in and turn the key so the rumble of my engine drowns out her judgment. Not really, but it makes it easier to ignore.

Before I know it, we're pulling into the mostly empty museum parking lot. Now that I'm faced with the museum, I'm not sure how to proceed. I chew my lip in uncertainty while I consider what to do next. I'm not exactly known for being subtle, but I don't want to come across as nosy.

CC's snorted laugh tells me I've once again said my thoughts out loud, and she thinks I'm nosy. Before I can chicken out, I climb out of my car and, with CC trailing me, head inside. I just hope inspiration will strike.

Ms. Clark is alone at the front desk. I decide to subtly pump her for information. "Good morning, Ms. Clark. It's lovely to see you again." I smile warmly at her. Her expression makes me think she is surprised to see me at the museum.

"Claire, I'm surprised to see you here," she says. I silently congratulate myself on correctly identifying her emotions. I'll make a great PI. Wait, I'm not going to become a PI. I'm going to open a bookstore.

Mentally shrugging, I continue. "CC and I just love the museum." I lie shamelessly to her face. "Ever since we were here for Pierre's art show opening, I find myself drawn back again and again." Well, at least that part isn't a lie. I do feel drawn back here, just not to view the art.

"It is such a shame. That poor man." Ms. Clark shakes her head sadly. "He was just beside himself." I cock my head in the international symbol for confusion. Maybe that's just for dogs. Oh, well, too late to change tactics.

"What do you mean, 'was'? Has his painting been found?" I ask, super casually. Ms. Clark looks like she's concerned, possibly for me. I guess my super-casualness isn't convincing.

"No, but I heard he just packed up and left early Monday morning." She leans closer and lowers her voice. "I think he just gave up. The poor dear."

I deftly steer the conversation to the real reason for my visit today. "How is Ms. Swanson holding up? This must be just terrible for her," I say, with a concerned expression. Ms. Clark frowns at me, making me think my expression may not be projecting concern like I hope it is.

"She's at her wits' end," Ms. Clark practically whispers, looking around to be sure we're alone. "I heard she isn't sleeping or eating. Her husband has been bringing her lunch every day, trying to get her to eat something."

Aha! I think, and fortunately do not say. "That's so nice of him. She is so lucky to have such a supportive and loving husband. Did I hear right that they got married just six months ago and only met last year?" I hope I'm finally able to pull off nonchalance. Ms. Clark's eyes light up with what I think is barely suppressed glee. She must have some good gossip.

"That's right," she confirms. "They met at a fundraising event and just knew." Her sigh is wistful as she stares off into space.

I give her a moment with her memory before pressing on. "He must have a flexible work schedule to be able to bring her lunch every day." I'm starting to see why Missy fishes for gossip; it's kind of fun.

"Oh, he isn't working right now," Ms. Clark tells me. "He wanted to spend time with Ms. Swanson and support her. With Pierre's big art show opening, he knew she would be busy, so he quit his job." Her smile makes me think she finds this romantic. I mull over this information. I kind of suspected Ian didn't have a job, but now that's confirmed, I try to fit the pieces together.

"CC, Claire, what are you doing here?" Dominic's voice comes from behind me. He does not sound happy. When I turn to face him, my suspicion is confirmed. He is frowning. At me. Why doesn't he ever frown at CC?

My eyes dart around the room as I try to decide what to say. The only possible distraction is a mailman exiting an elevator with a cart filled with several wrapped boxes, cartons, tubes, and large envelopes. He seems unlikely to help me distract Dominic. While I'm still trying to come up with a distraction, I'm interrupted by Dominic's next question.

"What are you doing here?" I guess it's the same question; he's just repeating himself. "I'm repeating myself because you aren't answering." He answers my apparently spoken thoughts with what I would describe as a mix of frustration and exasperation.

"CC and I enjoy the art. With the kids in school all day and with my office closed, we finally have time to see the exhibits," I lie.

"What a coincidence," he says. "I was going to tour the whole museum just to be sure I didn't miss anything. We can see all the exhibits together. You don't mind company, do you?" Uh-oh, he apparently sees through my lie and is now trying to get me to crack and admit the truth.

"Well, we are having a *girls'* day, so ..." I trail off, trying to deflect his request.

"I insist," he says in a tone that tells me he won't be denied. I feel my shoulders slump in surrender. I know I can just admit the truth, listen to his lecture on staying out of his investigation, and go home, but I'm unwilling to admit defeat.

We spend the next several hours walking through the entire museum and staring at the art displayed. It is beyond tedious, but I have to pretend to be fascinated with everything I see. After what feels like days, but probably hasn't been that long, I realize CC is missing.

"Where did CC go?" I ask, looking around frantically.

"She went to the bathroom," Dominic says.

"Alone? Doesn't she know women go to the bathroom in groups?" I march off to the bathroom. Or at least I try to. I only get two steps away before I'm pulled up short by Dominic's grip on my arm.

"Don't be silly," he says with an evil smile. "You wouldn't want to miss the next exhibit, it's early Greek pottery." He *is* evil. We stroll with mind-numbing slowness through approximately nine thousand nearly identical pottery pieces. Every time I try to hurry us along, he comes to a complete stop, and since he's still holding my arm, I'm forced to stop too.

"I think I'm going to skip on ahead to the next exhibit," I tell him, trying to pry his fingers off my arm. "I saw this one last time."

"Oh, good," he says. "Then you can tell me all about it."

I give up trying to pry his fingers off my arm and glare at him. "Fine," I say grudgingly, "we weren't coming to look at the art. I was trying to find out more about Linda and Ian's relationship. I just think it's crazy that they got married after only knowing each other for six months, and that Ian doesn't have a job, and I find it interesting that he's the one who convinced Linda to host Pierre's art show here." I glare at him, even though I'm the one butting in where I don't belong. I've never let that stop me before, and I'm not going to let it stop me now either.

"I knew it!" he says as if he solved some great mystery. "I knew you weren't here to see the art."

"Well, duh!" I counter, folding my arms. I belatedly think that maybe I shouldn't antagonize him, but it's too late now, so I continue. "I only came to the museum the first time for Kyle, and he's in school. It's not like you solved some great mystery." He looks like he's counting to ten to regain control of his temper. I wait, but he's taking a long time.

Losing interest, I wander away. Well, I tried. He apparently gave up on counting and grabs my hand. We proceed through the rest of the museum, but much faster than before. Instead of pausing to look at each display, we keep up a steady walking pace. None of the art we pass is large enough to conceal the missing painting, even if it was rolled into a tube. There are very few doors in the galleries, and all of them seem to be locked.

"How did you get the keys?" I ask him as he unlocks the first door we come to and quickly searches inside. It appears to be a supply closet full of paper towels and toilet paper. He closes and locks the door before we continue.

"I'm the sheriff," he tells me. "It's my job to investigate." It's like he's trying to point out that it's not *my* job to investigate. When I'm a PI, it will be my job. (Wait, I decided to open a bookstore, not become a PI.)

"And for that, I am thankful every day," he mutters, making me think I was thinking out loud again.

"Rude," I tell him, but he ignores me.

"Sheriff Armstrong, any updates on the investigation?" Ms. Swanson asks from behind me. When I turn to face her, I'm shocked speechless by her appearance. Her complexion is waxy and has a sheen of sweat. Her pupils are dilated. She sways slightly on her feet, and Dominic and I both reach out as if to catch her.

"Are you okay?" I ask her, perhaps stupidly, because it's obvious that she's not okay.

"Yes, I'm fine," she answers, as if by rote. "I just haven't been sleeping well." I'm unconvinced, but not sure what to do to help her.

"Maybe you should see a doctor," Dominic suggests.

"No, I'm fine. I just need a little rest," Ms. Swanson says. Before we can do or say anything else, she stiffens and then falls to the floor. Luckily, we're able to catch her and ease her down, so she doesn't get hurt.

"Ms. Swanson, can you hear me?" Dominic asks while he checks for a pulse. "Ms. Swanson? Call 911," he tells me, returning his attention to her.

As I pull my phone out, her arms and legs begin jerking. I call 911 and relate what is happening.

Everything seems to happen in a time warp, both fast and slow at the same time. In what feels like both seconds and hours, an ambulance with paramedics arrives. They lift a still-unresponsive Ms. Swanson onto a gurney and wheel her away. Dominic and I trail them as they rush to the parking lot and the waiting ambulance. CC rushes to join us. "Oh my gosh! What happened?" she asks.

"Ms. Swanson had a seizure," I tell her. "The paramedics are taking her to the hospital."

"Oh, how terrible! I hope she's all right," CC says worriedly.

"Linda?!" Ian calls, dropping a container as he rushes toward the gurney. Apparently, he arrived to bring her lunch. "What's happened? Is she okay? Linda? Can you hear me?" He clutches her lax hand. "What happened?" he asks the paramedics again. "I'm her husband. Is she going to be okay?"

"Her vital signs are stable, but she's still unconscious, so we need to get her to the hospital immediately. You can follow us there." They quickly load her into the ambulance and slam the doors behind them. Ian watches the ambulance drive away, then turns and rushes to his car.

Something about his expression seems wrong. "Does he seem off to you?" I ask Dominic, frowning after Ian's car as it pulls out of the parking lot.

"Yeah," he agrees, also frowning after Ian's car.

Dominic walks over to the container Ian dropped, picks it up, and opens it. I follow him and try to peer over his shoulder. Since his shoulder is too tall to see over, I end up leaning around him to see what's in there. It's a salad.

"Huh," I say, not sure what I was expecting, but somehow disappointed by what I see. Dominic scowls at me, apparently upset that I'm butting into his investigation, but he doesn't say anything about it.

"I have to go," he says. "I'll see you later." He looks a little distracted, but also a little unsure, as if he doesn't know if I'd like to see him later.

"I'd like that," I tell him. His eyes warm, and he smiles slightly at me.

"I like your shirt," he adds, turning to go. I look down as if I don't remember what shirt I'm wearing. Today's shirt of choice has a picture of two cartoon beakers. One of them is bubbling over, and the other one has the words YOU'RE OVERREACTING in a speech bubble. I like that he likes my shirts.

Now that the commotion has calmed down, the small crowd that gathered to watch the tragic spectacle disperses. CC and I head toward my car slowly.

"Ian didn't seem as surprised or as upset as I would expect," I muse as we walk.

"He seemed pretty upset," CC counters, but I'm not convinced. I mull over why I'm questioning Ian's behavior as I drive home.

Somehow, we end up at the hospital instead.

"Huh," I say, surprised to find myself parking in the hospital parking lot. "Well, since we're here, we might as well offer our sympathy to Ian." CC looks like she's torn between offering sympathy to Ian and reminding me to butt out of the Sheriff's investigation. I wonder where this desire to steer clear of his investigation was a couple of months ago, when she dragged me into a murder investigation and almost got us killed.

"Where was this desire to steer clear of Dominic's investigation a couple of months ago when you dragged me into a murder investigation and almost got us killed?" I ask her, perhaps with a judgmental tone.

She frowns at me. "In hindsight, we might have gotten in over our heads and put ourselves in a dangerous situation." Ignoring her reticence, I climb out of my car and head toward the entrance.

I immediately spot Ian in the waiting area. He's scrolling through his phone like he doesn't have a care in the world. He must feel my stare because he looks up and glances around until his eyes land on me.

As soon as he recognizes me, his expression becomes one of worry, frustration, and sadness. "They're running tests, but they won't tell me anything," he says. "I feel so helpless. I was just looking at old photos of us together."

He's volunteering information, a common sign of lying. His eyes get a slight sheen like he's fighting not to cry, but I'm not buying it. It feels very manufactured. Everybody can see through his theatrics.

"Oh, you poor man," CC says, sitting beside him and taking his hand supportively. Apparently, not everybody can see through his theatrics after all. "I'm sure she'll be all right. The doctors will figure out what's wrong, and she'll make a full recovery. I just know it."

"Does she have a history of seizures?" I ask gently in a concerned manner. (The fact that CC frowns at me before returning to comforting Ian tells me I might not actually have asked with gentle concern.)

"No. I mean, I don't think so. She never said anything about them, and she hasn't had any since I've known her," Ian answers.

"So, she hasn't had one in the past year?" I press further. "It seems weird that she would suddenly start having seizures for no reason."

"I'm sure there is a reason, and the doctors will find out what it is and fix it," CC says, glaring at me while she pats Ian's hand. I glare back at her. Maybe I should have filled her in on my suspicions and plan before we got here.

Dr. Young, the hospital's ER doctor for the last thirty-plus years, enters the waiting room. As usual, his white hair is standing straight out from his head in all directions. His bushy eyebrows look like two oversized furry caterpillars marching across his forehead, and his liver-spotted hands are tapping his legs in a rhythm that only makes sense to him.

"Mr. Swanson?" Dr. Young asks, somewhat needlessly, since Ian is the only person besides CC and me in the waiting room, and is, therefore, Ms. Swanson's husband.

Ian stands up. "It's Mr. Newman, but Linda is my wife," he says. Not exactly an important detail when your wife is dying, I think. Luckily, I don't say this out loud.

"She's stable, and we expect her to make a full recovery," Dr. Young tells Ian. He wilts, in what should have been relief, but I think more closely resembles frustration. "We gave her some anti-seizure meds and are running blood tests. The good news is she's conscious. She's very tired and is showing signs of confusion, which is very common after a seizure. We're giving her IV fluids and will continue to monitor her overnight. Hopefully, the blood tests and a brain scan will help us determine what's wrong."

As if suddenly remembering his lines, Ian reaches out and shakes the doctor's hand. "Thanks, Doctor, that's great news," he says. "Can I see her?" He sounds like a worried husband, but I'm still suspicious.

"For just a couple of minutes, then I'm afraid you'll have to leave. She needs her rest, but you can come back in the morning."

Dr. Young leads Ian through the doors. I debate waiting for Ian to return and questioning him further, but I decide he's unlikely to reveal anything now.

CC and I are quiet on the way home. I'm not sure what she's thinking about, but I'm trying to figure out how all the pieces fit together. What does Linda and Ian's relationship have to do with Pierre's missing painting? What does the missing painting have to do with Linda's health? (It's getting easier to think of her as Linda, and not Ms. Swanson.) Why do I suddenly find Ian so suspicious? Why wasn't Dominic at the hospital? How does Dominic always know when I lie to him? Why did Dominic look like he wasn't sure I wanted to see him later? I might have thought of some other things besides the pieces fitting together.

"Do you remember when the only crimes committed in our town were accidents and harmless pranks by kids?" I ask CC as I park my car in my driveway.

"I'm not sure I would describe the incidents with your car and Mr. Johnson, Mr. Russell, Mitchell, and Ralph as accidents. I'd describe them more as avoidable mistakes," CC says with a heavy note of censure in her voice. "Also, I think the swim team would disagree that adding dye to the pool was a harmless prank." I crack up, remembering how the swim team was blue for almost a month during our senior year.

I'm still chuckling as we enter CC's kitchen. She starts making dinner, and I plop onto a barstool to watch. It's like witchcraft. She starts with random things like potatoes, cabbage, flour, and chicken, and before I know it, she's made fried chicken, coleslaw, mashed potatoes, and gravy. If I started with those things, I'm pretty sure I would make a fire or maybe a poison.

My stomach grumbles, making me realize all we had for lunch were brownies. CC hands me a bag of chocolate-covered pretzels on one of her many passes around the kitchen. She knows me so well! I happily munch on the pretzels as my mind wanders. It's prone to wandering; focus isn't really my strong suit. This time, it wanders from Pierre's missing painting to Linda's hospital visit.

"What do you think Ian used to poison Linda?" I ask CC. Based on her expression, she hasn't even considered that possibility.

"What?! What makes you think he poisoned her? He's such a loving husband." Her shocked words are also a clue that she hadn't even considered that Ian had poisoned his wife.

"Come on, CC," I say in a tone that says she's being naive. "You're being naive." (Oops, it wasn't just the tone that said it.) She frowns at me, but I push on. "They got married right after meeting each other. He doesn't work. She's rich. Two and two make four. He married her for her money, and now he's getting rid of her. It's like a black widow but in reverse."

"He's shown nothing but kindness to her," CC says, stubbornly clinging to her belief that he is a decent guy. "He has supported her through the theft and brings her lunch every day to try and get her to eat something. I think you are seeing things that aren't there." Her mulish expression tells me I'm not going to convince her that Ian is a bad guy.

"Don't you find it the least bit suspicious that Ian's the one who convinced Linda to host Pierre's show?" I ask. "What if he's using her for more than just her money? What if he wanted the painting too?"

"Where would he hide the painting if he did steal it? I'm sure Ms. Swanson would have found an eight-foot painting if it was lying around their house," CC counters in a tone that implies I'm being ridiculous. "How would he even have gotten it out of the museum? Put it in his pocket?" Now she's just being ridiculous. We would have seen an eight-foot painting in his pocket.

"That's the part I'm stuck on. How did he get the painting out of the museum? Actually, now that I think about it, I don't remember seeing Ian at the opening. Do you? Wouldn't you think he would be there? He's a huge fan of Pierre's work, and his wife is the host of the evening. It seems like a loving, devoted husband would be there."

"We don't know that he wasn't there. We didn't know who he was at the time. We might not have realized we saw him." CC thinks she's being logical and making sense, but I disagree.

"I remember seeing Linda after the painting was discovered missing, but Ian wasn't with her. If something like that happened to you, wouldn't it take a crowbar to pry Jake away from you?" I counter.

She tilts her head in thought. "You're right. Jake wouldn't leave my side."

"Of course I wouldn't," Jake agrees, coming in the back door. He demonstrates by wrapping her in a hug and thoroughly kissing her. Sadly for him, she's still cooking dinner, and after only a few seconds, she gently pushes him away. As a consolation prize, CC hands him a potato masher and a huge bowl of boiled potatoes.

"Here, mash these for me, please," she says. While Jake is mashing potatoes, Jane comes to set the table. She has a crow with a wrapped wing on her shoulder like a pirate's parrot. It's uncanny how they always know when to appear to set the table or eat dinner. It's also uncanny that Jane collects wild animals like some people collect coins or stamps.

"What's his name?" I ask her.

"Edgar. He hurt his wing, so I had to wrap it. It should be as good as new in no time." I nod like this is normal, which for Jane it is. "Just don't leave anything shiny lying around," she continues. "He has a habit of borrowing shiny things."

"It's true. I spent hours searching for my keys the other day, only to find them in Edgar's nest," Jake says. He acts like having a crow with a nest in his house is a normal occurrence. I guess with Jane as a daughter, it is.

The rest of the children filter in and find places at the banquette. I hop up and grab a spot between Frank and Eve. Before we can start passing bowls and plates of food around the table,

Dominic comes in the back door. I wonder when he began letting himself in like he's family. It seems like it's a big step, and it went unremarked.

"When did you start letting yourself in like you're family?" I ask. I guess it didn't go unremarked after all. Everybody freezes and stares at me.

"Claire!" CC admonishes. "Dominic, I'm so glad you made it. I was worried work would keep you." She smiles at him, apparently trying to smooth over my question. My unanswered question. When did CC start calling him Dominic? She's always called him "Sheriff." I debate asking this question, too, but I doubt I would get an answer, so I remain silent.

"When did you start calling him Dominic? You've always called him 'Sheriff'!" I guess I didn't remain silent after all. CC ignores this question, too. How come she gets to ignore questions she doesn't want to answer, and I always have to tell everybody everything?

"Hey, Eve, can I trade spots with you?" Dominic asks and waits for her quick nod before scooping her up, sliding into her spot, and depositing her on his other side. Now I'm sitting between Frank and Dominic. I'm not sure how I feel about this. On one hand, I like sitting next to Dominic. On the other hand, sitting next to Dominic sometimes makes me feel edgy. On the other other hand, Eve sometimes steals my food. On the other other other hand, it was a smooth move that was well executed. Serving platters and bowls start circulating the table before I run out of hands or make up my mind on my feelings.

"How's Ms. Swanson?" CC asks Dominic. "Her husband must be so worried."

"She's stable and being monitored," Dominic tells her, instead of his standard I-can't-discuss-an-ongoing-investigation response.

"What happened to Ms. Swanson?" Kyle asks, brushing a stray blond curl out of his eyes. It bounces back into the tangled mess that is his hair.

"She had a seizure," I tell him. "It was awful. First, she was gray-tinged and sweaty. Her eyes were dilated to the size of Mars, and then she just dropped. Before we could do anything, she started having a seizure. I had to call an ambulance and everything."

Kyle fidgets with his fork. "Do you think her husband did something to her?" he finally asks hesitantly. I'm shocked! Why would he think that? I mean, *I* think that, but why would he?

"Why do you think that her husband did something to her?" Dominic asks. He asks like he really wants to know, not just to pacify or distract Kyle.

Kyle shrugs his shoulders, but then flips through his ever-present sketchbook, tears out a sketch, and hands it to Dominic. I lean over to get a better look. This presses my body against Dominic's. The change in his breathing tells me either Kyle's sketch is really good or he's noticed I'm pressed up against him.

The sketch shows Linda in her taffeta dress from the art show opening. Her expression is a mix of happiness, focus, and serenity as she walks toward us. (I guess it was toward Kyle since he's the one who drew it.) In the background, Ian stares after her. The expression on his face is disconcerting. He stares at her intently, but it isn't with love. The best word I can think of to describe it is malice.

Dominic studies the drawing for a long time. "When did you draw this?"

"A couple of days ago. I saw them at the art show opening and couldn't get it out of my mind, but it wasn't until later that I realized they were married. That made his expression even weirder." He straightens his perpetually crooked wire-rimmed glasses, leaving a smear of something green on the frames. "Why would he look at her like that? It's like he despises her."

Dominic seems to be struggling to look away from the drawing. "Can I keep this?" he asks Kyle, ignoring his question. Kyle nods.

"What does it mean?" I ask, but Dominic ignores my question. I'm getting really tired of people expecting me to answer their questions, but feeling free to ignore mine.

Ann takes the brief lull in conversation as an opportunity to relate, in excruciating detail, how she beat the neighborhood kids at a soccer free-kick goals competition. Even when she let them combine all their goals against hers, she still beat them. I'm surprised anybody will still play her at anything.

When she winds down her story, Dean jumps in with a technical synopsis of his automatic swing pushing machine. By the time he finishes talking, everybody has finished eating, and they are leaving to do whatever it is kids do these days.

The dinner time conversations have become monotonous, I think. "You weren't contributing to the conversation," CC tells me as she clears the table. I guess I said it instead of just thinking it.

I sigh deeply. "It's not like I could have. I don't think either of them even paused for breath."

Jake and CC, having finished putting the food away, rejoin us at the table with beer bottles. The four of us silently sip our beer and solve the mystery of the missing painting, Linda's poisoning, and quantum physics. Just kidding—we have no more answers than we did earlier. Plus, quantum physics sounds really hard.

"I still can't figure out how he got the painting out of the museum," I say. "If he'd stolen a smaller painting, he could have smuggled it out in a bag, or a box, or his coat, or something, but he stole the eight-foot-tall one. Even after he got it out, how did he drive away with it? It would be pretty conspicuous in a car. A rental van would have drawn attention and left a paper trail. I guess a minivan or truck could hold it."

"What if he folded it so it wasn't eight feet long anymore?" CC asks.

Dominic shakes his head. "Folding it would damage the painting. Whoever took it wanted it intact. If they only wanted to ruin it, they could have done so at the museum. It would have been a lot easier."

"Well, they had to get it out of the museum somehow," I say. "Otherwise, we would have found it by now. We've searched every inch of the museum."

Dominic's scowl tells me he doesn't like me saying "we" and he thinks he's the only one who should be investigating. When he opens his mouth, probably to yell at me, I decide to try to distract him. I place my hand on his thigh under the table and give it a friendly squeeze. He covers my hand with his and stares deeply into my eyes. I feel victorious. I've distracted him, and now he won't lecture me on butting out of his investigation.

"Don't think this will get you out of a lecture on butting out of my investigation," he tells me. Dang it! Sometimes I think nothing goes my way. "Come on," he says, standing up and pulling me out of the banquette. "It's been a long day. Let's call it a night."

CC and Jake don't even try to stop us as we leave. "If I'm ever kidnapped, they'll be no help," I grouse as I'm pulled along in Dominic's wake. He ignores me until we're in my kitchen.

"I want you to stay out of my investigation," he says in a stern no-nonsense voice, with a stern no-nonsense expression. Jaws mirrors his stare, and I feel ganged-up on. "This isn't just a missing painting anymore. Linda is very sick, and I have a strong suspicion it wasn't an accident." Although his expression is stern, his eyes hold concern, and something I'm not sure I want to name. "I mean it," he continues when I remain silent.

"I know," I say. He seems relieved I've agreed. Silly man, I didn't agree to stay out of his investigation. I agreed that I knew he meant it. He gives me a quick but thorough kiss before leaving. I take a minute to strengthen my knees from their jelly-like consistency before I attempt to climb my stairs. Jaws watches from his counter perch. He looks like he's judging me, but I might be projecting.

Chapter 20

I wake up feeling well-rested and refreshed, having slept soundly without Agatha snoring in my ear or Blackbeard claiming my pillow. Not really—I wake up contorted around Agatha and Blackbeard, with the echoes of Agatha's snoring bouncing in my skull. I drag myself upright and stagger toward CC's and coffee.

There's a slight traffic jam in the doorway as I try to enter while CC's children try to exit to catch the school bus. Luckily, nobody gets hurt, and I make it inside for my coffee. I drain my mug and hold it out for a refill, grabbing a muffin out of the pan. I mentally review my to-do list while I eat my still slightly warm muffin. I feel overwhelmed by the number of things on my to-do list.

"Finish your breakfast, and then we're getting started on your to-do list," CC says. I might be dawdling over finishing my muffin to delay the inevitable. CC refrains from commenting on my delay tactics, but her expression tells me she knows what I'm doing. Also, her fingernails impatiently drumming on the counter tell me she's annoyed at my delay tactics. Eventually, I can delay no longer, and I finally pop the last bite of muffin in my mouth. CC snags my coffee cup and refills it. Instead of handing it to me, she turns and walks out the back door.

"What? Where are you taking my coffee?" I ask, jumping up to follow her. She doesn't answer me. She just continues through our yards and into my kitchen. I hurry after her, or more accurately, after my coffee.

Only once I've entered my kitchen does the thought that I could have just grabbed a different coffee cup and avoided tackling my to-do list occur to me. I sigh, knowing it's too late to change plans, and I'm stuck with adulting.

CC is already settled on my couch, flipping through my pile of papers. Benji is overjoyed that we're here and brings me a pen to celebrate. "See, even Benji wants you to get to work on this," CC says pointedly. "No more avoidance."

I wilt as I accept the pen from Benji, give him a distracted pat on the head, and plop onto the couch next to CC.

The next several hours are productive but laced with anxiety and panic, at least for me. CC seems to be handling it better. "There. We got several things done, and now you have a timeline for checking the remaining things off your list." She seems pleased and not at all overwhelmed. "Time for lunch."

I feel as if I've gone ten rounds in a boxing ring. I half expect to see bruises marring my skin as I trail CC back to her house. "I'm exhausted," I mumble, plopping onto a barstool.

"It wasn't that bad," CC says. "Besides, now you're that much closer to starting your bookstore." I drop my head on the counter. "We should hear back on your offer on the storefront in the next couple of days. That will really get the ball rolling."

"That just makes it worse," I say into the counter where my face is resting.

"Buck up, you decided to open a bookstore, and now you have to do the work to make it happen." When I don't lift my head, she continues. "It's a good decision, and you can do this." She gives me a quick reassuring pat on the shoulder, continuing to make lunch.

"What if I can't?" I whisper to the counter.

"Here, you'll feel better after you eat something," CC says, setting a plate in front of me.

I finally lift my head. "Your lack of sympathy is making me question if you are really my best friend," I tell her, pulling my plate closer. I fidget with my fork, running it through my fingers. I feel like I need to say or do something, but can't figure out what it is.

"Please, I've been your best friend since kindergarten, and you know it. Besides, *you* are the one who decided to open a bookstore. *I'm* just supporting you." The emphasis she places on her words implies she thinks she's helping me and not pushing me outside my comfort zone.

I remain quiet, possibly for the first time in my life. My silence seems to concern her greatly.

"Claire, if you really don't want to open a bookstore, it's okay to change your mind. It's not too late, and even if it was, I'd help you anyway." She reaches out and holds my hand.

"I know you would," I say. "I do want to open a bookstore. I'm just afraid I won't be able to do it. What if I fail? I don't have a great track record of success."

"Don't be ridiculous! You're very successful. You graduated from college with honors, you single-handedly saved Brown Insurance from going bankrupt when you were a new graduate, you have enough money in your savings account to buy an island, and you're vital to my family." CC's vehement defense of me brings tears to my eyes, but I refuse to let them fall.

I hug her, perhaps a little desperately. "Thanks, I needed to hear that," I tell her, sniffing back the last of my tears. CC pulls back from my hug. I may be reluctant to let her go, but she's slippery and is soon free of my embrace.

She moves to answer the knock at the back door. I'm not surprised to see Dominic standing there. I mean, who else would it be?

When Dominic sees my possibly tear-stained face, he rushes toward me. "What's wrong? What happened? Are you okay?" he asks rapid-fire, staring at me intently, as if he can somehow determine the reason for my tears.

"What are you doing here?" I try to deflect. "Don't you have some investigating to do?"

His quick frown implies he doesn't appreciate me ignoring his questions. "Why have you been crying?" he asks, ignoring *my* questions. He looks a little worried.

"It's nothing. Just a little panic about opening my bookstore," I tell him. He relaxes slightly, making me realize he was very worried.

"You'll do great at it," he says. "I have no doubts." His blind faith is touching. It's probably misplaced, but it's touching nonetheless. "I just stopped by to make sure you remembered our conversation from last night. Stay out of my investigation," he reminds me, with a glare.

"I remember our conversation," I tell him. He seems suspicious of my ready acceptance, but nods as if I agreed. Silly man, I didn't agree, I just acknowledged I remembered what he said.

"Dominic, can I make you some lunch?" CC asks.

"No, thanks. I have to go." He casts one last look at me. I can't read his expression, but it seems to be mostly disbelief that I have agreed to stay out of his investigation.

"Finish your lunch. We need to leave soon, too," CC says, once Dominic leaves.

"Leave? Where are we going?"

"To visit Ms. Swanson." She says this like only an idiot would need to ask. I want to say something scathing about her implication that I'm an idiot, and her assumption that I would go to the hospital to visit Ms. Swanson, but I'd like to talk to Ms. Swanson, so I refrain.

We finish lunch silently. I'm not sure why CC is silent, but I'm silent because I'm contemplating Ms. Swanson's health issue. I apparently contemplate so strongly that I don't even remember finishing my lunch, but CC suddenly whisks my plate away.

"Hurry up and get dressed," she says, practically pushing me out the door and toward my house. "I'll wait for you in your car."

I choose a dark blue shirt with a picture of an atom and the words NEVER TRUST AN ATOM, THEY MAKE UP EVERYTHING printed around it. It's perfect, since I think Ian is making up his concern for his wife. CC frowns slightly at me but doesn't comment on my shirt as I join her in my car.

"What are we going to say to Ian?" I ask as I drive to the hospital. "I mean, we don't even know Linda, and we're visiting her again. Doesn't that seem like something he might find strange?"

"Don't be silly," CC counters, unconcerned. "Visiting somebody who's sick is normal, and I'm sure Ian will appreciate the support."

I'm unconvinced. I think Ian is going to be annoyed that we're butting in. That reminds me of Dominic. He also gets annoyed when I butt in. Well, at least he won't know about it this time. I'm not sure what I'm going to do, but I will probably butt in somehow.

CC confidently walks into the hospital while I trail behind her. "Hi, Marge. How's Luna?" she says to the receptionist at the front desk.

Marge was a couple years ahead of us in school. She's slightly overweight, and she styles her hair in what most closely resembles a helmet, but when she smiles broadly—as she always does when talking about her show dog, Luna—she transforms into a beauty.

"She's great! She won Best in Show last month," Marge brags. "How are your kids?" I ignore the rest of the required polite chit-chat and look around the waiting room. It's empty, so I tune back in to their conversation in time to hear CC explain the reason for our visit.

"We're here to visit Ms. Swanson," CC tells Marge. "We were at the museum when she collapsed, and we wanted to check in on her."

"That's so sweet of you," Marge says, tapping a few keys on the computer in front of her. "She's in room 218 just down that hall." She points to our right.

CC smiles her thanks and guides us down the hall to Linda's room. She knocks on the open door and waits for Linda to call out "Come in!" before stepping over the threshold.

"Ms. Swanson, I don't know if you remember us. My name is CC, and this is Claire. We were at the museum when you collapsed. We just wanted to check on you and see how you're feeling." CC presents her with a bouquet of flowers.

Where did she get a bouquet of flowers? Has she had them the whole time? I don't have time to ask her where they came from before Ms. Swanson recovers from her surprise and confusion at our visit.

"Oh, that's kind of you," she says, a little uncertainly. "I guess I'm feeling as well as can be expected."

"Where's your husband?" I blurt out. Subtlety isn't my strong suit. CC looks both shocked and annoyed at me. Linda just looks shocked.

"Ian? You know Ian?"

"Uh, we've met. I just assumed he would be here with you. I mean, you collapsed, had a seizure, were admitted to the hospital, and are waiting for test results. Where else would he be?" I don't even sound sympathetic to my own ears.

"I'm sure he'll be here soon. He's probably taking care of something important at the house." Linda sounds defensive. Maybe I should have tried harder to be subtle.

"Of course he is," CC soothes. "He was so distraught yesterday while he was waiting to talk to Dr. Young."

"What are you doing here?" Ian asks from the doorway. He looks mad.

"See, I knew he would be here soon," Linda says. "Darling, I'm glad you're here."

Ian enters the room and sets a small container down on Linda's table. He leans over and places a chaste kiss on her cheek. "I brought you some soup. You should eat to keep your strength up."

"I'm not hungry now. I'll have some later," she says, holding his hand.

Ian's face tightens. "Just a couple of bites," he coaxes, reclaiming his hand and opening the container. He tries to spoon-feed her a bite, but I interrupt him.

"Did the test results come back? Is she even supposed to be eating anything? Doesn't the hospital have food service for its patients?"

He glares at me before schooling his expression. "I'm just so concerned about you," he says, transferring his now concerned gaze to Linda. Linda looks like a love-struck teenager, and Ian tries to spoon-feed her a bite of soup again.

"What's going on here?" Dominic asks from the doorway, distracting Ian from his efforts. Ian's face tightens again in what I think is frustration. Dominic takes in the scene and quickly moves to intercept the soup. He must be suspicious of Ian as well. "CC, Claire, it's nice of you to stop by, but I need a minute alone with Ms. Swanson."

"Of course, we'll go now. Ms. Swanson, I hope you feel better soon," CC says, turning to go. She walks several feet down the hallway, then turns and walks back into Linda's room to grab my arm and escort me out with her.

Once out of the room, I pull up short, forcing her to stop as well. Before she can say anything, I press my finger to my lips in the international sign for quiet. She rolls her eyes at me but stays quiet.

"Have the test results come back yet?" we hear Dominic ask.

"Not yet," Linda answers. There's more mumbled conversation, but I can't hear it.

Unfortunately, I also don't hear Dominic saying his goodbyes, and I'm caught loitering outside the door. His expression indicates that he's not surprised that I'm meddling, but he *is* displeased that I was meddling.

"Why am I not surprised?" he asks, grabbing my arm with the hand not holding the container of soup, and marching me down the hallway. I guess his words, as well as his expression, told me he wasn't surprised.

"What? I wasn't eavesdropping. I had to, um, tie my shoe," I lie. He doesn't bother to reply.

"Sheriff, I'm glad I caught you. I have Ms. Swanson's test results," Dr. Young interrupts before Dominic can drag me out of the hospital.

"Was she poisoned?" I ask. Dr. Young doesn't get a chance to answer.

"It is not your business," Dominic grits out between his teeth. He continues to glare at me while directing his next words to CC. "CC, please take Claire home before I arrest her."

CC takes his threat seriously. She quickly grabs my free arm and tugs me outside.

"Well, that didn't go well," I say, scowling through the glass sliding doors at Dominic. I can't hear what Dr. Young is saying, so I read his lips.

"Bug best fur income glue give." Either Dr. Young isn't making any sense, or I might not be as good at lip-reading as I hoped. I sigh heavily and give up on trying to read his lips as he continues speaking to Dominic.

"I feel terrible for Linda," I tell CC as I drive us home. "Her husband stole a painting from her museum, he's trying to kill her, and she doesn't even know it."

"Honestly, Claire. I don't know why you keep trying to blame Ian for her getting sick. I mean, he even brought her soup!" She seems exasperated with me. "Besides, if Ian did do what you're accusing him of, don't you think Dominic would arrest him?"

"Dominic can only arrest him if he has proof," I counter, then pause. That kind of reinforces her argument. There isn't any proof that Ian stole the painting or poisoned Linda. Unless, of course, Dr. Young was telling Dominic the test results show she was poisoned.

Now I wish I'd stayed at the hospital to see if he escorted Ian out in handcuffs. Impulsively, I whip a U-turn, narrowly avoiding sideswiping the mail truck. Earl, the mailman, shouts angrily, but his shouts are mostly drowned out by the rumble of my car's engine, so they're easy to ignore. Besides, I didn't even hit his truck, so he shouldn't be mad.

"Claire!" CC shouts, bracing herself as if expecting an impact.

"What? I missed the truck. Why are you so upset?" My questions don't seem to pacify her, but before she can answer, a thought occurs to me.

"He mailed it!" I shout, swerving slightly into oncoming traffic in my excitement. Luckily, I avoid the hatchback coming my way. "Ian mailed the painting! It's brilliant! He wrapped it and left it with the outgoing mail in the basement. Then, he waited for the mailman to pick it up and walk it out of the museum. Nobody would pay attention to the mailman and his various packages. By the time Dominic searched the basement, the painting was already gone!" I might be shouting it all out in my excitement.

"That is a genius plan," CC concedes. "But where did he mail it? If he mailed it to their house, Ms. Swanson would have seen it."

I chew my lip while I consider this. "There has to be a record of packages somewhere. They should all be insured and have tracking numbers, right? I bet there's a record at the post office." I take a sharp left at the next intersection, causing CC to slam into her door. Before she can recover, I pull into the post office parking lot.

I hop out and rush toward the counter. "Hi, Ms. Scott, I need to see the tracking information for the packages picked up from the museum on the twenty-third," I say in a rush. Ms. Scott looks surprised. I'm not sure if it's because I'm there, or that I'm asking for package information from the museum, or that I ignored the social expectation of chitchat before anything else.

"I can't give you that," she says, apparently recovering her wits. She looks past me. "Hi, CC. How are your kids?"

CC smiles warmly. She's always happy to talk about her kids. "They're great, Ms. Scott! Nell is having a wonderful time at college and has a new boyfriend. Frank …"

"It's really important, Ms. Scott. I need to know where a package went." I cut CC off before she can go through all the kids' accomplishments.

Ms. Scott looks back at me and frowns. Her white hair is in a perfectly cut and styled bob, but her face is free of wrinkles, belying her age. "I really can't tell you. I could lose my job." I wilt. I don't want to be the reason she loses her job.

"Maybe you should tell Dominic what you think happened. He could probably get a search warrant or something," CC suggests. I wilt further. I don't feel up to a lecture from Dominic, but I know she's right.

I pull out my phone. It rings twice before he answers.

"Don't be mad," I blurt out as soon as I hear the call connect. His sigh communicates his exasperation at me, but I continue before his words can also express his exasperation at me. "I know how Ian got the painting out of the museum. He mailed it. After stealing it, he took it to the basement and wrapped it up for shipping. Then he put it with all the other packages waiting to be mailed. It would have been picked up by the mailman and delivered to wherever he wanted."

I say it in a rush so he can't interrupt me with lectures about butting into his investigation. However, there's only silence on the other end of the line. I pull my phone away from my ear to look at the screen to check if I've been disconnected.

"Where are you?" he finally asks.

"I'm at the post office," I answer softly. He sighs again, but again refrains from yelling or lecturing me.

"I'll be there soon," he says, and hangs up. I'm not sure if it's a statement or a threat.

"Well, that went better than I thought it would. He'll be here soon," I tell CC and Ms. Scott. CC and Ms. Scott fill the time by continuing to list their children's and grandchildren's accomplishments respectively, but I ignore them and stare out the window, waiting for Dominic. I'm both dreading and eagerly anticipating his arrival. Once more confirming that I'm a complex person with complex emotions.

When Dominic arrives several hours later—okay, it's probably only several minutes later—I rush out to meet him. "Finally!" I grab his arm and half drag him inside.

"Tell Ms. Scott you need the shipping information from the twenty-third," I say, pushing him in front of her.

"Sheriff, as I told Claire, I can't give out shipping information. I could lose my job," she says before he can say anything.

"Can you tell me if an eight-foot-long package was picked up from the museum in the last two weeks?" Dominic asks. "If so, I'll get a warrant for the information, but if not, I won't waste everybody's time."

"We don't record package dimensions, just if something is oversized. Many of the packages coming from the museum are oversized, so I don't think that would be helpful, even if I could tell you," Ms. Scott tells him. We are all glum-faced as we consider this. I'm starting to think Ian might get away with stealing the painting.

"What about delivery addresses?" Dominic asks. "Most of the museum packages would be shipped to other museums. Have any packages been delivered to private residences or PO boxes?"

"That's a great idea," I say. I must have sounded surprised, because Dominic glares at me.

Ms. Scott saves me from a lecture. "Let me check," she says, typing on the computer.

After the longest search in the history of the world, she looks up. "You might want to get that warrant," she says.

"I knew it!" I crow. Dominic is already on his phone talking to someone, presumably about the warrant.

The wheels of justice don't move as fast as they seem to on TV, and we stand around for what feels like hours waiting for Dominic's deputy to bring us the warrant. It's boring.

I don't do well when bored; things tend to go awry. In my boredom, I may have accidentally knocked over the display cabinet full of mailing packaging. Luckily, Dominic is strong enough to right the heavy cabinet, and we have plenty of time to clean it all up before the search warrant finally arrives. Ms. Scott may have banned me from the post office, but I'm pretty sure that she can't enforce that, so I don't worry about it.

"Deputy, please escort Ms. Miller home." My gasp of outrage interrupts him. He glares at me. "If she gives you any trouble, arrest her."

"That's a fine way to thank me for solving the case," I say, crossing my arms angrily.

His deputy looks unsure. He doesn't seem to want to come close to me, let alone escort me anywhere, but he also doesn't seem to want to ignore Dominic's command. When Dominic transfers his angry gaze to him, he musters up his courage and slowly approaches me, much like I imagine somebody would approach a bear.

"Don't even think about it, Ollie. You've never been able to beat me before. I doubt you can now. Remember your senior trip?" I half taunt, half warn him. He stops his slow approach, proving he does remember the trip and that he doesn't want a repeat. Let's just say his senior trip involved an attempt to spy on me, a patio umbrella, and him riding in an ambulance. I'll never again plan a vacation without double-checking where the high school trip will be.

"You're a grown man, and a deputy," Dominic says, but it's no use. Ollie is terrified of me.

"Go home, or else *I* will arrest you," Dominic tells me. Somehow, I don't think I'll be able to intimidate Dominic, so I huff my way out the door and toward my car. CC follows me silently.

"He is infuriating! Here I am trying to open a bookstore, and I take time away from that to help him solve his case, but does he appreciate it? No! He just yells and bosses me around. The nerve of him!" I rant, slamming my car door.

I glare at him through my windshield and the post office window. He's pinching the bridge of his nose as though he has a headache. As if feeling my gaze, he looks up and meets my eyes.

When he starts walking toward me—more like stalking toward me—I decide that some space between us would be a good idea.

I start my car and shift into reverse. He reaches me before I can back out, but I ignore his attempts to get me to roll down my window and quickly back out of my parking spot. His shout of pain makes me think I ran over his foot again. I don't stop to check before I drive away.

"I can't believe you ran over his foot again. And you didn't even stop to check if he was okay," CC admonishes me. I take a peek in my rearview mirror and see Dominic give my car one final glare before he limps back into the post office.

"He seems fine," I defend myself. "Besides, he threatened to arrest me if I didn't leave, so I left. Why is everybody mad about that?" CC frowns at me but doesn't comment.

Somehow, my car drives itself back to the hospital instead of home.

"Huh," I say, surprised to find myself once again in the hospital parking lot. "Well, since we're here, I guess we should talk to Linda again."

CC seems torn between trying to convince me to go home and wanting to check on Linda. I don't give her time to decide. I hop out of my car and head inside. She follows me like I knew she would.

I wave to Marge as I head straight toward Linda's room. She looks like she wants to stop me, but I breeze past too fast for her to do anything.

"Please, sweetheart, just a couple of bites." Ian is trying to coax Linda into eating the soup he brought. It looks like he has a new container; the bowl is different from the one I saw earlier.

"You heard what the sheriff and Dr. Young said. I'm not supposed to eat anything besides what the nurse brings me," Linda says.

"Am I interrupting?" I ask, entering the room without knocking. Ian glares at me, but quickly recovers and morphs his expression into one of polite greeting with a touch of concern. I find his ability to transform his expression so convincingly deeply disturbing.

I move farther into the room and "accidentally" knock over the bowl, spilling the soup. I'm not subtle about it, and not even a blind man would think I did it by accident. "Oh, no! How clumsy of me," I say, with false contrition. Ian's face reddens in anger, but he swallows back his retort.

"Don't worry, I'll find someone to clean it up," CC says in full-on concerned-mom mode.

"Why do you keep trying to force-feed her soup?" I accuse in what some might call a belligerent tone.

"I'm just concerned for her. She hasn't been eating much. There's no need to be belligerent," Ian says. I guess he's the one to call it belligerent.

Linda looks back and forth between us like she's watching a tennis match. "What's going on?" she asks.

"Why don't you ask Ian what he put in your food?" I say, glaring at Ian with my hands on my hips.

"Ian, what is she talking about?" Linda asks Ian.

"I have no idea. She's obviously crazy. I even caught her in the basement at the museum," Ian says, trying to paint me as a crazy person. The joke's on him; everybody already thinks I'm crazy. Wait, that doesn't show me in a good light. Nonetheless, I soldier on.

"There's no point denying it," I tell him. "I talked to Dr. Young and he told me everything. About how Linda's been poisoned. If I hadn't called the ambulance when I did, she could have died. And, most important, they've identified the poison you used and have already started her on the antidote."

"That's impossible," he scoffs. "There's no antidote for hemlock poisoning."

"Aha!" I crow, pointing a finger at him accusingly. "I knew you did it, and now you've admitted it in front of witnesses."

Ian's face darkens in anger. "You've ruined everything!" he shouts angrily. His face contorts into a truly terrifying sight, and I belatedly think that confronting an attempted murderer might not have been wise. When he stands and advances toward me menacingly, I instinctively back away.

"Wait, can we talk about this?" I ask, perhaps a bit desperately. He lunges at me, his hands reaching for my throat. My survival instincts kick in, and I turn to flee. Sadly, my coordination isn't great, and one of my feet slips as I turn, causing me to drop to my knees. Ian isn't able to slow his lunge, and he hits me with such force that he flips over me and slams into the floor. Happily, at least for me, he seems to have knocked himself unconscious. Uncertainly, I stare at his prone and unmoving body as I straighten up.

"Well, that worked perfectly," I say, as hospital staff arrives, having been drawn by the commotion.

"Oh, my gosh! Claire, are you okay? Are you crazy? What were you thinking?" CC asks in a flurry as she grabs my arms and stares intently into my face.

"I'm fine," I assure her. "Everything worked out just like I planned. We should restrain him," I tell the nurses who are checking on Ian. "He admitted to poisoning Linda and tried to attack me." They stare at me as if I have two heads. "Also, you might want to call the sheriff. He'd probably like to be informed about what happened here."

"I would like to be informed of what happened here," Dominic says from behind me. I close my eyes in resignation. I was hoping to escape before he got here. I've been counting on the delay in seeing me cooling his anger toward me.

"No chance of that now, so you'd better start talking," he says.

Gathering my courage, I turn to face him. "Well, you see, after we left the post office, we thought we should check on Linda. We didn't really get a chance to earlier, and I feel connected to her since I basically saved her life by calling the ambulance and all." His expression remains steely, but I continue anyway. "Ian was here again, trying to convince her to eat some of the soup he made, and out of nowhere, with no provocation at all, he admitted to poisoning Linda and then tried to attack me. Luckily, I was able to avoid his completely unprompted and unexpected attack. He accidentally, and through no fault of mine, fell and knocked himself unconscious."

CC, Linda, and the hospital staff all stare at me flabbergasted. Dominic stares at me like he can read my mind. I fidget self-consciously. It would be best for everybody, but especially me, if he didn't read my mind. My mind is kind of scary, and some parts are embarrassing.

"Do you want to tell me what actually happened?" he asks. "Or should I check the security cameras?"

"Security cameras?" I gulp.

When he continues to stare deeply into my soul, I crack. "Fine. I suspected Ian was poisoning Linda, and when we walked in on him trying to convince her to eat the soup, I knew I had to do something. So, I might have hinted that he put something in her food. I also might have implied that Dr. Young confirmed poisoning and had started Linda on the antidote. Ian called me a liar because there isn't an antidote for hemlock poisoning. I calmly and discreetly indicated to CC that we should call you to tell you he had admitted to poisoning Linda. Out of nowhere, and with no warning, he suddenly attacked me. Luckily, I used my self-defense training, and I was able to use the force of his attack against him, and he knocked himself out."

"Let me see if I've got this right. You butted into my investigation and recklessly accused Mr. Newman of poisoning Ms. Swanson. Then, when he accidentally admitted to it, you dramatically let him know you had caught him, which drove him into a rage that caused him to attack you, and somehow you accidentally caused him to knock himself out," Dominic says.

"Yeah, pretty much," I admit.

I'm torn on how I feel about him knowing me so well. I don't want to take the time to examine my feelings right now. That's what nighttime is for, so I move on quickly. "The important thing is that he admitted to poisoning her. In front of witnesses."

Dominic takes a deep breath as if trying to regain control of his emotions. I'm not sure it works. He grabs my hand and drags me to an empty room. When the door closes behind us, I'm the one who takes a deep breath to try to regain control of my emotions. It doesn't work.

"Okay, I'm ready," I say. "You can yell at me now." Instead, he pulls me into his arms. I'm not sure what to think. I was thinking he was mad at me and he wanted to yell at me in private.

"I *am* mad at you," he tells me. His face is buried in my hair. "You insist on butting in where you don't belong. You're reckless and continually put yourself in danger with a complete disregard for your own safety and well-being. You drive me crazy. I live in fear that something is going to happen to you, and you do nothing to protect yourself." Well, when he puts it like that, I sound deranged, or simpleminded; maybe both.

Not wanting to examine my lack of self-preservation skills, I turn the conversation. "What did you find out at the post office?"

Dominic sighs deeply, and I fear he won't answer me due to that whole I-can't-discuss-an-ongoing-investigation nonsense.

"You were right," he finally says. "The painting was mailed to a rental house. Mr. Newman rented it the same week he and Ms. Swanson rented the house they shared in town. My guess would be that he planned to steal the painting whenever the opportunity presented itself, and he wanted to be ready with an address. The painting was in the house. As was Mr. Newman's wife."

I pull back, shocked. "What? Linda was in the hospital. How was she at the house, too?"

"Not Ms. Swanson. Mr. Newman has another wife. I think they were in on the theft together, but I didn't have time to question her fully. Something told me you wouldn't go home like you were supposed to, and that I should take Mr. Newman into custody as soon as possible."

I ignore his not-so-subtle insinuation that I always butt into his investigations, and that I'm likely to need rescuing from a killer. Just because it happened on his last investigation doesn't mean it would happen on this investigation. Although, since he's being so calm, I decide not to start an argument over it.

"Did he marry the other wife before or after Linda?" I ask. Either way, it will be terrible news for Linda to hear.

"I'm not sure, but if I had to guess, I'd say he was already married when he married Ms. Swanson," Dominic answers. I'm surprised I'm getting so much information out of him. Usually, he's pretty closed-mouthed about his investigations. I wonder what else I can get him to answer. Unfortunately, a commotion in the hall stops me from asking any other questions.

"Let me go! You have no right to hold me. Arrest that woman. She attacked me!" Ian has regained consciousness and is shouting in the hallway. Dominic releases me to go do his sheriffing stuff. I follow him into the hallway in time to hear him read Ian his rights.

"Ian Newman, you are under arrest for attempted murder and theft. You have the right to remain silent. Anything you say can and will be used against you in a court of law. You have the right to an attorney. If you cannot afford an attorney, one will be provided for you."

"Wow! It's just like on TV," I say. This draws Ian's attention to me, and he tries to lunge for me. I might have ducked behind the teenage hospital volunteer standing next to me, but I wouldn't admit to that even under oath. Since Dominic has a firm grip on Ian's arm, he isn't able to do anything except yell and kick out at me. Luckily for me, and the volunteer I'm using as a shield, he's too far away to reach us. His rage-filled shouting echoes in the hall, and in my head, even after Dominic drags him out.

"I think that went well," I say, straightening from my half-crouched position behind the teenage volunteer. Everybody turns to look at me incredulously.

"What's happening?" Linda interrupts from her room. That seems to kick the medical professionals into gear. Several of them rush into her room, and I can hear quiet murmuring from within.

"What? No! That's impossible. He wouldn't do that to me. He loves me!" Linda yells. She seems to be struggling with hearing the truth about Ian, and she doesn't even know all of it yet. I feel bad for her. Dr. Young joins the nurses in Linda's room and closes the door behind him. Since I can't hear what he's saying to her, I decide I might as well head home.

"Dominic found the painting," I tell CC, as I link my arm with hers and we walk toward my car. "But that's not all he found." On the car ride home, I fill her in on what else Dominic discovered.

"I can't believe it," CC says, looking a little shell-shocked. "He was married to someone else the whole time? He only pretended to love Linda so he could steal the painting? They seemed so happy, and he was just pretending the whole time. He tried to kill her. I just can't believe it." CC tends to see the best in people.

She moves around the kitchen as if she's on autopilot. I sit on a barstool and watch her gather ingredients and start cooking. She murmurs "I just can't believe it" every couple of minutes, but she keeps on cooking, so I don't worry about it. In no time at all, she's prepared the world's largest pot of spaghetti and meatballs.

Ann arrives to set the table, so I move to claim a seat before the other children join us. Jake and Dominic come through the back door in time to help bring the pot of spaghetti and meat-balls, bowl of salad, and platter of French bread to the table. I'm sitting in the middle of the bench, so Dominic can't sit next to me. I'm both relieved and saddened by this. His expression tells me he's aware I've done this on purpose. He doesn't get a chance to say anything about it, though, because the children talk over and around each other about contraptions, sports events, rescued ani-mals, and princess movies.

"Pierre's painting has been found," Dominic tells Kyle when there's a lull in the conversation.

"Really? That's great news," Kyle says. He has a streak of what appears to be flour on the left side of his head. Small puffs fall off every time he moves. "Who stole it? Where was it? Does Pierre know?"

"Ian, Linda's husband, stole it," I answer. "He mailed it to a house he rented, where his wife was staying. His other wife," I clarify. "I figured it out and got Ian to admit he was poisoning Linda. I would have made an amazing PI."

Dominic shoots me a look. If I'm interpreting it correctly, he disagrees with the idea that I'd be an amazing PI. The look also seems to imply he thinks I've glossed over how I got Ian to admit to poisoning Linda and the danger I put myself in.

"I contacted Pierre to let him know about the painting. I expect him back in the next day or two," Dominic answers Kyle.

"Is Linda going to be okay?" CC asks.

"Dr. Young seems to think she'll recover. Even though Ian was poisoning her, she wasn't eating much, so she likely ingested very little of the hemlock he was putting in her food. If she had been eating more, she would be dead."

Hearing how close Linda came to dying is a sobering thought. I must be thinking hard about this possibility because I don't realize everybody left until Dominic tugs me closer to him. "What? Where did everybody go?" My crack observation skills let me down again.

"CC went to put on her boots for line dancing night, and the kids went with Jake for ice cream," he answers, staring deeply into my eyes. I swallow hard against the feelings his gaze stirs.

"Ice cream? They went to get ice cream without me?" I'm hurt. I love ice cream. Why wasn't I invited?

"Jake said he'd bring you back some. Now, you'd better go put your boots on or you'll be late for line dancing." Dominic pulls me out of the banquette and walks me home, still holding my hand. He only releases my hand at the bottom of my stairs so I can go change into my boots.

I can feel him watching me walk up the stairs, but I don't look back. I take the time it takes to put on my boots to calm my emotions. Just kidding—I need significantly more time than it takes to put my boots on to calm my emotions, so they're still out of control when I head back downstairs.

Dominic is petting Benji, but when he hears me coming, he straightens up to lean against the counter next to Jaws' bowl. He smiles warmly when he sees me. He seems perfectly at ease in my house, like he belongs here.

"Are you ready?" he asks. He probably means am I ready to go line dancing, but my overthinking brain wonders if he means something more. Something deeper. I hesitate to answer.

"I think so," I finally say, answering both possible meanings, as I come down the last of the steps. He smiles that smile that makes my insides mushy, and takes my hand again.

About the Author

Writing has always been a hobby for Amanda Nelson. However, it was not always something she thought she could make a living with. After years of teaching elementary school, she finally sat down and wrote her first book, a cozy mystery about best friends solving a murder in their small town, the first book in the *Claire's Chaos and Crimes* series.

Since turning her passion into a profession, she is never happier than when she sits down at her desk and puts the opening words to a new book or story on paper.

Amanda lives with her husband of over 20 years, her two grown children, and a lot of pets. When not writing, she likes to spend time with family and friends, walk on the beach with her dogs, read, and take photographs.

Follow Amanda on Amazon for notifications when new books release and connect with her directly at amandanelsonauthor.com.

About Laurel Elite Books

Laurel Elite Books partners with authors who have meaningful stories to tell and important ideas to share. We provide publishing services that combine professional editorial care, beautiful book production, and personalized marketing strategy so authors can move from manuscript to published book with clarity and confidence.

Every Laurel Elite title begins with the author's unique voice, vision, and lived experience. While technology continues to change the publishing landscape, we believe the most impactful books are still created by humans with something real to say. Our role is to help shape, polish, and position those stories so they reach the readers who need them most.

Laurel Elite Books was founded on the belief that publishing should feel collaborative, transparent, and empowering, not confusing or out of reach. Whether an author is pursuing personal legacy, professional visibility, or long-term readership growth, we provide the structure, guidance, and expertise to help them publish with purpose.

Announcing Our New Division: Inner Light House

Laurel Elite Books is proud to support a growing division dedicated to amplifying women's voices, stories, and leadership through publishing partnerships that honor both creative expression and professional ambition. We believe women's stories deserve to be heard, valued, and widely read, and we are actively seeking new titles that bring fresh female perspectives to the page.

If you'd like to publish with Laurel Elite or apply for our newest division, Inner Light House, we welcome thoughtful, well-crafted work on our website.